SPITE YOUR FACE

An absolutely gripping crime thriller full of twists

EMMY ELLIS

Detective Carol Wren Mysteries Book 1

Originally published as *Biding Their Time*

Revised edition 2023
Joffe Books, London
www.joffebooks.com

First published in Great Britain in 2022
as *Biding Their Time*

This paperback edition was first published
in Great Britain in 2023

Cover art by Nebojša Zorić

ISBN: 978-1-80405-888-6

PROLOGUE

21 Larch Lane — Scudderton

She cowered in his presence, always did, afraid, wishing her mother hadn't gone off and left her. Dad hadn't been right since, and he drank a lot, raised his hand a lot and told her mean things. If she could fly away like the bird that was her namesake, she'd do it in a heartbeat. Wren. Little eight-year-old Carol Wren with the tatty clothes, the unkempt hair, and people around her who turned a blind eye because she smelled a tad musty and looked like she would eat a scabby dog.

When she was a big girl, she'd save all the kids like her, ones without a voice strong enough to be heard. Kids without a helping hand who weren't *seen*, their circumstances swept beneath many a carpet. Folks didn't want to step in and have a word with an alcoholic fella who'd likely punch their face in.

Yes, best to pretend it wasn't happening.

Except it was.

In the untidy living room, Carol quivered, anxious about what he'd say next, this father of hers who struck her more often than not. He liked the drink, had taken to guzzling straight out of the whisky bottle instead of using a glass like before. So many things had changed since her mother had gone.

"You're a thief," he slurred. "A filthy, rotten thief."

She didn't know what he was talking about. She was always too scared to steal *anything* — except a slice of bread when her tummy hurt — yet he believed what he'd said, that was clear from his widened eyes. The devil's eyes, that's what they were: all red around the edges, bloodshot, the brown so dark it could be black.

"I didn't steal nowt," she said.

"Liar!" He advanced towards her in the middle of the room, his hand held high. "You took my ink pen, didn't you? Stole it. Thought: *I'll have that!* Well, it's mine, not yours, and if you don't give it back, I'll wallop you to kingdom come."

She shook her head, her body turning cold. "I haven't got it, honest!"

He slapped her around the face, and the force of it sent her to the crumb-speckled carpet. The pain of violent, skin-on-skin contact burned, and her eyes watered. Her hip hurt from where she'd landed so hard, but she didn't dare move. She couldn't get up until he said so.

"Fucking bitch," he muttered and kicked her in the back.

Carol didn't cry out. If she did, he'd hit her again, kick her again.

"Why couldn't your mother have taken you with her, eh? What the fuck do I want with a snivelling, thieving wretch like you? You're a chain holding me down, that's what you are."

Carol stared beneath his favourite chair, the one with the stout wooden legs and the comfy seat. His pen rested beneath — probably dropped off the arm when he'd placed it on top of his newspaper. Some things had stayed the same; he still did the daily crossword.

She didn't reach under, didn't stretch her skinny arm to clutch the pen and bring it out. If she did, he'd say she'd hidden it, seeing as she miraculously knew where to find it, and she'd get a slap for that an' all. She stared at the fountain pen, with its silver nib, a dash of navy-blue ink on the tip, and the word *Parker* on the lid, which he'd popped on the end of the pen.

"I'm going," he said. "Off to The Lion."

She closed her eyes. Waited for the sound of the front door closing. The sound of his footsteps thumping down the path then along the pavement.

The sound of her sobs.

CHAPTER ONE

59 Wexford Close — Scudderton

It could be considered weird, staring through windows at people, but Martine did it just the same. The family didn't know she stood between their elder hedges most nights, drawing the leafy branches across so only her head popped out. If they did, they'd have surely phoned the police, at the very least coming out to shoo her away, but so far, she'd remained undetected. It gave her a sense of power, that she was invincible, and that whatever force out there governed justice, it was helping her, agreeing with the plans, keeping her hidden from sight. For hours, she watched the people interact inside, their life a movie with the sound turned down low, her straining to pick up the conversation through the gap the open window afforded, although if the man in *this* house got angry, his voice sailed through and into her ears well enough.

He got angry a lot — well, snippy, perhaps frustrated whenever he didn't get what he wanted. He should have been a headmaster, that was what he reminded her of. People got scared if he called them to his office, mainly because of the way he barked at them and the thought of losing their jobs. But if he hadn't done what he had, she'd see him as a typical boss, someone who had to maintain order, and if that meant being a bit grumpy, then so be it.

But he *had* done what he had, so she hated him.

The family never closed their lounge curtains, giving the impression they were the sort of people who wanted to show off their wealth. Leather sofa. Expensive sideboard. Real wooden floorboards, not laminate, polished so the furniture reflected on the surface. The room stretched all the way to the back of the house, a number seven in shape, the left-hand top part the kitchen. If she craned her neck, she got a good view of that area — the sink under the window, one of those posh taps that boiled water but also spat out filtered cold, a few cabinets below — but not the far wall where the cooker stood, nor the one opposite the sink. She had to go around the back to see that. Stand in the garden beside the potted yucca.

The sun had been a hot bugger for five weeks running, no rain to give everyone a break. Lots of complaining: "God, could we just have a good old downpour? Even a short shower would do. I'm boiling."

Her scalp itched from the evening heat.

Sue, the woman of the household, usually came out into the back garden around eleven to water her plants, hefting a large green watering can around with her, going inside twice to refill it. She had all those flowers in the borders, didn't she, and some small shrubs she clipped by the light of her phone torch. She also used a spray attachment on a hose, giving the grass a much-needed drink, despite there being a hosepipe ban at the minute.

Rules like that didn't apply to this lot.

Martine reckoned Sue took that time to reflect on her day — or, more likely, get some peace from her boisterous family.

Her bossy husband.

He was the reason Martine stood on their property night after night, biding her time — *their* time — until the right moment came for them to strike.

5

Although it wasn't *them* as such but Martine, doing Dad's dirty work for him, like she'd done before. She didn't mind. Just because the Bad Time hadn't happened to *her*, didn't mean she couldn't get justice. It *had* affected her for much of her life, so why shouldn't she help him?

Dad wasn't well, although he thought she didn't know. He sat in his desk chair every day in the living room, his gaze glued to the monitor, clicking through images, photos she'd taken while out and about.

Photos of this family and a few other people.

He regularly coughed up a lung, blood speckling the tissue held at his mouth, him stuffing it down the side of the chair beneath his thigh, thinking she hadn't noticed. Hard *not* to notice scarlet splodges, but if she mentioned it, he'd only get arsey, so she pretended she hadn't got a clue. A proud man, her father, one who since the Bad Time had lived off Disability Allowance — and a pension given to him by his then employer, though the correct term would be paying him for his silence, an extra-early retirement fund to stop him from blabbing. Two grand a month the payment for losing a hand sliced off then mangled by machinery. His left hand, and wasn't that a mercy? Dad wrote with his right. Still, a hand was a hand, no matter which one was missing, something that belonged to him once but had ended up in a hospital incinerator, unable to be sewn back on.

Dad was still bitter about it ten years later; it had happened on Martine's eleventh birthday. From the moment he'd come home from hospital, she'd grown up captivated by the fact his hand was missing, fascinated by the stump of his wrist, the way the skin puckered like an arsehole. He'd had a graft, a slice of his bum cheek used to patch him up. Martine hadn't seen *that* scar, of course she hadn't, but one day soon, she might well have to look at it. With Dad clearly unwell now and refusing to see a doctor, she reckoned he'd end up bedridden with some kind of lung disorder. Maybe he had cancer. She'd have to care for him, wipe his backside or whatever. Turn him in bed so he didn't get those sores she'd seen on Google. Ring for an ambulance when shit got bad and she couldn't cope anymore, but she'd have to hide a couple of things before she did that. Couldn't have anyone in authority poking about and adding two and two.

It would help if Mam hadn't buggered things up, getting herself into a life of deception. Martine wouldn't have to cook and clean, sort the bills, be there for Dad, although saying that, what else would she be doing other than going to work then sitting in her room night after night, a loner?

Mam had gone funny on them three years ago; she couldn't stand Dad's depression any longer, his rancid moods, and another man had taken Dad's place. Martine had known all about it — she'd followed her like Dad had asked, waiting outside the Bode Hotel for her mother to come back out, her hair not quite the same sleek style as when she'd gone in. A button not done up at the top of her blouse. Her cerise lipstick gone.

Signs of an affair.

The lipstick had been her downfall. She hadn't used it for years, then suddenly had; she hadn't left the house of an evening for years, then suddenly had . . . And Dad knew then, he *knew* what she was up to.

"She's got a pink mouth, Mart. She's got high heels on. Dirty woman."

From then on, after Mam had been confronted, Martine was his eyes in an outside world he no longer wanted to be a part of; he disliked the stares, the comments, the pity that a missing hand brought. She became his tool, one he manipulated to fulfil his desire to get his own back. That business with his hand had warped his mind, and Mam copping off with another bloke had turned him further, showing Martine a side of him she'd always known was there, a side he'd previously only shown to her, coming fully out to play when . . . when *that* incident had gone on and someone they called Guest had come to visit shortly after.

A relieved Martine had rejoiced at not having to hide herself anymore either; pretending to Mam she was a good girl had worn thin. A burden, keeping Dad's secrets, her secrets — *Mam must never know who we are*, the mantra Dad had always chanted. They still had to cover up for outsiders, but in their house, they could say whatever they liked now. Dad said if Mam heard them discussing things, tough. Anyway, her mother had kept her opinions to herself for three years, Martine had seen to that.

She didn't mind doing this for him, standing in bushes or behind fences, down alleys. It gave her something to do of an evening. A purpose. Life had been getting boring anyway since . . . well, Martine's first foray into properly embracing her dark side. So at least she had stuff to do instead of going over and over her first unlawful act. Google said people did that. Psychopaths and whatever. Imagined their crime a million times, did it, then afterwards, thought about that a million times, too, before going out and doing it all over again.

She jolted out of her thoughts. Her boss, Gary Cuttersby, stood from the sofa and walked towards the window. Martine held her breath, same as she had the first time he'd done this. Back then, she'd shit herself, thinking he'd spotted her head poking out of the elders, that he'd recognised her, but it soon became clear, night after night, he rose at nine o'clock to look outside, tip his head back and examine the sky.

Tonight, streaks of pink candyfloss sat on top of the grey-blue remnants of the summer day, and above that, darker pink topped by bruise purple. She wasn't in the right location to see the sun going down, the top of its head staining the horizon orange. She had to be on the moors to get a good view of that — a majestic vista, one she only witnessed when she walked out there to take a bunch of flowers and place it on the grass. When it rose, she'd have to be at Scudderton Cove to get the best effect.

If Gary wanted to see the stars, he'd have to wait for a while. He remained at the window, pushing it open wider. The house must be stuffy, the fan doing fuck all except waft hot air about. He closed his eyes. Breathed deeply. Perhaps tuned Sue out, who chattered in the background.

Martine didn't have to cock an ear. Sue's voice was loud tonight, the woman animated, her hands flying up to emphasise her point.

"Oh, I've just remembered!" she said.

"Hmm?" Gary frowned.

She's disturbing his thinking time.

"Betty Tavers," Sue said.

The old bag at work. She gives me the creeps. I've seen her on the moors when I put the flowers down.

". . . and I said to her, 'Will you *stop* doing that?' Of course, she didn't, she carried on after I walked away, but that's no surprise. The woman's a law unto herself, doesn't like someone younger telling her what to do — for example, me. Can't stand the fact I have authority now. She's as old as the bloody hills and going deaf, too, so should she *really* be on our books? Is there any way you can move her out of cutting and back to sewing? She's winding up the other workers. At least in sewing, the machines make enough noise to drown her mutterings out. She's taken to spouting rubbish, some witchy business — did you know she dances on the moor when there's a full moon? I mean, for goodness sake, who *does* that? I've half a mind to phone the police next time she's out there. She'll get done for indecent exposure because she flounces about *naked*."

"Hmm," Gary said.

"She's what, seventy-one? Past retirement, so why have we kept her on?"

"Hmm."

"Is that a yes, or are you humming to make me think you're listening?"

"Hmm."

They always talked like this. Any minute now, if they stayed true to form, one of their children would pipe up. Put in their two-penn'orth, as Dad would say, but Martine called it winding their parents up, their sole aim to get a rise out of them. The Cuttersby twins weren't the most pleasant. One of them, Jack, gadded around as though he owned the town, the brat. He probably had an inflated sense of his own importance because his father employed so many residents. Cuttersby Clothing was going strong, had been since the day Gary had taken over the failing business from his drunk father, a year after the Bad Time.

That was the only issue Martine had about this particular part of the plan. Gary hadn't been in charge when it had happened, so it wasn't really his fault. But he'd been in the cutting room, so . . . yes, he *could* be classed as to blame. Being caught up with someone else, wedged into a corner, meant he hadn't witnessed the accident, but he *should* have — could have prevented it if he hadn't been so distracted by a pair of tits. His father, long dead from his liver packing up from too much brandy, was the man who'd overseen the business as a whole, so it wasn't like they could kill *him*, was it?

Dad wasn't bothered about that, though. Apparently, Gary still had to suffer. Dad liked to keep some things close to his chest, and she followed his orders regardless, but "sins of the father" had been mentioned once or twice, and she kind of got the gist.

Someone had to pay, so why not Gary?

* * *

The Back Garden

Martine stood by the yucca in the back garden, her heart thrumming away, the thuds seeming to inflate her taut chest, the drumbeat a pounding rhythm in her ears. Tonight was different to all the others. She had her tool bag, a beige fabric one her father had made. He'd taught himself to use the Singer in the back of their living room one-handed, and the bag had turned out lovely. Compartments, they were key. One side for each of her tools, a large one opposite for when she'd used them — that section was lined with plastic sheeting, easily wiped or replaced, no trace of her work left behind. Work, that was what she called it. Better than naming it what it was: breaking the law.

Gary and the twins had gone upstairs around ten. Sue had sat alone ever since, looking at a blank TV screen for a while. All that time, Martine stared through the patio doors at the back of her head, then Sue put a film on. *Love Actually*, Sue's all-time favourite. Martine, well aware of the pattern, only had to wait until Emma Thompson cried, then Sue switched off, wiping her tears, trotting off to the kitchen to open the tall cupboard and take the watering can out. Fill it. Wipe her cheeks again.

Gary had been a naughty boy, so did the scene from the film hit a raw nerve? People gossiped at the factory, and Martine soaked it all up. She worked in the pressing department, ironing the finished products using the big machine with the two hotplates. She'd thought about putting someone's head in there and closing it as much as she could while her victim screamed in pain from the burn. That would get her into trouble, though.

She shrank back into the darkness, wedging herself into a corner created by the edge of the house and the high wooden fence separating the garden from the one next door. No light from inside reached her, no chance of it revealing she was there, watching — a creeper.

Sue hauled the patio door aside and stepped into the garden. Took a deep breath, one that shuddered, a result of pent-up emotion. Was she imagining Gary in the material storeroom, kissing one of the young women against the wall? That was apparently what he did, sampling the newbies. If they agreed to more than a bit of slap and tickle, he took them into the small office.

He'd never done that with Martine. Maybe she wasn't pretty enough, but like Dad had said, Gary wouldn't dare add fuel to the fire. Couldn't risk feeling Martine up when her father was being paid off.

Sue turned on the hose and watered the grass. Martine could just do with standing beneath that spray. She was hot in her all-black suit beneath her leggings and T-shirt, sweat beading at her temples.

Sue wound the hose around the holder on the wall, picked up the watering can and headed for the yucca. Martine wondered why the woman didn't use the hose for the plants when she was out in the dark and no one could see her; it seemed silly to traipse in and out of the house with the can. She held her breath for the sixteen seconds it took for Sue to water the yucca — *she's so close I can smell her.* Next, Sue went to the fence and, as usual, reached halfway down, then had to go inside for a refill. Martine waited until Sue had watered the bottom — another trip inside — then half of the opposite flowerbed, her back to Martine.

Time to make her move.

Martine picked up the tool bag in her latex-gloved hand, gripped the weapon with the other. Glanced into the living room to ensure Gary hadn't got up. Walked over to the kitchen window, ultra-aware that if Sue looked her way she'd see a silhouette, the light from inside behind her. Martine would appear as a man — she'd scraped her hair into a low ponytail and bulked herself out with a padded suit Dad had made for her.

Sue wouldn't be alive to give a description, but someone else might.

Head down, empty watering can held beside her, Sue made for the patio doors. Martine slowly lowered her bag to the ground then took a long step towards her, hammer swinging, the claw end disappearing into the left eye socket. No scream, just a strange growl of shock. She fell backwards onto the grass, both hands over her face, a low moan seeping into the night.

Why wasn't she screeching? Martine had prepared herself for that, anticipated laughing at the sound, and Sue had denied her the pleasure, the thrill of having to get the job done quickly then run in case Gary or a neighbour came to investigate.

Angry at her imaginings not matching reality, Martine stormed over, straddled her but remained standing, and clasped the hammer in a two-handed grip. Lifted it high. Brought it down, the claw end entering the top of Sue's head.

Sue's hands left her face. Brushed Martine's shins then landed on the grass. Martine bent, wrenched the hammer out — it took a lot of effort as it had got stuck — then hammered the other eye. Sue wouldn't be able to see anything bad now. The pale swath of light from inside highlighted blood and some mush on the silver prongs. Martine wiped the tool on Sue's blouse then embedded the claw in the grass to get as much gunge off as she could. She inspected the hammer, deemed it clean enough and smiled.

"Sorry, Sue," she whispered. "You were an all right sort, but Dad wants Gary to suffer. Maybe this'll take your Jack down a peg an' all. He really is a self-righteous prick."

Martine returned to her bag and placed the hammer in the plastic-lined compartment. Took out her phone and snapped some final pictures of Sue. These were so different from the usual, where she sat on the sofa watching the telly. Maybe someone would spot the flash and come out now, confront her so she could get the thrill she'd missed out on earlier when Sue hadn't screamed.

No one came, and with images taken from all angles, Martine pressed the sole of her boot onto the grass, twisting her foot from side to side to make things difficult for the coppers, adding more of her weight so it made a skewed impression on the damp earth beneath. Two sizes larger. Men's boots not women's.

It was the small details that made all the difference.

"All gone now," she whispered. "Sue is dead."

She left the garden. Clomped down the little fenced alley between houses. She smirked on the pavement — no one at any windows that she could see — then made her merry way home in Mam's old car, eager to tell Dad she'd been a bad girl.

The best bad girl.

CHAPTER TWO

3a Robottom Street — Mollengate

Trying to get a full night's sleep when living on a main road was a challenge. Robottom Street, the busy thoroughfare of Mollengate, a village just outside the northern coastal town of Scudderton, had traffic coming along at all hours thanks to a slip road nearby that led to the A170. Granted, there were fewer vehicles than in the day, but enough that a lorry trundled past every five minutes, sometimes one after the other, as if a fleet had blown in, their engines too loud, intruding on what should be a silent home.

DI Carol Wren stared at her bedroom ceiling, asking herself for the fifth — or maybe the hundredth — time whether it was better to get up at 3.20 a.m. than lie there pondering the whys and wherefores of life, driving herself around the bend while she was at it.

There was a murder lull in Scudderton at the moment, killer criminals perhaps taking a breather, enjoying the summer, so she'd had a relatively peaceful month with her team, taking on other serious crimes instead. She reckoned they were due another dead body, though.

To stop herself tempting fate, she rolled over onto her side and closed her eyes. Concentrated on the sound of her breathing, forcing it slower, deeper, drifting towards that heavy moment where she'd sink into sleep. Imagined her life with a permanent man in it, a boyfriend or husband, and smiled at the futility of that. Her past relationships had crashed and burned, all of the blokes citing she worked too hard, for too long, and they felt neglected. Whinge, whinge.

She was better off alone anyway. Had a few weird quirks no partner ought to put up with. Mind you, she'd got a handle on one of them — untidiness to the point she might have been taken for a hoarder. She'd had a week off a while back, visited the tip umpteen times, let go of some stuff that held emotionally crippling value and brought on tears if she looked at them — crap from an equally crappy childhood she'd rather forget. She'd even bought some throw cushions and new bedding. Got used to the pick-up-as-you-go mentality.

Her mind had cleared somewhat along with the flat.

But a permanent fella? No, she saved herself the hassle of a proper relationship by visiting a certain someone to scratch the type of itch down below that crept up every so often — she didn't need *that* much in her busy life, so her current behaviour suited her fine. Besides, she had her work partner, DS Dave Waite, if she wanted to chat outside of work. His wife had kicked him out recently — she was of the whinge-whinge variety — so he had more time to spend with Carol.

They were a pair of sad sacks to be fair, moping into their drinks in The Lord down the road here. They ate there a couple evenings, too, but sometimes Carol had him over at her upstairs flat, or she nipped to his. Funnily enough, he lived on the ground floor in her block. He'd moved there once his missus had stated her intention of keeping their four-bed in Scudderton. The village of Mollengate was far enough away that husband and wife wouldn't bump into one another at the shops — like Carol, Dave stuck to the local

Co-op, and if they were going out on a bender, they parked their backsides in The Lord so they didn't have far to stagger home, plus the villagers took no notice of coppers bending their elbows and laughing inappropriately at the dark side of their jobs.

Outsiders didn't get how death could be funny.

She drifted again, inching towards sleep, and lost herself in the black void in front of her closed eyelids that reminded her of the infinity of space. It sparked her to imagine stars, nebulas, a red planet in the distance, growing bigger as she sped towards it.

* * *

She woke to the sound of her phone going off. Took a moment to figure out if it was her alarm, which she'd set for midday, or a call. Old-fashioned ringing — a work call, then. She fumbled on her bedside cabinet, pushing herself up onto one elbow, cursing the fact it was Saturday and she was supposed to get the whole weekend off, as was her small team.

Fuck it.

She pressed the icon to answer. "What can I do for you?"

The daytime desk sergeant, Joy Parsonage, chuckled. "Did you think you were getting a lie-in?"

"I'd hoped so, yes. Big night with Dave in The Lord last night. What bloody time is it?"

"Seven-fifteen."

"Balls. What's happened?"

"A murder. The wife of the bloke who owns Cuttersby Clothing. You're needed at fifty-nine Wexford Close, Scudderton. Woman's in her forties. Back garden. Rib's already there. I tried phoning you earlier . . ."

I must have slept through it.

She thought of the shaven-headed pathologist, who went by the name Rib Shears. He was fond of telling people he used that tool enough in post-mortems and it was better than calling himself Scalpel. Carol privately wondered why

16

he couldn't just go by his normal name like everyone else, but it took all sorts. He rubbed her up the wrong way more often than not, and no matter how hard she tried to remain calm, he always succeeded in pissing her off. On purpose.

She sat up, her head gooey from one too many lemon gins. The room spun. "Right. SOCO en route, I take it?"

"Probably already there by now. The DCI actioned it — he was in my vicinity when the call came in. You know how he likes to poke his nose in."

"Don't I just." *He's new, letting everyone know he's there, in charge, yet he doesn't want to know about getting his hands dirty.* "Who was first on the scene?"

"Pitson and May."

"Okay, I'll get hold of Dave and be there in about twenty minutes."

"I wouldn't rush," Joy said. "It's not like the woman's going anywhere, is it?"

"Have you been taking bad joke lessons from Rib by any chance?"

Joy tittered. "Have a nice day!"

Carol stared at her phone for a few seconds then called Dave, who took a while to answer.

"Fuck," he said. "Don't tell me, the weekend off is a no-go."

"Hmm. Murder."

"Jesus. Give me ten."

"I'll give you fifteen. I need a shower and some toast."

"Make me some while you're at it."

She laughed. "Cheeky bastard. Jam or Marmite?"

* * *

59 Wexford Close

Protective suits on, masks over their mouths and nose, hoods up, Carol and Dave stood side by side on evidence steps placed on a yellow-and-pink chequered patio. A tent had been erected over the body, the front flaps pinned open. Officers worked in the surrounding garden, uniforms out the front going door to door.

Carol stared at a watering can on its side to the left. Green. Plastic. Forlorn.

Dropped? Thrown when she'd been attacked?

Had the woman been watering her flowers early on before the sun came up? Had she been hit from behind or the front? Carol glanced around the tent to the bottom of the garden. A flowerbed, raised, a stubby Cotswold stone wall keeping everything tidy. It ran around three sides, an upside-down U, the ends abutting the patio that spanned the width of the house.

To her right, in the corner close to the patio doors, stood a large yucca tree which was so high it should, by rights, belong down south on the coast, not somewhere like this. The closet beach was two miles away at Scudderton Cove.

She pulled her gaze away from it and her mind from sitting on the sand, which she'd intended to do this afternoon. Scarborough. A visit to North Bay, quieter than Cove, with its chalet-lined promenade and altogether more serene feel, away from South Bay, chock-full of arcades, shops, her favourite chippy. Castle Headland to the right, a visible speck in the distance from Cove. She'd planned to sit and watch the sea, but that had gone down the pan with the ringing of her phone earlier.

Rib, inside the tent on his knees on a step beside the body, peered into the victim's messy eye sockets.

Carol nudged Dave with her elbow. "Suppose we ought to go in there, then."

"I've got beer tummy," he said. "The blood . . . can't guarantee I'll stay inside."

"Don't you dare puke."

They entered the tent via the pathway of evidence steps, a halogen in the corner lighting up the gross sight on the grass. Poor woman. Who the hell imagined they'd end up like this? A yellow evidence marker with a number five on it perched on the grass to the right of the victim's shoulder.

Rib's slow drone of a voice poked into the early-morning heat. "Hammer, I reckon. The sort with two prongs, the curved type. If you look closely at those gaping holes of the eye sockets, you'll see where the curve went downwards, towards the underside of the cheekbones."

"I don't *want* to look closely," Carol said.

"Dave?" Rib smiled.

"Um, no ta. Don't want to bring my toast back up."

"Pair of babies. Right, the same end entered the top of the head, penetrated the brain. I should say that fucking hurt, but lights out would have been quick if the head wallop happened first, so she wouldn't have felt the ones in the eyes. If it was the other way around, can you *imagine* that? Ouch. Your eyes are killing you, then you get a whack in the head. Hardly fair, is it?"

"She must have screamed. Someone will have heard that," Dave said.

Carol sighed. "Maybe they did and that's why she was found so early."

Rib beamed one of his I know more than you smiles. "Err, no, it didn't happen around the time the triple-nine call was made. Rigor has set in, so at the very least, she died more than three hours ago. Based on the rigidity so far, I'd estimate around midnight, but her temperature is buggered up because of how hot the weather is, so . . . going by those three hours instead, would anyone be awake, as a rule, at four a.m. to hear her scream?"

"I was awake around three," Carol said.

"Not likely to hear her all the way over in Mollengate, though, are you, Bird?" Rib rolled his eyes then grinned, clearly knowing she hated it when he called her Bird instead of Wren or Carol.

"I didn't mean *that*," she said. "Just stating I was awake, so other people could also have been awake. Insomnia affects a lot of people, you know."

Rib brushed her words aside. "Whatever. Didn't you get the memo that I'm a facetious bastard? I swear you did . . ."

19

Carol suppressed the urge to give him what for. "If she died around midnight, it's more likely someone heard something." She glanced at Dave. "We'll use the timeframe of between midnight and six for now." She switched her attention back to Rib. "Owt else apparent before we speak to the husband?"

"Entry into the eyes from the front, same with the head."

"How can you tell?" Dave asked. "Regarding the head, I mean."

"The curve I mentioned." Rib winked. "It goes towards the forehead. If she'd been attacked from behind, it would have pointed to the back of the skull."

Dave's blush crept past the top of his mask. "Obviously. Sorry, not thinking straight."

"That'll be the booze-up you two had last night in The Lord," Rib said. "Friend of mine saw you. Recognised you, Bird, from the newspapers about your last big case, Miss Celebrity Detective that you are."

She stopped herself blurting that what his friend saw was none of his fucking business — and that her celebrity status was a hindrance; but if she admitted the latter, Rib would keep mentioning it. "No idea why your mate would give a shit what we get up to."

"He doesn't."

"Then why bother telling you?"

"Said it in passing, didn't he? He'd nipped into the pub to pick up some pork scratchings before coming to mine. Said, 'I saw that Wren woman knocking one back.' You know the kind of thing. Bullshit conversation."

"Bullshit is right," she muttered. "Owt else?"

"Nope, he didn't say more than that."

"I meant to do with this body." She gritted her teeth. Told herself to get a grip and not let Rib knob her off. Not ask him whether he lived in Mollengate now, too — he must do if his mate had gone into The Lord. That was all she needed, to bump into Rib in the Co-op, him making quips about dead bodies while holding a packet of lamb chops.

"I'll know more when she's on the table. Her husband and kids are over the road at her mother's, by the way, so good luck with that. Lots of wailing, by all accounts."

"I'm not surprised," Dave said. "What with a family member being dead."

Carol internally cheered his sarcasm, not to mention reminding Rib that wailing was par for the bloody course in these situations. But Rib didn't view things like they did.

"Death is nowt but a transition," he spouted, "from one realm to another. Hopefully, she's sunning herself poolside in Heaven, knocking back a drink of her own."

Carol glared at him. "Piss off, Rib, and do what you do best — dealing with dead bodies."

"Oh," he said, "but I also do something else best — winding you up." His grin spread. "Far more than you'd like."

"Her blouse." Carol pointed. "Looks like blood's been wiped on it."

Rib shook his head as though she didn't have much up top. "Weapon cleaned on it, do you think?"

"That's what I was suggesting, yes. I thought I was quite clear."

He jabbed a finger towards evidence marker five. "I'd say the killer also used the hammer to kill the grass, but that would be silly. Based on there being blood on some blades, plus some grey matter and two holes, they hit the grass to get the rest of the mess off it."

"So I doubt we'll find the murder weapon tossed into the flowerbeds, then."

"I expect they took it with them. Also, I need a marker to put there." He pointed to the left of number five. "Boot print. I'll get SOCO to do a cast."

"Thanks." Carol groaned internally. The results would likely take a while to come back from that. No immediate help.

"Bird, do you have a hangover by any chance?"

Rather than answer Rib, she stepped out of the tent. Glanced at SOCOs drifting around the garden, searching for clues that might not exist if the killer was the meticulous sort. She sensed Rib in the tent behind her, waiting for her to bite, and for once, she wouldn't give him the satisfaction. Instead, she waited for Dave to join her and jerked her head at him: *We need to speak to the husband.*

He nodded.

They had work to do, and fucking about here while Rib tried to pull her into verbal sparring was a waste of time.

She'd rather chew glass.

CHAPTER THREE

62 Wexford Close

Gary's head pounded. He'd cried, of course he had, and this had set the headache off, but now his mother-in-law's wailing had taken it to a new level. Migraine territory. Flora was shrill at the best of times, but add in the murder of her daughter, and you had a hotpot of screeching that had Gary fighting the need to slap her face, bring her out of her self-pity party and think of someone else for a change. Like her grandsons, currently sitting at the table in the dining room off the far end of the lounge, easily seen through the doorway, heads bent over their phones while they played some game app or other. Gary had suggested it to keep their minds occupied, although in their shoes, he didn't think he'd be able to concentrate.

He laughed at himself. *Who am I to cast judgement on Flora? It's not like I'm exactly the selfless sort, is it?*

Finding Sue had been appalling. His worst nightmare. As he'd said to PC Alan Pitson, who stood by the window with one hand on Flora's shoulder, her sitting on the recliner doing her wailing, it had been surreal. Like, he'd *seen* Sue there on the grass, but his mind hadn't accepted it for the true horror it was. Thanks to a gentle reprimand from Pitson, Gary now knew he could have bodged up the crime scene by rushing over there, kneeling beside her, trying to shake her awake, attempting to revive her, but there was nothing he could do about that now. What was done was done, and to be brutally honest, he didn't give one shiny shite. All he'd been interested in was doing CPR, despite her chest being harder than usual, not much give in it.

PC Pitson had said something about rigor mortis.

Despite his wife having gaping holes in her eye sockets and another in her head, it was the blood and a glob of what he now thought might have been brain that had told him there was no coming back from this. He'd run inside and grabbed his phone off the kitchen worktop where he'd left it — God, how he'd like to rewind time to when he'd placed it there, pre-discovery, going to the kettle to flick it on, glancing out of the window, *not* seeing her; she'd have been in bed in the spare room — his snoring woke her in the night — and he'd have taken a cup of tea up to her, saying, "Wake up, sleepyhead."

All in an alternate universe.

Instead, he'd dialled 999, his hands shaking. The tears had come when he'd said, "My wife. Help me, please, help me. She's . . . she's dead."

Reality had hit, proper reality, and he'd bent over, heaving, an inner voice chirping in his ear, his mind selfishly going to how quickly he could fill her position at work, how the business would suffer without her there as she'd been more of a manager than him lately. Then he'd scrubbed that away, ashamed, and thought of their sons, Jack and Joseph, the kids they'd never thought they'd have — twins. IVF had come through for them, and while Gary hadn't been faithful — Sue spent *far* too much time wrapped up in the boys to give him the attention he needed, craved — he *had* loved her.

The person on the end of the phone had stayed on the line with him, asking questions, assuring him someone was on the way. Gary had gone out into the garden to wait, unlatching the gate like the woman told him to, using the sleeve of his pyjama top per her advice. He'd stared down the little alley, willing a police car to appear at the end, parking on the road, but it had taken fifteen minutes for PC Pitson and another officer to arrive, and all the while, the woman on the phone had talked to him.

Now, Gary couldn't remember what she'd said.

Pitson's colleague had checked Sue, stayed with her, and Pitson had told Gary to wake the boys, established Flora lived opposite, then advised Gary to take some clean clothing with him as the pyjamas would be needed as evidence — and to leave via the front door so the kids didn't see their mother like *that*. Pitson had assured him someone would take photos of his bloodied hands and acquire scrapings from beneath his fingernails later — maybe to scare Gary into thinking he thought he was a suspect — and had gone on to say that perhaps DI Carol Wren, who would be arriving shortly, would allow that to be done at Flora's instead of the station.

"It'll depend what side of the bed she's got out of," Pitson had said. "She bends the rules if she's in a good mood."

I'd rather go to the station. Anything to get out of this house.

Flora let out a humdinger of a screech, staring at the ceiling, her eyes bulging. "I can't . . . *breathe*. Oh God, I can't breathe. I need to see my baby . . . This is all some big mistake. It should never have happened . . ."

"Oh, shut up, Flora, for fuck's sake," Gary muttered. "The boys . . . If you've got an ounce of compassion in you for someone other than yourself, please, keep it together for them."

She glared at him. "Like *you've* got compassion? Like *you've* kept it together? Your marriage?"

Irritation prickled. "That's irrelevant at the minute."

"*Everything's* relevant," she seethed, her top-knot bun wobbling. "Every. Thing."

"Let's calm down, eh?" Pitson patted Flora's shoulder then checked out of the window. He headed for the living room door. "DI Wren's here, and she'll be wanting to get to the heart of the matter, not listen to any spats, so you'd be well advised to keep a lid on your emotions."

Is he allowed to say stuff like that? Sounds a bit rude.

The bell rang, and Pitson went off to open the door, his low voice filtering in, indistinct words, him probably telling Wren this was a hotbed of feelings and unstable people: "Watch this lot, they're on the edge."

Flora narrowed her eyes at Gary and whispered, "You'd better come clean. It could be one of those bitches who's done this. Jealous. Wanting my Sue out of the way." *Way* went up an octave, and she slapped her hands over her face and sobbed into them.

Bitches. Sue must have found out. Must have known. She shared most things with her mother, much to Gary's annoyance, and now he'd have Flora on his back, possibly causing grief on top of the grief he was already experiencing, grief he was battling to keep at bay for the sake of his sons.

But did Sue know about the other thing? The worst thing?

He flicked his gaze over to the boys. They had earbuds in, fingers dancing over their screens. Jack looked intent on what he was playing, focused only on that, but Joseph swiped at one cheek, drying his tears. The earbuds had possibly saved Gary's blushes, but what if Joseph had just inserted them and turned the game sounds off? He could have heard what Flora said.

Fucking woman. It should be her who's dead, not Sue.

What if the boys find out what I've done?

They'll hate me.

PC Pitson returned with two officers. He moved to the window again and laced his hands in front of him. Did the man not have any ambition to be more than a PC? Was it too late for him to climb the ladder? Or did he enjoy being hands-on?

The woman officer — middle-aged, sandy-blonde hair, her face weathered, perhaps by life itself, not time spent in the elements — stepped farther inside and sat on the sofa closest to Gary, while the man, a thickset sort in a grey suit, remained in the doorway, leaning on the jamb, arms folded, a notebook and pen in one hand.

"I'm DI Carol Wren. Firstly, I'm incredibly sorry for your loss, Mr Cuttersby, it must have been a terrible shock. Are you up to talking?"

Gary got the sense he had no choice, that even if he was in the same state as Flora, who sniffled loudly, *breathed* loudly, he'd be expected to spill his guts. "Yes, but can we close that door? My sons . . . This is awful for them."

Is that really why I want the door shut?

"We're just waiting on the FLO to arrive, and she can go in there, and yes, the door can be closed." Wren smiled.

Gary had no idea what she was talking about. "FLO?"

"Family liaison officer. Her name's Whitney Faulds. Lovely woman. She'll remain with you throughout the investigation, what with you having children. She's very well-trained when it comes to kids, so your sons will get all the support they need, as will you and . . ." She turned to Flora. "Apologies, I don't know your name."

"Flora. Flora Troy. I'm Sue's mother."

"I'm sorry for your loss."

"Believe me, so am I. It should have been *him*!" Flora sent Gary a scathing glance and took up crying again.

Wren appeared annoyed by it, the crying, or maybe she was working out her strategy; Flora blubbing could hold things up. "PC Pitson, would you mind taking Flora into the kitchen? I'm sure Gary could do with a cuppa."

"But I want to stay," Flora wailed. "She's my child, I have every right . . ."

Wren smiled kindly, although it appeared a strain to do so. "Please, I'd like to speak to Gary alone for the moment."

Gary chalked one up to himself in the battle they'd entered from the day he'd come into Sue's life. The war between him and his mother-in-law had worsened as time had gone by. Flora walked bent over, clutching her stomach in a hug, for sympathy he was sure, and PC Pitson led her from the room and down the hallway.

The doorbell rang again.

Wren sighed. "Can you get that for me, Dave?" She smiled at Gary. "Forgive me, I should have introduced my partner. DS Dave Waite. We'll do our level best to find out who did this to your wife. Ah." She stood and walked across to a woman who'd appeared at the doorway, Waite behind her. "Gary, this is Whitney. Whitney, this is Gary and his sons . . ."

"Jack and Joseph," Gary supplied.

This had all happened so quickly, he supposed Wren hadn't had time to get up to speed with who everyone was. He wouldn't hold it against her. He'd been in similar situations at the factory. Fights broke out, arguments, and he didn't know half of the new people he'd employed recently, just recognised their faces, so if he had to sort something out, he usually pointed at them rather than embarrass himself by revealing he hadn't a bloody clue who they were.

"Hello, Gary." Whitney smiled. Sad and wistful. "Would you like me to sit with your sons?"

"Please."

"I won't question them," she said. "But if they're inclined to talk, do I have your permission to chat with a PC present? An appropriate adult as they're under eighteen. Or do you have someone else you'd rather be there?"

Gary shook his head. There was no way he wanted Flora involved, poisoning them with her spite, and *his* mother wasn't mentally fit enough to be appropriate for anything except babbling her nonsense to the nurses in the care home. "A PC is fine, thank you."

"It'll be low-key chatter anyroad," Whitney said. "I understand they were asleep so . . . Best to keep the pressure off for now, you know? Too much at once . . ." She grimaced. "Could be detrimental."

"I understand." Gary nodded. "That's very kind of you."

Whitney glanced over her shoulder, past Waite. A woman PC hung around by the front door. "You're with me."

Whitney walked towards the dining room, the PC following, who closed the door once they were inside. It was the officer who'd turned up with Piston earlier, the one who'd stayed with Sue.

Wren retook her seat. "That's PC Helen May. I apologise again, we must seem unprofessional. The truth is, we rushed to the garden, viewed your wife, then came over. Information has been sparse as all the uniforms are doing house-to-house enquiries, but still, that's no excuse. I should have got up to date with the scene sergeant, but my main aim was to be here with you."

Gary waved her excuses away. "I get it. You're human."

Will they view me as human if they discover what I've done? Or will they think I'm a bastard?

"Thank you," she said and glanced at Waite, who stood straight and held his notebook in front of him. "Okay, talk me through things, starting with last night."

"Last night?" Gary frowned.

"So I can get a picture of Sue's final movements."

"Right. Um, right. Okay, we sat and had dinner about half six — she'd made pizza and chips as it was a Friday; it's normally healthy stuff on all the other days."

"Were Jack and Joseph present?"

"Yes. It was just the four of us. Flora comes over for a roast on Sundays." *Much as I hate it.* "I helped with the dishwasher and kitchen clean-up while the boys had a shower — it's movie night on Fridays, as a family. Sue insists on that." He winced. "Insisted."

"Don't worry. If it helps to talk in the present tense, do so. What film did you watch?"

"*Shrek.*" He laughed, a sob catching in his throat. "One of Sue's favourites. About three-quarters of the way through, she must have let her mind wander, as she got a bee in her bonnet about a woman from the factory."

Wren perked up. "Problems there?"

"Only that the woman — Betty Tavers, her name is — likes to dance on the moors with no clothes on. But the main

29

bugbear for Sue is that Betty's distracting other employees with her stories. She's apparently taken to acting like some old witch, spouting nonsense about sage and whatever, and people are getting spooked by it."

"So it's nowt that would result in what's happened."

"Good God, no. I'd planned to just have a word with Betty, get her to pack it in, and move her back into sewing so no one can hear her over the machines. She's seventy-something, no harm to anyone."

"So what happened next?"

"The film ended. Jack and Joseph went upstairs to play on their Xboxes. Some game where they can play together against others online — you'd have to ask them what that is. I went to bed, as Sue wanted to watch *Love Actually*, her ultimate favourite. I've seen it too many times to count, so I left her to it. Now I wish I'd stayed downstairs . . ."

"Why would she have been in the garden during the night?"

"She usually goes out there about eleven to water the plants — it's been so hot, she waits until it's cooled down, then she does it again around six a.m. She loves her back garden."

Wren smiled. "We have a tentative timeline — she died after eleven p.m. and prior to the six o'clock she'd have gone out to water the plants this morning. Could she have perhaps fallen asleep on the sofa, woke, then gone out to do the eleven p.m. watering much later than usual?"

"I suppose so, but owt past two a.m., and I think she'd have just left it until six, doubled up the water. Although saying that, I really can't call it. Who's to say whether she even looked at the time?"

"So you didn't hear her come to bed?"

"No, I slept right through until sixish, turned over, and she wasn't there."

"Is that the norm?"

"I assumed she'd taken herself off into the spare room." A blush heated his face. "I snore. It drives her mad." *Or maybe*

30

she definitely found out what I've been doing and couldn't stand to sleep next to me.

"Have you noticed anyone hanging around in the street lately?"

"No more than usual. People coming and going to work . . . no, it's all been the same." It had, hadn't it? He searched his mind and found nothing but normality there — or hadn't he taken any notice because his head had been stuffed with the new contract he was on his way to securing? Clothes for a major high-street store. More profit. *Not to mention the other thing.*

"Okay. Now tell me what happened after you got up."

He relived it all in the telling, seeing it in the air like a movie, not stopping to think, otherwise he'd cry, and he didn't want to do that in front of these two. He brought them up to this moment, leaving out Flora's accusations — *It could be one of those bitches who's done this!* — worrying that she'd voice her suspicions again when Wren and Waite spoke to her next.

While Wren got up and paced, Waite scribbling in his notebook, Gary's mind wandered.

Where was that cup of tea Pitson had been sent to make? Gary's throat was dry, and it was painful to swallow. How were the boys faring? Had they seen anything out of the window? Heard their mother screaming? They'd said they hadn't earlier, but with them being teenagers, who knew if they were hiding something.

A cold prickle of fear danced down his spine.

Had one of *them* killed Sue? No, that was ridiculous. If his sons killed anyone, it would be him.

But another person in his life, *they* might have done it.

Fuck. *Fuck* it!

31

CHAPTER FOUR

62 Wexford Close

PC Pitson sat with Gary in the lounge. Carol and Dave perched at the kitchen table with Flora. This was where they'd find out whether the Cuttersby marriage had any cracks. Carol didn't suspect Gary — while he'd held his emotions in check, managing not to cry in front of them, she'd sensed him using all his strength to keep it together, possibly so his sons didn't hear him sobbing. This was a man used to presenting a poker face — he'd have to while running the clothing factory. He *had* been crying, though, evidenced by his red-rimmed, bloodshot eyes, and maybe he'd let rip tonight while he was alone.

How awful to find your wife dead in the back garden, then have to put your grief aside for the sake of others, keeping everything inside when you must want to scream. Even worse, sitting there with her dried blood on your hands and pyjamas.

Pitson should have got him to change out of them really, put them in an evidence bag. Maybe he hadn't felt it was appropriate to play it by the book when Gary and Flora were so upset. Carol would have to cover that up if it came to light, but she'd do her best to ensure it didn't.

Flora sniffled into a crumpled tissue. Offered Carol a scathing look. "Why are you here when you should be out there finding whoever did this?"

Carol smiled through her irritation. Why did most people ask that? Didn't they realise it wasn't as simple as haring around Scudderton in search of someone with a bloodied hammer? "How can we be out there before we have any information on who we need to search for? We have to question those closest to the victim first, gain some sense of who the deceased was, find out if there were tensions between Sue and her killer — if she'd argued with anyone recently, that kind of thing."

Flora lowered the tissue to her chest, her cheeks flushing. "Sorry. Yes, that makes sense. It just feels so wrong, us chatting while she . . . What *is* happening to her at the moment?"

"She'll remain in situ for a while, but don't worry, she's inside a tent. Forensic officers are there — they'll not only scour the garden but the house as well. Gary and the boys won't be going back there anytime soon."

Flora straightened her shoulders. "The boys can stay here, but Gary . . ."

Dave scribbled something in his pad.

Carol raised her eyebrows. "But Gary . . . ?"

"We don't get on. I find him overbearing. He snipes at me a lot. Sue said it's just his way, that he's a teddy bear underneath it all, but when all you've seen is a gruff, sarcastic man from the first time you met him, well, it's hard to believe he's got a soft side."

"Are you saying he's quick-tempered?" *Someone likely to strike out with the nearest thing to him, a hammer?*

"Not particularly, just sour. If you're asking if I think he's capable of doing . . . doing *that*, do you think I'd have him here in my house?"

"I suppose not." Carol hadn't found Gary sour, nor gruff or sarcastic, so she put Flora's view of him down to the fact Gary probably disliked her and vice versa. Some people just didn't gel. *Family dynamics. Sometimes utter bullshit.* "Why don't you two get along?"

"How do you know we *don't*?"

"From what you just said." And there it was, the reason Gary may well gripe at Flora. She was contrary, annoying. Sawing away at Carol's nerves.

"Well, I didn't think he was suitable for my Sue right from the off. Still don't. I'm not a fan of people who tell it like it is."

Carol almost choked on the hypocrisy. Maybe they clashed because they were birds of a feather? Or maybe Flora sensed Gary wasn't the type to put up with the likes of her, so she made out he wasn't a nice man to make herself feel better.

Flora went on, "She's due more than a man who . . . who doesn't cherish her as she deserves. She's wonderful, my girl, and it just about kills me inside when I see her worrying, upset, over something *he's* doing. After all she did, too, going through IVF when I had a sneaking suspicion it was *him* shooting blanks, not that *she* was the issue, like he'd insisted. They tried for years for a baby, and in the end, she chose to go private because going through all those tests with the NHS, well, she couldn't stand it. He agreed, probably so he didn't have to face the fact he's infertile."

"Did they use his sperm?"

"Of course they did."

"Then he isn't infertile."

Flora frowned. Must have realised how silly she'd sounded. "Whatever, he's a pig. Sue should leave him. Walk away and never look back."

She's forgotten her daughter's dead — just for a moment, she's gone back in time to before this happened. "In your opinion."

Flora bristled. "I'll have you know, Sue doesn't need someone who goes elsewhere."

Carol hid her spiked curiosity by getting up to flick the kettle on. "Goes elsewhere?"

"You know. Other women. One of his floozies could have done this. Killed her so she could have Gary all to herself. His money."

"Do you have proof of other women?" Carol busied herself with cups and teabags while the kettle rumbled, leaving Dave to watch the woman's expressions and make notes regarding them. This was a tactic they employed often — Carol acted casual, her back to the person so they let their guard down, didn't feel so stared at, inspected by the inspector, and more often than not, they let something slip. Something more than they'd originally intended.

"Not proof of the actual act, no, but Sue told me she suspects him of playing around. Girls at the factory."

"Girls?" Carol added sugar to each cup, her hackles rising as they always did when the word *girls* was used in those kinds of sentences. *We'd better not have a paedo on our hands.*

Flora cleared her throat. "Well, technically they'd be classed as women, but young ones. A few years older than his own sons, and that's just disgusting if you ask me. Eighteen-, nineteen-year-olds, wanting to have the boss's hands all over them."

"Hmm."

"Sounds a tad like cradle-snatching, or maybe he's having a midlife crisis." Flora sniffed again. "But I believe my daughter. There's no way she'd have come to me about something like that if it wasn't true."

Carol poured boiled water into the cups. "Why do you think she stayed with him if he's . . . seeing other people?"

"Because she loves him, thinks their marriage is worth saving." Flora chuffed out a wry laugh. "If I had my way, she'd leave him. Maybe then she wouldn't be *dead*."

A loud shriek followed, real life crashing back in for Flora, but Carol ignored it, leaving Dave to do the usual, probably stretching out a hand to hold hers or pat the back of it. She finished making the tea and passed the cups over, sitting as Dave pulled his arm away from Flora to scribble in his notebook.

"Any names?" Carol asked. "Of the women?"

"No. The majority are just flings according to my Sue, but the latest, she's got her claws into him. Here's where the proof comes in: Sue found hotel receipts that were nothing like those she files for the business — Gary goes away on conferences and to meetings, especially recently, what with the merger with that lot in London."

"Merger?"

"It's all hush-hush, but he's going to be supplying clothes for that trendy chain . . . I can't think what it's called now."

"Don't worry. So, about those receipts . . ."

Sue picked up her cup and blew on the tea. Sipped. Winced. She'd likely burned her tongue. "They're for a hotel not too far way. And if he's hidden them in his boxer shorts drawer and not the box folder, he's clearly planning to hand them to the accountant before Sue's done her usual with the books, so ordinarily she wouldn't be aware they exist. He's shagging the girl on the taxman's dime, because you can bet he'll put them through as expenses. He's sly; he'll be waiting to get the accountant on his own. Paul Gedds, a mate of his from old. Thick as bloody thieves, the pair of them."

"Which hotel?"

"Betterway, Runswick Bay. Officially, he only went to Runswick Bay once for work, some conference or other, and he didn't stay at Betterway, so why's he been going lately? Doesn't take much to work it out. Sue knows where all the conferences are, she's his dogsbody, so she knows damn well Runswick Bay hasn't been on the list for a good long while."

"Did Sue happen to mention the dates of when he stayed there?" Carol wanted a better understanding of how often Gary poked other people's fireplaces, if at all.

"Every fortnight on a Thursday. He's not in the factory on the Fridays after, but he's home by the evening as that's their family night. Movies and popcorn, that kind of thing."

"When do you think this started?"

"What, the movies? Ever since Jack and Joseph were old enough to watch."

"No, the alleged affair."

"The first receipt was for eight months ago."

"Okay, owt else you'd like to add to that?"

"No, just that he's a filthy pervert. A liar. I *hate* him."

They drank their tea in silence for a while, Flora letting her tears fall without wiping them away. She stared out of the window, perhaps seeing her daughter in her mind's eye, or maybe she imagined stabbing Gary.

"Other than the women, is there anyone else you can think of who may have wanted to kill Sue?" Carol leaned back and crossed her ankles. Cradled her tea on her chest, a move designed to inspire the feeling of safety in Flora, that Carol was someone she could confide in.

Flora flinched. "No. Sue's a lovely woman, wouldn't hurt a fly."

Many said that. The thing was, lovely people still had skeletons in their closets, folk who disliked them, and almost everyone had swatted a fly.

Carol eyed her. "So you're convinced it has something to do with Gary possibly having an affair?"

Flora barked a terse laugh. "There's no 'possibly' about it. He's dipping his wick, I'm telling you. Dirty bastard."

* * *

Carol and Dave swapped places with Pitson again, who'd shaken his head to Carol's silent, raised-eyebrow query to say no, Gary hadn't said anything, there was no other information he could pass on.

Carol sat on the sofa, and Dave leaned on the closed door.

Carol decided to just get on with it. "I'm sorry to bring this up, and it may well be embarrassing for you, but Flora has told us that Sue's been talking to her. While what you do wouldn't normally be important, nowt is sacred in a murder inquiry, and it could well be the link we need to proceed."

Gary blinked. "What do you need to know?"

"I'll be blunt. Are you having an affair?"

He closed his eyes. Bit his bottom lip. Opened his eyes and stared straight at her. "Not an affair, no — not like you might think. I've had a few . . . instances where I've messed about with people at work, but it wasn't the sort of thing where we planned to run away together. They were just . . ." He shrugged. "I don't know, quick fumbles?"

"These 'quick fumbles'. Why? Was your marriage going downhill?"

"No, we were solid other than the lack of regular sex." He glanced at the closed dining room door. Lowered his voice. "Sue was always busy, either with work or the boys, and I felt neglected." He sighed. "Bloody stupid of me, selfish, but I have needs, and I thought if she couldn't provide me with, well, you know, I'd give her a break and get it elsewhere. Believe me, I wish I hadn't. I should have helped her out more, shared the housework, took the boys out so she could rest, then she might have been more inclined towards the romantic side of things. Flowers, gifts, they'd become the norm instead of acts of love. But if I'd arranged time away, just the two of us . . . Hindsight."

"They say it's a wonderful thing," Dave said, "but it can actually be a right bastard. It torments you."

Carol glanced over at him. He'd be thinking of his own situation. How his wife had felt neglected. How, now he knew the score, he'd be beating himself up like Gary was, wishing he'd done things differently. Given his wife more time.

"It'll hurt for a long while," Dave said. "The what-ifs."

"Don't I know it. I wish . . . God, I wish I'd just talked to her, told her what I needed, that I wanted us to be like we were years ago. We had time for each other back then, especially before I took over the factory. Once Dad died and I inherited the lot, the boys needing attention . . ."

Carol believed Gary was contrite. *Of course he would be, his wife's bloody dead.* Time to up the ante. "Tell us about Betterway in Runswick Bay."

"Shit." His face drained of colour then immediately flushed.

"Hmm. Sue found receipts. Told Flora, who suspects you've been meeting someone there, doing what people do when they get together overnight in a hotel."

"*That* isn't what Sue thought though, what Flora thinks. Yes, I had a thing with someone in Runswick Bay, met her at a clothing convention a couple of years ago, saw her a few times after that at her house — Charlotte Majors, she's called — but I don't go to Betterway to have sex with her. That ended around seventeen months ago, and it was only fun, nowt serious on my part."

"Why *do* you go there?" Dave held his pen above his notebook.

"I . . ." Gary got up to look out of the window. Stared over at his house. Raised a hand to his forehead and turned to face them. "I . . . I stay there with someone, every couple of weeks on a Thursday, and I'm with them on the Friday until about five. Sue thinks . . . *thought* I was going out with one of my old friends, getting drunk, staying at his for the night, then on the Friday chatting about the business. Paul Gedds, lives in Whitby — he's our accountant, so it's feasible we'd chat shop. He's aware of why I have to go to Runswick Bay."

"You said you stay there with someone. Who's that?"

Gary swallowed. "My eight-month-old daughter."

Shit a brick. "Right . . ."

Gary staggered across the room and flopped back into his chair. All the fight seemed to have seeped out of him. "I couldn't tell Sue. Charlotte . . . she said if I didn't pay her over-the-top child support and have the baby one night every two weeks, she'd let my wife know. She has me over a barrel. When she told me she was pregnant, I ended it, came out with the nasty line that I couldn't even be sure it was mine — I feel rotten about that, but I panicked. She forced a DNA test on me, said if I didn't do *that*, she'd tell Sue. Everything to do with Charlotte results in her threatening to tell."

"What's classed as over-the-top payments?" Carol asked.

"Two grand a month."

Christ.

Dave whistled. "That's a lot, but if she's going by how much you earn, it's probably spot-on, or as close as."

Carol's mind ticked over. "Is that why you've gone for the merger — Flora called it that. Did you need to bring more money in to cover those payments?"

"No, I take cash from one customer, always have, siphoned the money off that. Hid the deficit by telling Sue I'd given the bloke a discount for being with us for so long."

"Weren't you worried she'd mention it to the customer and the customer wouldn't have a clue what she was talking about?"

"Yes, but what else could I do?"

"Two *grand*, though?" Carol couldn't hide her incredulity.

"When you consider the customer usually pays us thirty a month . . ."

"Hmm, two grand isn't such a massive discount, then."

Carol rose and went to the window. A SOCO came out with several evidence bags and placed them in a van. Closed the door. Patted the van, which then drove off.

Is it just the usual, or have they found something significant?

No, I'd have been told if they had.

"So you pay Charlotte in cash?" she asked.

"Yes, on the second visit of every month when I pick the baby up."

"That's twice you've referred to her as 'the baby'. Can't you stand to say her name?"

"She's called Starbell. Bloody ridiculous. That's why I never said it."

"The things people name their kids these days . . ." Carol itched to go to Runswick Bay. "What's Charlotte's address?"

Gary rattled it off. "Will Flora and my boys need to know about . . . the child?"

"*Starbell*? Maybe not. It depends on whether Charlotte's the one we're after." She turned to him. "Let's hope for your sake she has an alibi, otherwise, your *activities* will have to come out in the open during the trial. If she's in the clear and it can be kept quiet, you might have to get a story together to explain to Flora about Betterway, because she's going to ask, you can guarantee that." She walked towards the door.

"Talking of receipts. I'd advise you to get them off Charlotte from now on if you don't already. With no proof you've been paying her, she could fleece you later down the line."

Gary paled. "Fuck."

Carol smiled. "I rather think a fuck is what got you into this mess, don't you? No need for any more of that, eh?"

* * *

Out on the front step, Carol sighed. PC Helen May was in the lounge with Gary, Pitson still in the kitchen with Flora. Jack and Joseph had asked to be left alone for ten minutes. Carol, Dave and Whitney stood in a close huddle in case neighbours either side listened through their open windows. The sun had risen higher since they'd been inside — it had to be ten o'clock by now — and the heat was once again heading towards unbearable.

"Did you get owt of significance out of the boys?" Carol asked Whitney. "I didn't want to chat with them just yet, if at all, in case it traumatises them more."

Whitney wiped sweat from above her top lip. The stifling air really was a bugger. "They were asleep before eleven last night. Didn't wake until Gary went up there after he'd found Sue this morning. I don't believe they had owt to do with it. Jack is harder, has a handle on his emotions, but Joseph's a little teary and worried about his mam being in the garden with strangers. Once I've spent some time with all of them together as a family, I'll get more of a sense of how they work as a unit. Is there owt I need to know?"

Carol whispered about Starbell and that they'd be visiting Charlotte once she'd had a word with the sergeant to check on how door-to-door chats had been going.

"Bloody hell!" Whitney's eyes widened. "The webs people weave, eh?"

"From what I could gather, only him, his friend Paul and this Charlotte are aware of him being the father, but who knows, Charlotte could have informed her family. We'll find out later. Whatever, act like you don't know owt. If Charlotte's nowt to do with the murder, I'll not be the one to poke the hornet's nest — it's Gary's decision whether he informs his sons they have a sister."

"Wouldn't want to be in his shoes," Whitney said.

Dave chuckled. "Me neither, but if he hadn't let his dick wander, this wouldn't be an issue."

"Right, we need to crack on." Carol stepped back. "If you hear owt, Whit, give me a ring. Otherwise, you know the drill. Listen, watch them and see if owt crops up. I need to get someone to take Gary down to the station, get his nails scraped, fingerprints taken, plus we need his pyjamas. He could probably do with getting out of that house for a bit. Flora's . . . unpleasant."

Whitney pulled a face. "Hmm, I gathered that much. Okay, now we're done with chatting to them separately, do you want me to ask Helen to take Gary to the station? It'll be interesting to see how Flora acts with Jack and Joseph without their father around."

"That'd be great, thank you. Ask Helen to wait and bring him back, too — we need written statements from them all at some point. Although, Flora's given the impression Gary isn't welcome, so perhaps suggest to him that he takes his boys elsewhere — and you go with them."

"They have a holiday house at Cove. Jack was saying he'd rather be there."

"Give the address to Dave while I go and natter to the plods. Them going to Cove is an excellent idea. They'll be more relaxed by the sea, safer away from this street — who knows, the killer might come back for another bloody go. Plus, Gary might confess some other gems if Flora isn't around."

"You don't think it's *him*, do you?" Dave asked.

"No, but he might recall something that helps us if Charlotte isn't in the frame. Someone, somewhere, had a beef with Sue, and I'll be damned if I'll let them slip through the net."

* * *

The one night they needed a resident to hear a scream and no one had.

Carol smiled grimly at the sergeant dealing with uniforms in the street. Richard Prince, in his forties, hair greying at the temples, always did a bang-up job, so if there was any information to be had, he'd find it via his officers. So far, he hadn't told her anything much, hence her grim smile.

"So out of all those who've been spoken to so far, no one heard or saw owt?" she said.

"Not during the time frame we're working with, no — midnight to six."

"You little sod, teasing me. What *do* you know?"

Richard grinned. "A few doors down at fifty-one, a lady called Mrs Lethe leaves her house for work every evening at quarter to seven — she's a barmaid round the corner in The Lion. Most nights lately, she's seen a woman in black walking towards her — dark hair, ponytail, around five-nine — and when she gets closer, the woman dips her head like she doesn't want her face seen. Mrs Lethe wondered whether it was a self-conscious thing, as the lady is about a size twenty-six — Lethe has lost a lot of weight recently so understands what it feels like to be stared at for your size."

"Right . . ."

"Lethe always looks over her shoulder once she goes past her, maybe thirty or so seconds after, and the woman just disappears."

"She could be visiting someone and has gone up the path or inside a house in that time."

"That's what I thought, until I tapped at a few doors closest to where the woman might have gone. No one recognises the description, nor do they know anybody like that. None of them have even had a visitor at that time recently."

Carol frowned. "So where would she have gone?"

"I thought she might have parked down here, worked in the parade of shops by The Lion, and got into a car, but just in case, I checked the hedge in front of the Cuttersby home. There's four bushes in a row, only they present as one because

43

of all the branches and leaves knitted together. I knelt, saw the individual trunks — they're like trees. Next door but one says they're elders — nice of her to shout that across at me. Anyroad, between two of the bushes . . ."

"Don't tell me there are footprints, because unless Sue watered them, that ground will be dry as a bone with the weather we've been having. Gary said she loved the *back* garden. The front is just those bushes."

"Not footprints. Sweet wrappers. Loads of them."

"What sort of sweets?"

"Chocolate bars. Snickers. A couple of Mars and Twix. There are even some stuffed into the bushes either side of the gap."

"So the woman is standing in the bloody bush scoffing Snickers, having a snack while she spies?"

"Could be. We've got sod all else."

"Those wrappers need bagging up, so make sure you do that. Keep prodding the neighbours. Someone must have seen her there."

"Not if she crouched."

"Whatever, it's a lead. Chase it up. Actually, have the leaves checked for hairs and fibres off the clothing, grab a SOCO. I'd say call my DCs in, but I want them to have their weekend off — saying that, I really need someone to do the social media checks and all the other bollocks like that, so one of them will have to come in. Me and Dave, we have to go somewhere, but first I'm going back in to speak to Gary. Christ, that's given me the creeps if that woman's been standing there watching them."

She patted Richard on the shoulder and left him to it, walking past Dave on the doorstep, twirling her finger for him to follow her. Helen sat with Gary in the living room, and Carol waited for Dave to join her, then she closed the door. Whitney must be back in with the boys.

"That lady we discussed. What does she look like?" Carol asked quietly, ignoring Helen's frown.

Gary rubbed his chin. "Blonde. Thin. Five foot nowt."

"Okay, thanks. Have you noticed a dark-haired woman hanging around outside your house? Size twenty-six, something like that?"

"No, and I would. I always look out about nine o'clock."

"Why?"

Gary appeared uncomfortable. "It's a silly thing."

"I'll have to hear it."

"My dad." He sighed. "He died at nine o'clock, and I always stare at the stars, waiting for the twinkle. Him, letting me know he's still there."

That doesn't sound like something an arsehole would do. Yep, Gary is a teddy bear underneath, albeit a philandering one. "And you've never seen anyone in your bushes eating chocolate?"

"What?" He laughed in confusion.

"Don't worry about it for now. We're off to speak to that *other* lady, so I'll be in touch as to whether it affects you or not."

He nodded in understanding. "Thank you."

"Helen, did Whitney mention going down to the station?"

Helen nodded. "We're just waiting for a car."

Carol left with Dave, then she phoned her DCs on a three-way call and broke the bad news — one of them needed to come in. Katherine Anderson was already sunning herself at Scudderton Cove with her little boy and girl, but Michael King, a singleton, had "bugger all to do, so I'll nip to work now."

"I'll get Dave to email you the details while we're en route to Runswick Bay," she said. "Then there's Joy on the front desk if you need owt else. If you get bogged down, ask Richard for a uniform to help you. I really don't want to get you off that beach, Katherine. You barely see your kiddies as it is."

"Thanks," Katherine said.

"We'll be back by this afternoon."

Carol and Dave got into her car, and she took a moment to breathe.

"What the actual fuck?" Dave said.

"I know. A secret child, a woman eating Snickers in the bushes, the mother-in-law fresh from Hell. I'm already looking forward to a gin in The Lord later."

Dave groaned. "Don't . . . The thought of alcohol."

Carol set off. "It'll pass, and you'll be wanting a bevvy come this evening. Gary's got his work cut out if Charlotte's our girl."

Dave sniffed. "His problem. I've got no sympathy for him on that score. He sounds like a right Lothario. I'm actually jealous — Sue kept quiet about knowing what he gets up to because she felt their marriage was worth saving."

"Whereas your wife . . ."

"Yep, my wife gave up, didn't want to save owt, yet I was faithful and treated her well. Got home as soon as I could. I know I was late a lot, and she was lonely, but I worshipped her."

Carol sighed. "I'm sorry."

"Don't you dare feel bad." Dave slapped his thigh. "She's been doing a Gary on me."

Carol's heart skipped a beat. "What, having an affair?"

"Yeah."

"That's got to bite, pal."

"It does. Christ."

He won't help you.

She patted his arm and continued driving.

CHAPTER FIVE

Smithy's Cottage

Dad had gone through the new photographs of Sue when Martine had got in, and she'd told him all about her evening: hiding in the bushes, going round the back, doing the deed, driving away. Mam had sat in the armchair in the corner, not saying anything, but then she wouldn't, would she? Martine had taught her a lesson a long time ago, and the silly woman knew from the second Martine had given her *the news* that she would never be allowed to mutter her opinion again.

Cheaters weren't entitled to one.

Martine had gone to bed wondering whether that applied to Gary. He was a cheater, but he'd surely have an opinion or two on why his wife was dead. Who would he think had done it? Certainly not her.

She'd slept well and got up to find Dad still sitting at the desk, his cheek on it, the computer monitor dark. He'd snored, and she'd made coffee and toast, taking it in to him, waking him up. His ever-increasing weight concerned her. Maybe that was why he was ill? Pressure on his chest? That was why he'd made her a padded suit, so it'd look like *he* was doing the killing, as if he was really there and not stuck at home, waiting for her to return.

He'd eaten then shuffled himself off for a shower in the wet room he'd had installed in what used to be a big larder. So much easier than traipsing to the bathroom upstairs, although they still had to go up there for a soak, and Martine preferred that loo so she got some privacy. The cottage sat on the edge of the moors between Scudderton and Mollengate, owned by Nan, Dad's mother. Mam had never liked it, said it was too remote, eerie when nighttime crept in. Martine loved it, and so did Dad — and only their happiness mattered. He'd been brought up here and had never liked living in Scudderton when he'd first got married.

Now, Martine and Dad sat together in the garden, leaving Mam by herself in the living room, tied to her leather armchair.

"How are you feeling today, Dad?"

"All right, lass. Better now I know he's suffering like I have to."

"Some would say death is worse than losing a hand, but we know better, don't we?"

"We do. It's still a loss, the hand. Still got mourning attached to it, just like Sue's death has. Will you be going back to see what's going on?"

"Not today. I expect the police will be all over the place by now. Gary will have found her."

"Good. I hope he's crying, missing her as though he's lost a part of himself like I did. I still feel it there sometimes, the hand. Phantom something or other. Gary will forget, too, think she's there, and he'll go to speak to her like I go to pick something up, and he'll realise he can't. It'll crush him all over again." Dad laughed so hard he wheezed, lost his breath, then coughed into his tissue.

Larger scarlet splodges today.

"I'll do the second one like we discussed, then." She stared out past the garden to the moors beyond.

"Yep."

"Will you watch?"

"Yep."

"Lovely. It'll entertain you for years to come."

Only she doubted he had years, but there was no sense in reminding him he was poorly, would die earlier than he'd thought. Besides, she didn't want to think about that. It hurt too much and would bring her all manner of quandaries.

* * *

Fifteen years old and eager for her first time. Martine listened to her body, how it seemed to hum with anticipation. She'd waited for so long, had gone through it ever since Dad had brought the victim home, planning, imagining, getting up the courage. Now it was time, and she carried the shoebox and the pellet gun across the moors, far enough out that Dad would see her from an upstairs window. Mam was in bed, so Martine was safe from her prying eyes.

She placed the box down, a bit sad as she'd grown fond of the victim; Dad had warned her not to, but she'd become attached anyway. She'd talked to it every day, getting it to trust her, to eat out of her hand.

The pellet gun felt at home in her grip. She'd practised with it, but if she missed, she could just break the thing's neck.

In the light of the moon, she crouched and took the lid off the box. Dad had helped her to secure the target inside with rubber bands. They'd cut them into long strips and fed the ends through holes in the back, across the body, the neck, the twiggy legs, the wings tucked in tight, and tied knots.

The budgie trilled at her. They'd named him Baby Smith, seeing as he was the youngest member of the family.

"It's time to die, little fella," she whispered.

She stood and fired the gun. Baby Smith let out a pitiful string of chirrups, its wings straining against the thickest rubber band, then he went still. Martine got down on her knees and put her head so close to the box her face was almost in it, her nose a centimetre away from Baby Smith's rotund belly. A belly that bled. Martine sniffed in the scent of blood, stuck her tongue out to taste it.

"All gone now," she said. "Baby Smith is dead."

She scooped loose mud out of the hole she'd dug last night, popped the lid on the box, and placed the cardboard coffin inside. Covered it over. Patted down the mud. Sucked her tongue to regenerate the taste of blood.

What a good time to be alive.

* * *

"Where did you go to just then?" Dad asked.

"To the Land of Darkness."

"I thought so. Which one did you think about?"

"Baby Smith."

"Not classed as an unlawful act in my book," Dad said. "A bird, it's nowt. No one misses birds."

"Sometimes, no one misses people either."

They laughed, tears streaming, and stared at the spot in the distance where the budgie still remained. She must go and put some flowers down. Dad had drilled it into her that the first one was the catalyst for better things and should be honoured. He'd always put flowers on Nan's grave beside the budgie's, but the job had become Martine's since he'd refused to leave the cottage after the altercation with Mam. He had to stay with her, watch her, saying if he didn't, she might get up, walk out and never come back.

She belonged to him, and no other man was allowed to have her.

Martine didn't remind him Mam wasn't in any position to leave, tied up as she was. He'd get angry, dive into one of the rancid moods Mam had hated so much. Martine hated them, too, so she did as she was told at all times to prevent the boat rocking.

It was better that way.

CHAPTER SIX

2 Marble Close — Runswick Bay

Charlotte Majors' house was likely paid for with the two grand Gary gave her every month. All right, Carol was guessing on that and might be proved wrong, but she was going by the information they'd received.

Twenty minutes into the half-hour journey to Runswick Bay, giving Michael time to get to the incident room, Dave had asked him to do a quick search on the woman. The results had come back that Charlotte worked for a fabric manufacturer, Material World, was probably still on maternity leave and her position, when he'd cross-referenced it with other wages at the same level, wasn't anything that could afford her a place like this, so unless she came from money, she'd ordinarily only be able to shell out for a small house or flat. This gaff, well, it had three storeys and sat on its own plot of land away from the neighbours. She rented through an agency, the house belonging to a Mr Valour, who resided in Spain.

If Gary stopped handing over the cash, Charlotte was most likely fucked — although Carol would bet Charlotte's hold over Gary would still remain, even though Sue was dead. Instead of threatening to tell his wife about Starbell, she'd maybe mention his sons instead. That was if she was as manipulative as Gary had made out. Oftentimes, someone else's opinion of a person didn't match hers. Take Flora's aversion to Gary, for instance.

Carol parked on the drive behind a silver Audi and left the car, stretching out the kinks the journey had stitched into her body. Sitting in her Kia with Dave having a catnap had given her time to think things through without outside influences steering her off course.

A woman, possibly standing in the Cuttersby bushes for nights on end, waiting for the right moment to strike. If Flora was to be believed, this woman was a floozy who'd killed Sue so she could have Gary to herself, yet Gary had insisted his flings were just that — no strings, no promises to set up home together — so unless this particular woman had read the signs wrong and expected more, why else would she be standing in the bushes?

What if Charlotte had sent someone to kill Sue?

What if Charlotte and the bush woman weren't anything to do with it — who else would want Sue dead? Or was it just a random killing?

Michael was busy looking into Sue now, so hopefully they'd have more to go on other than knowing she'd been convinced her husband was having affairs, she wouldn't hurt a fly and she liked romantic comedies and tending to her garden at set times. What a sad state of affairs that someone's whole life could be boiled down to those few things.

Carol knew none of the important stuff about Sue that made a person tick. What had she laughed at? Cried at? What had she dreamed of, wished for, strived to be? What had her favourite memories been? What had she looked forward to? The rather bland image Carol had of Sue wasn't enough to create a solid picture of her personality.

Maybe I ought to chat to Jack and Joseph after all if Whitney thinks they can handle it so soon after the death.

Dave joined her on the driveway, and they approached the blue front door. Carol took her ID out and tapped using the fancy gold knocker. She glanced to the lintel, where a grey stone in among the red bricks claimed the house had been built in 1817. Listed? Possibly.

A shadow came towards the frosted glass. A lock disengaged, a chain scraped across and the door inched open. A pretty blonde woman poked her head into the gap. Maybe twenty or so. Gary definitely liked them young.

"Hello?" She sounded wary.

Carol held her ID up. "Charlotte Majors?"

"Yes . . . ?"

"DI Carol Wren and DS Dave Waite from Scudderton. Can we have a word?"

"Scudderton? Is it Gary?"

"It involves him, yes. May we come in?" Carol had asked politely enough but in a way where she'd made it clear she didn't fancy discussing this on the doorstep. "It's a bit delicate."

"God, okay." Charlotte stepped back and pulled the door wide, revealing a shiny-floored hallway, small mustard tiles with gaudy turquoise patterns, something that really ought to never see the light of day, old-fashioned. So yes, this house was listed if they were still in place — or if not, the landlord actually *liked* them. Her floaty white skirt wafted, and the pale skin of her arms stood out against the red of her spaghetti-strap top. "My baby is asleep, so if we could be quiet . . ."

Carol and Dave entered and followed Charlotte into a large, everything-beige living room, Starbell flaked out on a sofa with a fabric bed guard preventing her from falling off. Charlotte was conscientious, then — no cushions near the child. She led them into the rear garden, where she gestured for them to sit on the rattan furniture.

"Would you like a drink?" she asked.

"A cold one would be lovely," Carol said, her tongue parched from the air-conditioning in the car.

"Same for me, thank you." Dave would undoubtedly have cottonmouth from napping. He sat on a chair and stretched his legs out, basking in the sunshine. "Nice garden you've got here. A right old suntrap. Nice house, actually."

Charlotte smiled, perhaps a bit slyly? "Yes, I'm very lucky. I won't be a tick." She disappeared back indoors.

Carol sat in a chair beside Dave, leaving the sofa opposite for when Charlotte returned. They'd be able to watch her then, although if Carol needed to get up and let Dave do the expression-inspecting, she would. It depended how open Charlotte was. The woman might be one of those people who'd gladly sit there slagging Gary off, no problem with revealing secrets.

"You'd think she'd let Gary kip here every other Thursday so the baby was in familiar surroundings, wouldn't you?" Dave whispered. "There's plenty of room. Why would she want her kid cooped up in a hotel?"

"Maybe she hates his guts, what with him saying the child probably wasn't his, so she can't stand to look at him, let alone have him sleeping here. And maybe Charlotte needs a break. If he stayed here, she'd likely end up caring for Starbell with him if he played the incompetent father card. 'Oh, what do I do, she's crying?' That kind of thing."

"Your view of men is seriously messed up. There *are* fathers out there who do their bit properly, you know."

"My experience of that says otherwise."

"Yours is an extreme case."

"Hmm. *Shh* now."

Charlotte appeared carrying a tray and placed it on the small table in the middle. Tall glasses of cloudy lemonade. Ice. Straws. She sat and picked one up. Didn't sip. "So what's happened?"

"First of all, I'd like to ask where you were and what you were doing between the hours of midnight and six a.m." From the corner of her eye, Carol caught Dave taking his notebook out.

"Pardon?" Charlotte blinked several times, her false lashes flapping. "I was here. Why?"

"Was anyone else here?"

"My mam and dad. We had a barbecue, and they stayed over — both had been drinking. They only live ten minutes' walk away, but still. They left about nine this morning. We were up a lot with my daughter — she's teething, didn't want to sleep or maybe she couldn't. Calpol didn't touch the pain she must have been in."

"Could we have their address, please?"

Charlotte gave it, frowning all the while. "Look, I don't want to sound rude, but what's going on? When you ask someone what they were doing . . . it's unsettling."

Carol debated going down the soft route but ditched it in favour of being flat-out blunt. "Gary's wife, Sue, was murdered."

She stared at the woman for any signs of deceit. Didn't find any. Only shock, her cheeks paling, a hand going to her chest, fingers fluttering.

"What?"

"She was attacked in her back garden. Gary found her early this morning."

"Oh my God!"

"We're aware your daughter is his and that he's hiding that fact from his family. What's your relationship with him like?"

"We've never really had one, we just got together over the span of a few months, then I found out I was pregnant, thought he might be a little more forthcoming with wanting Starbell in his life. Instead, I had to force the responsibility on him. I can honestly say we didn't speak about owt significant, like the state of his marriage — I assumed it couldn't be all that if he was seeing me. It really was just flirting and sex."

"How did you meet?"

"At a conference. At the end of the speeches and whatnot, we all went to the bar. I got chatting to Gary — well, *he* struck up the conversation, I was fine on my own. He was suggestive, made it clear while he was away from home he could do what he liked, and I took him up on the offer. I was between men at the time, so what was the harm if his missus didn't find out about it? What you don't know can't hurt you."

But she did know or at the very least suspected. "Didn't you ever feel guilty about his wife and children?"

"*Children?*" Charlotte widened her eyes.

"He has two sons. Twins. Fourteen years old."

"Bloody hell! I had no idea. He just said he was married, wanted some fun, and so we had it."

"Would knowing he already had children have changed things?"

"Only that I'd have taken less child support from him. If he's got two others to look after . . ."

"How much does he pay you?"

"Two thousand a month. I looked on Companies House, saw what his business was worth, and decided he could stump up that much." She paused. "Actually, no, I *wouldn't* have asked for less as he can well afford to pay for three kids. What a pig. Starbell has brothers who have no clue she exists. I'm going to have to speak to him about that."

"I wouldn't advise it at the moment," Carol said. "Obviously, he's grieving, and owt extra on top of that really isn't necessary."

"But he's due to have Starbell overnight next week."

"That may also have to go on the back burner. He can't exactly leave his sons to come and stay at Betterway now he has no one to watch them."

"Did he tell you all this, about Betterway and Starbell?"

"Only after we discovered it from another source." *He'd have kept it to himself if Flora hadn't opened her mouth.*

"So he's told someone else he has a child with me? He said he didn't want anyone to know."

Carol wasn't about to get into the ins and outs of how they'd come to know things. "That's not relevant at the minute. What is, is us establishing your alibi."

"It wasn't *me*! I don't even know where he lives or what his wife looks like. Okay, I know it's Scudderton because he's said so, but as to *where* exactly, I have no idea."

"I didn't say it *was* you, but it's something we have to scrub off the list all the same. Do you have any information that would help us?"

"I have no clue who'd want to kill her. Gary certainly wouldn't. He's a charmer, he's been a bit blunt with me on occasion, but I don't see him as a killer. Even when I told him I was pregnant, he was more stunned than angry. Calculating, too — I could see the cogs working, him scrabbling to see how he could get away with not admitting to anyone what had happened. If I had even the slightest inkling he was odd, though, I'd never let him near our baby. He takes her every other Thursday, for goodness sake."

"Did you tell him that if he didn't pay you two grand a month you'd tell Sue?"

Charlotte nodded. "Yes. He was balking about taking responsibility, so I pushed him to. Sometimes, you have to do that to make people do the right thing. I wasn't going to sit back and cope with the baby on my own. We both made it, so we both have a responsibility."

Where was either of your responsibility in ensuring you didn't get pregnant in the first place? Or did you trap him? "When did you move here?"

"What has that got to do with owt?"

"Please just answer the question." *I'm goading her on purpose. Will she snap? Lose her temper? Show us she's capable of murder?*

Charlotte sighed. "My parents rent it for me, have done since I was eighteen — so, two years. Dad's on about buying it but wanted me to live here first, see if I liked it enough. I haven't decided because I wouldn't be allowed to do owt about those hideous tiles in the hallway — there's some rule or other where the structure and whatever can't be changed. Not sure I could permanently live with them, but maybe I could carpet over the bloody things. Then I got pregnant with Starbell, and all thoughts of moving went out of the window."

"What does your father do?" *This place must cost a pretty penny.*

"He owns a business. Material World."

"Ah, so you work for him?"

"Yes."

"You don't have to answer this, I'm just curious. Does Gary know about your financial situation? Is he aware you can live here without his monetary input?"

"I suppose so because he came here whenever we got together before Starbell, plus he picks her up from here. Why do you ask?"

"It doesn't matter." *Was Gary so afraid of Sue finding out that he agreed to the two grand, even though he must have known Charlotte didn't need that much?* "I think we're done here. We'll nip to see your parents now. Thank you for your time — and please, leave Gary alone for a bit. Let the dust settle."

"I'll give him a month, but no more than that. I don't want Starbell to forget who he is. He might be a user, but he's still her father, and she deserves to know him." Charlotte rose and gave another sly smile. "*And* her brothers."

Carol sighed and stood. Drank all of her lemonade then put the glass back. "Well, that's for you to discuss with Gary." *I'll be warning him the shit might hit the fan if he doesn't watch it.* "We'll see ourselves out."

Carol waited for Dave to guzzle his drink, then they tiptoed past Starbell, who sucked her bottom lip in her sleep. Her cheeks were flushed, so the teething story might be true. Either way, they'd speak to Charlotte's parents, check if her father knew anything about Gary that would assist them, seeing as they probably ran in the same business circles. Other than that, it was back to Scudderton and the incident room, catching up with Michael, then another trip to see Gary and his boys.

* * *

Orchard House

Mr and Mrs Majors, in their late fifties, had clearly enjoyed the finer things in life for some time. Their home was a smorgasbord of wealth, everything too posh and white to go near.

Carol didn't trust herself not to break something — lots of glass sculptures — so she remained standing in the centre of the large living room, thankfully on oversized marble tiles so she didn't have to take her shoes off. Dave braved it and sat on one of the suede sofas. Husband and wife had chosen the other one, and a small dog — white again, its eyes and button nose dark beads — flopped on top of Mr Majors' slippered feet.

"Sorry for intruding on your weekend," Carol said. "We just need to confirm your whereabouts last night and that of your daughter, Charlotte."

"Oh, we had a barbecue at Charlotte's, darling." Mrs Majors — "Please, call me Edith!" she'd said at the front door — sat so straight she might well have a rod up her arse.

Did Charlotte phone them, warn them we were coming? "When was the last time you spoke to your daughter?"

Edith smiled. "When we left this morning, around nine. I must say, you caught me on the way to having a nap. Starbell was the devil during the night, wasn't she, Frederick? I got up to help Charlotte out. Paced with Starbell while Charlotte slept on the sofa. Then we switched over. Poor baby, she couldn't sleep. Grizzled a lot."

"What time was that?"

"I first got up about midnight, then Charlotte woke at three and I napped in the chair until six. Charlotte then had a little sleep for an hour. Why?"

Charlotte could have gone to Scudderton while her mother slept. "Unfortunately, Gary's wife was murdered."

Edith slapped her chest. "Oh my goodness."

"And you think Charlotte did it?" Frederick laughed, a great big bellow. "My God, you police, you take the biscuit, you do."

"We have to rule people out, it's our job," Carol said. *And I would take the biscuit if you bloody offered one. You haven't even asked us if we'd like a drink.* She'd found that. In her experience, people with loads of money were crap hosts. Not including Charlotte, who might be young, but she had manners. Step into a lower-income family home and you had the offer of a cuppa thrust at you first thing. "How well do you know Gary, if at all?"

Edith sniffed, her nose in the air. "I don't have owt to do with the man." She flapped a hand.

Frederick snorted. The dog rolled off his feet onto its back and appeared to grin. "Daft bugger, Taffy. Stop wrangling for attention." He addressed Carol. "I've met him a few times — business, you know — but as for whenever he comes to pick Starbell up, not really. We saw him once or twice, happened to be at Charlotte's when he was due, and it was awkward to say the least, Charlotte ushering us out into the garden until he'd left. Now, we stay away. It's for the best."

"Why?"

"Because I'd give him a piece of my bloody mind, that's why, and Charlotte doesn't want any tension in front of the child, so we respect that, hence allowing her to shuffle us outside."

Fair enough. "Other than your feelings towards him fathering Starbell, what's your impression of him?"

Frederick grunted. "Nowt like his father — which is a blessing. That man was a drunkard come the end and ran Cuttersby Clothing into the ground — I don't supply material to them anymore because of him. Owed me a bloody fortune. Gary has paid it back since he's taken over, so he's not all bad — a lump sum, none of this instalment business. I'll give it to him, he's brought it round well, can't fault him there. The times I've met him at conferences, he's come across as a tad brash, a know-it-all, somewhat unpleasant to be around. You know the type, where they override owt you have to say, wanting to get their point across — I'm the same sort myself, so I'm told." He glanced at Edith, making it clear she'd said similar to him at some point. "Maybe that's why he annoyed me. I saw far too much of myself in him. No one likes to admit they have faults, do they? Still, I stand by my first impression — a bit of a bolshy prat. At least he pays Charlotte and looks after Starbell, although that's not as often as we'd like, but it's none of our business, so . . ."

"Would you say he was capable of murder?"

Frederick boomed another laugh. "Gary? No, he's all bluster. I know from Charlotte that the minute his world is threatened, he caves. A snivelling wreck was what she called him when she told him he had to pay her child support. Makes a change from when she informed him she was pregnant, I suppose. No emotion in that instance. The shock must have rendered him mute. So, a prat, yes, but he's no killer."

"And Sue. Did you know her?"

"No, afraid not."

"Okay, thank you for your time." Carol sighed.

They weren't getting anywhere by staying here.

CHAPTER SEVEN

The Incident Room

Lunch, purchased from Greggs and eaten once they'd got back, sat heavy in Carol's belly. She'd overindulged to combat the nausea from her hangover, having not only two sandwiches but an iced doughnut as well. Dave had gone for pizza and a chicken slice. She'd bought sausage rolls and a baguette for Michael, who was still wolfing it down while she wrote on the whiteboard from the notes he'd passed to her. Dave browsed some of the findings, his feet up on his desk.

Sue had only used Facebook. She'd created the account eight years ago. From the initial glance Michael had cast over her posts, given the amount of time he'd had so far to pull everything together, he'd noted only two people commented regularly — friends, going by the familiarity and obvious in-jokes. Sue's preference was memes about motherhood, specifically involving lazy teenagers, and the odd profound quote that appeared on a monthly basis, maybe in line with her reproductive cycle. Had she been emotional while on her period? Were her feelings scattered, her temper more likely to flare during this time? Had she had a run-in with someone?

Had she reprimanded someone at the factory and that person had taken umbrage?

They'd have to ask Gary to offer more regarding her temperament. Perhaps tomorrow, as today was so raw.

Carol added Sue's early life history to the board: her place of birth, schools she'd attended, things like that. A normal existence, as far as Carol could see. No criminal record. Her financial footprint wasn't in yet, but digi forensics had some basic info from her phone, text messages and the like. She had one game app. Carol had no idea what that was about.

"Can you look up a game for me?" she asked Dave, pausing with the marker held midair. "*June's Journey.*"

She moved to her recent text messages, provided on a piece of A4, the latest conversation between Sue and Gary drawing her interest. Last week. A Friday, the first one coming in at six in the evening.

Sue: *Where the bloody hell are you? We're waiting.*

Gary: *Got held up with Paul. Be about half an hour.*

Sue: *The dinner will spoil. And I'm getting tired of you doing the fortnightly Paul thing. Why can't you discuss the business without staying at his overnight?*

Gary: *It's the new contract, I told you that. Lots to sort. I'm coming now, so can't text as I'll be driving.*

Carol imagined Gary having to pull over to answer her texts as he'd have been on his way back from Runswick Bay. The "we're waiting" would have been the family night they always stuck to. What exactly was Paul's place in this dynamic? If Gary had told him about Starbell, they must be pretty close if Paul was willing to give Gary an alibi. And did that alibi include Paul staying at home, out of the way, for not only the Thursday night but all day Friday, just in case he'd bump into Sue? He lived in Whitby, but that meant on Fridays he couldn't go to Scudderton.

That was some friendship.

Could the accountant have killed Sue? Maybe she'd confronted him about the so-called business chats and things got out of hand? If so, why would Paul have turned up at the Cuttersby house close to midnight, knowing Gary was home? Wouldn't he have suggested Sue met him for lunch or something and killed her elsewhere?

Carol checked the other recent text messages and those from Messenger to see if Sue had contacted Paul — she might have asked him round after thinking about things and getting angry.

That late, though? Really?

But there were no messages between the pair, nor any phone calls — Michael, meticulous as always, had found out who all the numbers belonged to and had written their names beside them in the call log.

Sue's main contacts were Gary, Jack, Joseph and Flora. Two others, her friends from Facebook, were Karla Dodds and Julie Rivers.

Maybe we should speak to those two. They may know things about Sue that Gary wouldn't. Did she have a work phone?

"Michael, can you message Whitney and get her to ask Gary if any of them had work phones. We'll need them — and Gary's personal one, come to think of it."

"Will do, but Gary's was checked when he came in to get his nails scraped and whatnot. Nowt on there of any importance, so it was handed back to him."

"Well, if there are work ones, nip over to collect them, then give them to digi."

"Okay." He thumbed his mobile.

Carol wiped her forehead. Her skin was clammy. She loved the summer, but this one was evil. What she wouldn't give to be in a swimming pool.

"*June's Journey* is one of those hidden object games," Dave said. "Might give it a go myself now I don't have a wife to deal with anymore."

"Right." Carol placed the marker on the lip of the whiteboard and leaned on the wall beside it, arms crossed. God, her head was fuzzy from last night's drinking, and it didn't help that the air in here was thick, too warm, despite the windows being open and a fan whirring. "Charlotte, Edith and Frederick Majors are out of the running. Gary . . . I don't think it's him, but he could be a good actor. Paul Gedds?"

"Why would an accountant want to whack her with a hammer?" Michael asked. "Whitney got back to me. She said the work phones are at the house and SOCO have already bagged them." He scrunched up his food wrappers. "*That* was a nice lunch. Doubt I'll want owt else for the rest of the day, but I'm not complaining." He threw the ball into the bin. "I mean, think about it: Paul. Unless Sue was so annoyed about him taking Gary away from her every other Thursday, and she spoke to him about it at ridiculous o'clock, and Paul got the hump and went round to murder her . . . Come on, seriously?"

"It does sound daft. Probably best we speak to him any-road." Carol glanced at the time. "It's one o'clock. Dave, d'you reckon we can fit in Paul, Sue's two friends, plus go to see Gary again, all before, say, five?"

"If we don't fuck about gassing too long, yeah."

"What you call fucking about gassing, I call police work. Michael, can you carry on digging — poke into Gary now, just in case. If you don't find owt by three, go home."

"Do you want me in tomorrow?" he asked.

"If nowt else crops up in the meantime, take the day off like you were supposed to, but I'll let you know if you're needed. We'll try to get on by ourselves until Monday."

"Okay." Michael grinned a grin that spoke of having the devil inside him. "If we're on the subject of absurd theories, what about this one: Flora, upset her daughter's married to a perv, goes over the road to murder Gary. She hears someone in the garden, assumes it's him, wallops him with the hammer, then goes home."

"Bollocks, her doing it didn't even enter my head."

"She's arsey enough," Dave said.

"Yes, but wouldn't she have checked it was him first before striking? Plus he's taller than Sue — Flora would have realised it wasn't him watering the sodding plants, surely."

Carol sighed. "But it's something to consider. We'll pop to hers, too . . . I wonder if Gary and the boys have gone down to Cove yet." She took her phone off a nearby desk and rang Whitney. "Have you relocated?"

"Give me a second to go outside . . ." A door creaked. Footsteps. "Yes. After Gary got back from the station."

"How did Flora take it?"

"She was angry, wanted the lads to stay with her. Said she'd be lonely without them. Sounded like a guilt trip to me. She lives by herself so she'd be used to it, but they live close so maybe she sees them all the time."

"I'd say it's a guilt trip. She struck me as the sort. How has everyone else been?"

"Gary's subdued but keeping up appearances for the boys. Jack's sullen, got his nose in his phone, and Joseph's crying a lot. He went to his bedroom half an hour ago. This is a lovely place, by the way, bloody stunning. Any news on Charlotte?"

"She's in the clear as far as I can see, but don't say owt. We'll be dropping in to you about half four, so I'll let Gary know he's off the hook with her then — sort of. We've got a few others to see first."

"Okay."

"Catch you later." Carol slid her phone in her pocket. "Right, Dave, let's get a move on." She glanced at one of the sheets and wrote down all the addresses they'd need. "Ta-ra, Michael."

"Yep, ta-ra. Don't do owt I wouldn't do."

* * *

The Starburst Inn

Carol and Dave sat waiting for Paul Gedds to turn up. He hadn't wanted them at his house — his wife was a nosy sort, and he didn't need her butting in, said he couldn't concentrate with her twittering on. Carol didn't mind as it saved them the journey to Whitby.

Karla Dodds and Julie Rivers had been shocked and tearful at the news of Sue's death. Carol had arranged to meet them both at Karen's flat — a poky effort, no room to swing a mouse let alone a cat. They'd crammed into her little living room for an hour, and Carol had gained a new perspective on Sue, so there was no need to probe Gary for pointers on her personality.

She apparently had a dry sense of humour, was a bleeding heart, her marriage was perfect (no mention of Gary's "fumbles") and she adored her sons. The only bad word she had to say about anyone was when they'd discussed the news and the various people who'd broken the law. All in all, the "wouldn't hurt a fly" flag was at full mast with those two as well, merrily flapping in the breeze and high enough to let everyone know what a good person Sue was.

That didn't help.

"We've got fuck all so far except ruling people out," Carol said to Dave. Condensation dripped down her glass of Coke, her back just as damp from sweat because the bloody place didn't have air-conditioning. "If we get nowhere with Paul, we're left with the woman in the bushes."

"Providing she actually stood in them."

"Right. Bugger, is that him?"

A man, whose beer belly swung in before he did, stopped and glanced around. Carol lifted a hand to get his attention — if it wasn't Paul, she just had minor embarrassment from waving at a stranger to deal with until he really arrived. The fella said a silent *Ah!*, going by the shape his mouth formed, and he headed over and stood by their table.

"Wren, is it?" He favoured the comb-over. And wet-look gel. His hair appeared black but was probably brown.

"Yes, and DS Dave Waite."

"Righty-oh, I'll just get a bevvy in. Two secs." He walked to the nearby bar and leaned on it, his back to them.

Carol sipped some Coke. "I'm tired."

Dave nodded. "Same."

"But you had a catnap in the car."

"Still tired, though."

"Are we bothering going to The Lord later now we've been at work all day?"

Dave shrugged. "Up to you. We could get a takeaway and sit in your flat."

"Or yours."

"Mine's not a home yet. I feel embarrassed when you're there, and anyroad, you've got a better TV."

"Fine. Did you notice the DCI when we were at the station?"

Dave shook his head. "Nope. He probably fucked off home for the weekend once he knew there was a murder to deal with."

"Lazy git. Ah, well, saves me having to update him. I bet he has tomorrow off."

"Yep."

"So I can avoid the boss until Monday. *Shh*, Gedds is coming back." Carol composed herself and smiled, waiting for Paul to sit opposite.

He got comfy. "I know you said this was about Gary, but what exactly is it regarding? I can assure you, no funny business is going on with the company. I can't think why else you'd want to speak to me if it's not to do with crunching numbers."

Carol put her glass down. "He hasn't contacted you, obviously."

"Err, no. Should he have?" Paul sipped his lager.

"Where were you between midnight and six a.m. this morning?"

He widened his eyes then frowned. "In bed, like normal people."

"Was your wife home?"

"Yes . . ." His eyebrows scrunched even more. "What's this about?"

Carol had another swig of Coke. Placed the glass down. "What are your thoughts on Sue Cuttersby?"

His face lit up. "She's a good friend, as is Gary. We get together as a foursome every couple of months, without the

68

kids. Go for a meal, a few drinks. I've known them both years, Gary since we were around five. Met at school, been mates ever since."

"So you like Sue?"

"Yes . . ."

"What sort of person would you describe her as?"

"Diligent and meticulous at work — she gets the books ready for me every month, and to be honest, there isn't much I need to do once she's sorted them. She's trustworthy, nice. Taken over a lot of the burden running the factory. She's good for Gary."

"So good that he plays around?"

Paul flushed. "Look, that's none of my business."

"But you made it your business by covering for him." Carol smiled. "Starbell."

"Shit. Has Sue found out? Is that what this is in aid of?"

"We don't know if she's found out because she can't tell us. She was murdered during the night."

Paul's mouth dropped open. "What? Sue? *Murdered?*"

"I'm afraid so."

"Fucking hell. That's bloody rotten, that is. And you think it's Gary, is that it?"

"No. However, we're eliminating people from our enquiries. Could I have your wife's number so Dave can make a quick call, check your alibi?"

"Of course, of course." He farted about taking his phone from his pocket, accessed the screen, and held the details up for Dave to see. "Fuck me. Can't believe this is happening. Christ."

Dave pressed the numbers into his mobile then got up and wandered to the far corner where no customers were sitting.

"Shit. I can't get over this." Paul smoothed a hand across his forehead then gulped more lager. He thumped the glass down a bit too hard. "Who the *hell* would want to kill her? She's the last person I'd expect this to happen to."

"That's what we aim to find out. Obviously. So, you'd say it wouldn't be Gary, despite the secret he's been keeping."

"Absolutely not. I told him to come clean about the baby right from the off, but he wouldn't have it. Sue's always been desperate for a girl, but with the IVF lark, she didn't want to go through that again — costs a ruddy bomb going private. Her knowing he has a girl with someone else . . . It would have broken her."

"Would she have got angry had she known?"

"No. She'd have cried, blamed herself for him going off with someone else. Thought she hadn't been enough for him."

"This is curiosity speaking here. How have you lived with yourself, knowing what you know, seeing her as often as you do for work?"

He puffed out air. "It's been a challenge. The times I've wanted to tell her . . ."

"But you didn't."

"No. Didn't feel it was my place. Dodgy situation, being asked to keep that sort of thing quiet. It's Gary's mess."

"Yet you've helped him clean it up by letting Sue think he's staying at yours. Interesting. So is your wife aware? She'd have to be, wouldn't she? Sue could have asked her about the times Gary supposedly slept over."

"Yes, my wife knows, and she's had a hard time keeping it quiet, too. But Gary pays our wages — my missus works in the factory, cutting, sometimes sewing. God, it sounds so bad, us conniving with him, but it's all so *awkward*."

Dave came back and nodded. Paul was safe from suspicion — unless his wife had lied about his alibi as well as lying to Sue.

"How . . . how is Gary?" Paul asked.

"Inside, probably devastated. Outside, trying to hide it all for his sons." Carol gave him a tight smile. "But then, he's good at hiding things, isn't he?" *Have I got this wrong? Is it Gary?*

"Still, forensics are brilliant these days. We'll work it out soon enough."

"I'm telling you, it wouldn't have been him."

Carol shrugged. "Time will tell."

* * *

Whitney wasn't wrong. The place *was* lovely. Magnificent. It perched on the cliff, a white-painted building with lots of huge windows in the roof, the sort of home you'd see on *Grand Designs*. Two more houses, to the left side, were the only buildings in this little street. The other homes nearby, sitting on an estate about two hundred metres behind, didn't command the eye as much, but they were nice enough, far more than Carol could ever afford on her wages. She *did* have money in the bank, enough to buy something better, but she didn't class it as hers and refused to spend it. Her father had left it to her, the only nice thing he'd ever done.

"Why the hell don't the Cuttersbys live here instead of the smaller house?" she mused.

Dave shrugged. "Maybe Sue wanted to be near her mother."

"But this place isn't that far away. It's what, two miles? Flora could walk it." Carol shook her head and turned to look at the view.

The North Sea, softly peaking, stretched out ahead. She cast her gaze to the right and picked out the distant Castle Headland in Scarborough, where she was *supposed* to be today. If she had the guts, she'd walk to the cliff edge and peer down into the Cove, where people sat on the beach soaking up the sun. To the left and around the corner, at beach level, was the promenade and the pier, the end of it obscured to her by the sharply rising cliff. She imagined the Ferris wheel turning, the kids at the mini fairground situated around it, all those holidaymakers enjoying themselves.

She might blame one of them for the murder, but it was highly unlikely someone visiting would have discovered Wexford Close, marched into Sue Cuttersby's garden and hammered her to death.

She swivelled to face the front door. Whitney stood on the threshold and smiled. Came out, closed the door to. Walked to Carol and Dave.

"Got owt?" she asked.

Carol shook her head. "Not really. My head is all swings and roundabouts. I suppose I'd better go in and let him know where we are with things."

Inside, Carol's footsteps echoed on the marble-like floor, although she'd seen her fair share of revamp programmes and reckoned it was more like polished concrete. It was open plan, one vast room with areas in each quadrant — kitchen top left, dining area top right, lounge bottom right, another seating area bottom left. Wooden stairs with no risers took up the middle, the balustrades some kind of thick steel wire, topped with metal handrails. A balcony landing. Carol stared directly above her. What a waste of space. There was no ceiling — that started halfway down the area in line with the stairs. This end, in place of a ceiling were slanted windows, and she imagined lying on one of the black leather sofas and gazing at the stars at night. It would be like the outside was inside.

She glanced at Dave, who came to stand beside her.

"Fuck me," he whispered.

She held back a smile. Spotted who must be Jack at the dining table if Joseph had gone to his room. He was playing on one of those Switch games consoles. She shifted her gaze to the large folding doors at the back, kind of like patio ones but not. Gary stood in the middle of the garden, looking upwards. Maybe he hoped he'd see the shape of his father in the white clouds. Sue, even. Proof of life beyond death.

Carol went outside, Dave following.

"How are you holding up?" she asked.

Gary stopped his perusal of the sky and turned to her. "Still can't believe this is happening."

"Walk with me." She led him farther from the house so Jack didn't hear them. The garden was a big one, not surprising. "Charlotte has a solid alibi." *Sort of. If she didn't leave her house in the night and drive to Scudderton.* "So, she didn't know about your boys, then?"

"No."

72

"She does now, I'm afraid. She wants Starbell to know them."

"For fuck's sake." He palmed his face. "This just keeps getting worse."

"At the risk of sounding unfeeling, you made your bed . . . Anyroad, we've spoken to Sue's friends, Karen and Julie. They had no idea she was dead."

"I haven't told anyone yet. Haven't even informed my mother. Not that she'd know who Sue was anymore. She doesn't even know who *I* am."

A touch of sympathy poked Carol. This man ran a business, had an ill mother by the sound of it, a kid he kept hidden, fumbles he didn't want anyone to know about, a dead wife, sons to navigate through grief . . .

"Sorry to hear that," she said. "Must be tough."

"Sue had it tougher. I mean, she got *killed*."

"I've told Charlotte to leave you be. She said she'd give it a month. So you've got time to decide what to do."

"It's too early to dump this on my boys, isn't it? Not so soon after . . ."

"Then explain that to her. Hold her off. Tell her you'll go and see Starbell during the day while Jack and Joseph are at school, at least until the summer holidays start. It'll do for now, until you sort something else out."

"She won't listen."

Then I can't help you. "We're going to visit Flora again in a minute, plus I want to go back to the scene, check in with the sergeant there — I expect he's still monitoring the comings and goings and will do that until shift change, but knowing him, he'll stop on for overtime."

"Why do you need to see Flora again?"

"We didn't establish her alibi."

Gary laughed. "She's the last person you'll want to accuse."

"Why isn't it feasible? Sue may not have been her intended target."

He paled, the bright sunlight glinting in his eyes. "You mean . . ."

"She knew about the fumbles. Betterway. Could have stewed on it. Became angry on Sue's behalf."

"No, she knows I don't water the garden. She'd know it was Sue out there."

"I realise that, but we have to check — plus, she could have asked someone else to kill you."

"It's pointless, but thanks for going down all the avenues."

"I wouldn't do owt less." She gestured around them. "Why don't you live here permanently?"

"Because Sue said we'd brought the boys home from the hospital to the Wexford house. That it's special to her." Gary sucked in a long breath. "I'm not going back there. I'll pay a firm to pack it all up and bring our things here once the police have finished. I can't . . . can't stand to be where she died."

She patted his arm. "This is an ideal place to heal. And you will heal. One day."

* * *

62 Wexford Close

Flora was at it again, crying, and it seemed to be for show, to prove she was upset. Mirror, mirror, on the wall, who's the most distraught of all? Carol had seen many reactions in her time and didn't need such a display of grief to show innocence, if that was what Flora was up to. But if it got the woman through the day, then who was she to question it — unless it was over the top for a reason.

They stood in her kitchen, Flora leaning against the sink unit. Light from outside basted her shoulders.

"Just a quick one." Carol smiled. "In the shock of everything this morning, I can't recall if I asked you where you were between midnight and six." She held her hand up. "It's a formality. I'm not accusing you."

"I was here, and before you ask, no, I can't prove it. I was doing crossword puzzles."

Like my dad. "When?"

"Until two, then I went to bed."

"So you didn't hear Sue scream at all?"

"I would have said if I did. And had I heard owt, I'd have been outside like a shot, seeing if someone needed help. Did you ask Gary for the names? Did you speak to the floozies?"

"I'm not here to discuss what we spoke to Gary about."

"But it will be him, I'm telling you! He'd have arranged this."

Carol sighed. *Is she trying to make me think it's him, when in fact, it's her?* "Right, we'll be off for now. Thanks for speaking to us again."

"That's it, take his side. Just walk away as if I don't exist, as if what I want doesn't matter! I'm fed up with people not listening to me, not listening to the voice of reason."

Carol ignored her.

In the street, they approached the sergeant, Richard, who stood with Pitson, their heads bent over a notebook.

"Ah, Carol." Richard smiled. "I was just about to ring you before you turned up, but when you went into the mother's house, I thought I'd leave you be. Pitson's been having a cuppa with the woman two doors down from the Cuttersbys, the one who told me the bushes are elders. She's solved the issue of the sweet wrappers."

"Oh right . . ."

"Jack or Joseph, she can never tell them apart, stuff them in the hedge every day after school. Takes them out of his rucksack."

Carol thought back to something Gary had said this morning. All other days apart from Friday night, they ate healthy food. One of the twins must be cheating and scoffing chocolate during the day, disposing of the evidence. Did that mean Sue was a snoop, likely to look inside their bags? Why bother putting the rubbish in his rucksack, though? Why not dump it in a bin at school? What was it, an act of rebellion? Hiding the wrappers where his mother might find them? A teenager's way of saying "fuck you"?

"Odd," she said. "While I can now scrub out the image of a woman gobbling choccies in a bush, she still could have been standing there."

Richard nodded. "I checked with Mrs Lethe again on where exactly she turns around when she sees the woman in the evenings. I timed it, paced it out, walking at average speed to where they pass. I stopped, then retraced my steps for the thirty seconds that go by before Lethe turns to check over her shoulder. The woman disappears either at the Cuttersby place or the house on the other side, which, as you can see, doesn't have bushes — therefore, nowhere to hide."

I wonder if Gary has chosen not to say they have a visitor every night . . . The woman could easily have just gone to their house, got inside before Lethe checked. "Has anyone along here got a camera doorbell or CCTV?"

"Unfortunately not," Pitson said.

"Sod it." Carol sighed. "I'm off to the crime scene." She stomped to her car, Dave keeping up behind her, and took two suits, booties and gloves out.

They dressed in the little alley beside Gary's house, signed the log, then entered the back garden. The tent had gone, as had the body, and all that remained were evidence steps and markers, plus two SOCOs who were clearly going over everything again.

"Found owt significant?" she asked.

Todd Butcher stood from his crouch by the back flowerbed. "The footprint Rib mentioned. Here." He walked across two steps and stopped beside marker five, where the hammer had entered the earth.

Carol went over there and stared down. Where Sue's head had been, about twelve inches above it, was a marker plus the obvious evidence of stamped-down grass and a shoe, trainer or boot tread in the mud beneath.

"We did a cast," Todd said. "Notice it's heavy on the front of the foot, as though they lifted their heel up to put weight on the toes."

Carol, alarmed at the thought of someone adopting a ballet pose or whatever, frowned. "Why would anyone do that?"

"Took me a while for the cogs to turn on that one, but once we'd done the cast, it was obvious. The treads are skewed, like someone purposely dug one foot into the ground and twisted."

"Like they wanted it to be discovered and have us running around trying to work out what shoe it is, frustrated because it's not a clear print?"

"Seems so." Todd shrugged. "If I had to put a bet on it, I'd say someone's playing with us."

Carol glanced over her shoulder at Dave. "Did you hear that? Playing with us."

Dave sighed. "Lovely. Just what we need."

CHAPTER EIGHT

Undisclosed Location

Sometimes, screaming was the only option. But sometimes, you couldn't scream because someone might hear you. Come to see what all the fuss was about. Fuss was the last thing you needed. There was too much of that as it was. Extra on top? No.

Please, no . . .

"You fucked up," Guest said into the phone.

"No, it went exactly to plan."

"How do you figure that one out? Look who died!"

"It's better that way."

"For you or for me? It wasn't what we talked about. Jesus Christ! What were you *thinking?*"

"My thought processes are perfectly valid, thank you. I lost a hand, not my brain."

"This wasn't what we agreed."

"Not what *you* agreed, no. *You* wanted Gary killed. I prefer it this way, it suits me better. Martine can watch him, watch the devastation and report back to me. I'll enjoy seeing him suffer."

"Killing Sue was evil. I'm heartbroken. You need to get things sorted. Do what I suggested instead of going off half-cocked and changing the rules."

"Rules? They're made to be broken, and if I remember rightly, never once did I agree to kill the person you want dead. *Not once.* You *assumed* it would be him."

People said slamming the phone down was so satisfying and swiping a finger across a screen wasn't the same.

Couldn't agree more.

Then the scream came, extra fuss be damned.

Oh no, my breath, it's in the air, on the furniture. No . . . no!

CHAPTER NINE

The Lord

Carol had persuaded Dave to have "just the one, love" in their village local. The Lord presented itself as a three-storey cottage from the outside — the large sign above the lower windows and the blackboard on the pavement, food prices written in fancy lettering, the only indications it was a pub. According to the older generation, it had belonged to someone of importance back in the day. A rich landowner in the times before commercialism had descended and other properties were built either side. Their facades were so out of tune with it, too young, grandkids standing next to their grandad. She imagined it sitting all by itself, the moors as a backdrop, horses and carriages of visitors clip-clopping up the driveway, which now didn't exist. In its place, Robottom Street with its annoying lorries trundling by.

Inside was a different matter. No comfy chairs placed at cosy-conversation angles, no fireplace with brasses hanging on the mantel. No ancient, panelled bar. Modernism had claimed the interior, all traces of the past removed. High tables in one corner, stools circling them. A couple of raised booths, the stairs in front hell to navigate for boozy customers.

One drunken stumble and you're on your arse.

Carol preferred where they were sitting, another corner with normal-height tables and carver chairs, although the backs were too low, so she couldn't lounge back in comfort while she sipped her drink. This was their preferred spot to talk, away from listening ears, especially if they were chatting shop; it was secluded enough for privacy, but Carol had a good vantage point to view all the customers coming in.

Two men played snooker a few metres behind in the games area, the balls clacking against one another, one bloke moaning because the white had followed the brown into the hole. "Fucking hell" from him, and "Loser!" from the other.

Carol wondered what it must be like to be them, the only thing on their minds winning the game. No images of a dead woman in a garden to contend with. No wailing mother, grieving husband or disappearing ladies. Then again, she *could* understand it if she thought of it like a game. Wasn't that what she was doing, wanting to win, to bring the killer to justice? To beat the other player?

Been doing it all my life, wanting to win, hating to lose.

"Hair of the dog, please work." Dave took a gulp of Guinness. "It's been one hell of a day. I expected to wake up around lunchtime, eat a fry-up, watch the telly all afternoon, then come here and get bladdered again."

"Same here, except I'd have gone to the beach. But someone had other ideas for our weekend." Carol glanced at the menu, a folded laminated card propped in a wooden holder. The idea of shifting her arse didn't appeal. "Shall we just eat here?"

Dave's shoulders slumped. "I really fancied a Chinese, though."

"Fair enough." She couldn't deny it, the family who ran the takeaway three doors past the Co-op cooked the best food she'd ever eaten. None of that MSG business. "Good job I bought that dishwasher, that's all I can say. Fuck washing up, or, as I would have done in the past, leaving the dirty plates in the sink, plonking more on top, then moaning days later when I can't find a clean one. I never did tell you why I started cleaning like a maniac." She sipped. Her glass of white wine was going down far too easily. Maybe it was a good thing they'd be leaving soon. She didn't have any booze at home. They needed a clear head for tomorrow.

Dave prompted, "So tell me."

"May as well. Better out than in, so they say. The thing is, I had this weird thing going on."

"Yeah? Like what?"

"This is going to sound stupid, and I don't expect you to understand . . ."

"Try me. We're mates. We've both said some stupid stuff over the years to each other. Still mates. Come on, out with it."

He's right. We talk so much shite it's unreal. She took a deep breath. "I tested myself to see if I could create a different past to make me feel better."

Dave frowned. "What do you mean?"

"All the stuff I kept was significant in some way, linked to what my dad did. So, say one day he punched me and I fell on the floor and stared under his chair while I got myself together. Spotted the pen he'd lost, the one he'd just accused me of stealing, the sort where you have to put ink cartridges in it. The type with a nib. When I brought it out on the day I was packing everything up — you know, from one of the many boxes his crap was in — and looked at it, I tried to convince myself he was a literary man and imagined him sitting there with the pen, creating away, instead of stabbing me with the nib after he'd come back from The Lion and telling me I was a useless bitch and he wished I was dead."

"Fucking hell, Carol. I'll never get over what he did to you."

With Carol's mum walking out on her and her father, Carol had spent the rest of her childhood, and indeed her adult life until his death, controlled by him. There had been something inside her that wouldn't give her the go-ahead to break free, to leave him to his own devices once she'd been old enough to walk out. What was it? A tether to the only parent she'd known at that time, the only one who'd stuck around, even if he had treated her appallingly? An abusive parent was better than none at all, that's what she'd told herself, but of course, she was better off without him. Once he'd died, she'd been able to breathe for the first time since her mother had lived with them.

"He wasn't the best of chaps, was he?" she said.

"He was rotten to the core, that's what he bloody was." Dave closed his eyes momentarily. "Whenever I think of you as that little girl, I get this rage that sneaks up on me. The thought of kids the world over being treated like you were . . . well, it's not on, is it?"

"No, and that's why I do what I do, you know that. I have to save people, maybe in order to save myself."

"Did it work, the test, you trying to con yourself that you'd lived a different life?"

She only wished it had. "Nope. I only saw the truth, so then I cried because my past wouldn't go away no matter how hard I tried to rewrite it." She thought about the hundreds of abused and neglected children she'd dealt with in her time as a police officer, how their souls seemed to have left them, all the light gone. Had she looked like that once upon a time? She must have, yet no one had stepped up to see if she was okay, apart from one of her father's friends, and that had only been the once. People wouldn't have wanted to face Harry Wren's wrath, so they'd crept back into the woodwork, leaving her to it. Leaving *Dad* to it. He'd had carte blanche, the tosser.

Dave scratched his nose. "You tormented yourself for no reason, that's what you did. It wasn't your fault, it was your dad's doing. So where's all his stuff now?"

"I took his things to the tip and threw them away . . . It hurt, but it was necessary. I feel better. Like, the past is still there but not so in my face now I can't see that pen, his slippers, his everything."

"I don't know how you hold it together. No one would know you're traumatised inside."

"I do that because we have people to save."

"That's why you work so hard. To forget. Trauma response."

"I can agree with that."

"I remember you phoning me to say your dad had snuffed it. As you know, my answer was 'Good!' Best thing that could've happened, him slipping in that bath, pissed as a fart, banging his head. Knocking himself out. Drowning."

She winced at the recall. Her feelings on the matter. Seeing his shrivelled skin, what with him being in the water for so long. She'd stared at it and couldn't believe she was free, then felt bad for it, then didn't, then felt bad again, then didn't, and . . . God, she'd had to run out of that bathroom and lean against the wall beside the airing cupboard to catch her breath and let the hot tears fall.

"Much as we're supposed to *not* think that way," she said, "I agree with you. It was a bloody relief, finding him. I thought: *Oh God, that's it, it's over. Gone.*"

"Except it wasn't over or gone."

She sagged then straightened her spine — *no more feeling downcast when it comes to him.* "Probably never will be over, but it'll fade. I'll move on enough that it doesn't crowd my head, the things he did. Who knows, maybe I'll settle down with a fella, but no kids, I don't want those. Too old for a start."

"Talking of settling with a fella . . ." Dave swivelled his eyes to the right.

Carol glanced that way. The man who scratched her itches had come in. Stood at the bar. Poked at his phone screen.

She swerved her attention to Dave. "Err, no. He's not proper relationship material."

"Too much of a bachelor, set in his ways?" Dave swigged more Guinness.

"Something like that."

Dave raised his eyebrows. "Which means?"

She lowered her voice. The bloke was far away, but still. "He's one of those people who invites you over then watches to make sure you take your shoes off, hang your coat up and generally behave yourself in his house. I only go there for a bit of you-know-what, which suits me because he's good at that, but as for something more . . . I know I've become a bit of a clean freak, but I hope you don't feel uncomfortable when you come to mine. Like, you *can* breathe in my flat, can't you?"

"Yep."

"Thank God, because how I feel at his . . . Like I said, not relationship material. I have visions of him peering over my shoulder when I'm cooking, telling me I've dropped a slice of onion off the chopping board. Sighing when he picks it up and puts it in the bin with a look that tells me I've been bad. Sod that."

"Why do you even go with him, then?"

"Because he's not like that when doing the business, plus it's convenient." *Or it was. Until he told me he wanted more.*

"He's staring over," Dave muttered.

"I know." She'd sensed his gaze on her ever since she'd turned away.

"He'll be texting in a minute, seeing if you fancy a bit."

She snorted. "Not tonight. I intend to be full of Chinese watching some shite on the telly with my best buddy. What do you plan to do, you know, about your situation?"

"I'm not jumping into owt else for a long while. Being kicked out tends to have a bad effect on the old self-esteem."

"You're going to lick your wounds."

"Yep."

"D'you think she'll come round, realise being with you is better than being without?"

"Not if the rumours are true."

"About her cheating?"

"Hmm, except they're not really rumours. A mate of mine saw her walking on the beach with some fella, holding hands, laughing, all that sort of bollocks."

"Shit. I'm sorry."

Dave shrugged. "I'm not. Said mate also found out something else. Yes, she's been at it behind my back — but also when we were together."

"Why didn't you *say*? I thought it was *afterwards*! Fucking hell, you know I'll listen. Whatever, whenever."

"I was ashamed. Had to get my head around it first. But now you know."

Carol's phoned beeped.

Dave laughed. "What did I tell you?"

She slid her mobile in her pocket. Drank the rest of her wine. "Come on, get that Guinness down you. I want my dinner."

Dave had another two gulps then conceded defeat. He stood. "Aren't you going to answer that message?"

She stood too. "Nope. I'm turning therapist. You, pal, are going to talk through your feelings regarding your wife having an affair."

"Why?"

"Because with Gary having it away with Charlotte and God knows who else, it must have brought your issues to the forefront today — and don't deny it, you're talking to a pro who knows how things get inside her head."

He draped a hand over her shoulder, and they walked to the door.

"You're a good sort, Wren." He kissed the top of her head.

She smiled, glad he'd done that. It meant her lover wouldn't get any ideas about asking her, again, to become more permanent, to be a couple.

Perish the thought.

CHAPTER TEN

The Moors

Martine stomped across the landscape, her tool bag smacking her thigh with each step. It was a full moon tonight, so clear and visible, no clouds giving it a beard or a weird hairdo. Ahead, Betty Tavers danced in all her naked, shrivelled glory, happily oblivious to what was about to happen. Martine liked that, the oblivion. The woman not having a sodding clue that this was her last dance.

Betty had to pay for her part in the Bad Time — *everyone* involved had to. No one was immune to Dad's brand of retribution; there was no escape, no talking themselves out of it. They were fucked, the lot of them. Unless they admitted responsibility, maybe added a sorry on the end — but even then, no, Martine would still kill them. Dad didn't think sorry was enough.

Betty, the stupid cow, hadn't put the safety guard back down after using the new cutter in a demonstration. She'd been teaching Dad how to use it, and when he'd been left to his own devices — Gary loitering in a corner with some young bint, not taking any notice whatsoever — well, one missing hand and plenty of blood later, Dad's life had changed forever. He'd never mentioned Gary with a woman, though, just that he had been there. Martine had found out from someone else at work that a woman had also been present.

Although Mam had at first played the part of the doting wife and pledged to look after him as he healed, she'd been averse to him touching her once his stump had got as good as it was going to get. Dad said that *she'd* said it felt wrong, gross, for her to be fondled by the end of a wrist, the skin puckered and ruined, churning her delicate stomach.

Dad had asked her, "What happened to in sickness and in health?"

And she'd said, "I can't. I just can't bear it . . ."

Fucking bitch. She deserved what we did to her. Not only did the accident ruin his life, but she did, too, so she also played a big part. Now she's stuck at home, never going anywhere, and serves her bloody well right. But if he squicked her out, why did she stay for so long after the accident? All those years with someone who turns you off is weird.

Betty still worked at the factory, and in the years Martine had been there, she'd avoided her until Dad had said to make friends with her.

"If she thinks you're her pal, it'll make it easier when the time comes to kill her," he'd said.

It was hard, though, to make out they were friends when Martine despised her. Still, it had been good practice, and Martine had taught herself how to present one face and hide another. Now, she reckoned she could be a chameleon in any situation if it came to it.

She was a bit naffed off about the wasted hours spent outside Betty's bungalow, though. Okay, at the time, Martine hadn't known about the naked dancing so had to spy on the old woman to get an idea of when she could off her, but it still rankled. Once she'd heard about Betty's penchant for stripping her clothes off on the moors, then seen her doing it out the back, things had changed. No more hanging around in a street full of ancient people living in bungalows. Particularly dangerous when you considered the elderly had fuck all to do but look out of their windows and spot her. Martine had taken to going around the rear in the end, out of sight, seeing as that's where Betty's lounge was, but it had still been dodgy walking down the street under the possible watchful eye of someone sitting in their chair and gawping out.

Maybe she ought to invest in a face-like mask.

"Cut them some slack. Not all old people are infirm, confined to their homes," Dad had said. "Some are bloody sprightly. I mean, you've only got to look at Betty to know the truth of that. Not only is she dancing for the devil or whatever, she zips about that factory. You've told me that yourself."

"There has to be at least one old fucker watching her street, though," she'd said.

"It doesn't matter now you know she dances virtually in our back garden."

True, but it didn't stop her being miffed about it all.

She wiped her brow with the inside of her wrist. The heat of the day still lingered. One of those late evenings where the air sent her skin clammy. No padded suit, though. Pointless when Martine didn't need a disguise until later. She walked onwards, mindful of the dips in the ground — twisting an ankle would mess things right up — although she'd done so many runs of this so was au fait with the lay of the land. She'd created a path, plus she put the flowers down every now and then for the budgie and Nan, so it wasn't as if she didn't know her way around like dog walkers or those people who hiked for fun.

Betty presented as a silhouette on the moonlit horizon, a strange, undulating creature waving her arms and spinning around, her voice floating over the moors. Singing. Something about "we'll meet again". What was she doing? Thinking of someone who was dead, telling them they'd get back together one day?

Ironic. She'd get the chance soon enough.

Martine drew closer, but Betty, in a world of her own, continued dancing. No witchcraft gear was in evidence, so the rumours going around about the old bag performing some kind of sacrifice were unfounded. Then again, what appeared to be a bag sat on the grass, perhaps containing Betty's clothes and shoes, so it might have some witch stuff in it. Martine would have a nose later if the fancy took her.

"Betty!" she called. "Betty!"

The old gal stopped dancing and stared. "Is that you, Martine?"

"Yeah. I live just over there, don't forget." She jabbed a thumb over her shoulder to indicate the cottage. "I saw you from the window." *The window Dad's watching from.* "Thought I could come and dance with you. Is that allowed? I mean, you're doing some sort of ritual, aren't you?"

Betty, clearly unabashed about being naked, beckoned Martine closer, her elongated boobs swaying as shadows. They were that lengthy they almost reached her waist. "I *knew* you'd join me eventually. It's so freeing. No clothes, the elements on your skin . . ."

Martine thought about that weird cult that had been in the news. Had Betty been a part of it? Had she escaped the net, avoided being caught? That bloke, a judge, and some of his fellow perverts had taken the kids to the forest on the moors a couple of miles away and got them to dance naked. Filmed them. She was sure there'd been something in the papers about being at one with nature, having the elements on your skin, just like Betty had said.

"Sounds like that cult," Martine said on a laugh.

Betty gasped, wavering, flinging her arms around. "It's *nowt* like that! I dance for myself, not for some paedophile, and there are *no* children involved, as you can see. That's a disgusting insinuation, that is."

"Sorry." *I'm not.* "It was only a joke."

"Well, it wasn't a very funny one, duck. Honestly! Now take your clothes off and dance or go home and leave me to it."

Martine smiled. She dropped her bag to the ground then stripped. It'd save her clothes getting blood on them. She took the knife out of her sock and placed it on top of her

T-shirt and leggings, then removed her shoes and socks. Put them beside the pile. She edged towards Betty and copied her movements, swaying to a tune the old bitch had taken to humming. Waggled her arms about. Held back manic laughter.

Martine estimated five minutes had passed, this daft business getting on her wick. Bored, she gritted her teeth. At last, Betty did her next usual thing and lay on the grass, facedown, and spread her limbs so she resembled a star shape. She pressed her cheek to the ground and faced the horizon, giving Martine the perfect opportunity to nip over and pick up her knife without being seen.

"What's this bit?" she whispered, lying next to Betty. "You haven't told me about this before."

"We need to allow the vibrations of the earth to enter our bodies and infuse us with energy and life. We'll be reinvigorated."

"Right."

If it worked, that'd be nice, to be invigorated. Martine was a bit tired, if truth be told. All that standing around and spying on people, taking pictures, watching Mam for a time, caring for Dad, going to work. Her life was full of doing things for other people and nothing for herself, and she craved to only be worried about what *she* was doing, not catering to other people's needs. Still, when this was all over, when everyone involved in the Bad Time was gone, she could think about her needs more. Dad would be settled with everyone dead, and as for Mam . . . Maybe he'd consider letting her go at some point.

Martine clutched the knife tight. Waited for Betty's breathing to slow. She needed the woman's arms in a different position for this to work, so suggested, "Wow, if you put your arms down by your sides, you can really feel the energy rising."

Betty slid her skin-covered bones into the right place, and Martine rose to her knees, then to a crouch. She waited again for the heavier breathing, for Betty to be so relaxed it'd take her a moment to realise what was going on. Martine imagined Dad whispering, "Do it, do it *now!*", and that was all she needed to spur her into action.

She straddled Betty and sat at the small of her back, pinning her arms to her sides with her knees. Grabbed her wispy white hair and wrenched her head up. Betty let out a shriek, and Martine placed the blade at the crone's neck.

"Be quiet. Look at your precious moon." Martine wanted to laugh but stopped herself. "It'll be the last thing you see."

Betty struggled as much as she was able in the circumstances. She kicked, and Martine closed her eyes, her mind's eye switching on a light so she could view the scene perfectly. Betty's feet making shallow gouges in the hard ground. Dried mud on her toes. And if it had rained recently instead of everything being baked, the earth kicking up, she'd see fingers sinking in, clutching. As it was, Betty must be slapping the water-starved grass, palms upwards.

Feel the moon's vibration in that, bitch!

Martine gave in and howled out her laughter, staring at the sky, pretending Dad stood at her side, looking down instead of waiting behind a pane of glass at home in the spare bedroom. He said his stump itched whenever she was doing something bad, and he'd known the second she'd killed Sue because it had burned. Was it itching now? Was he scratching at it like some mad beast?

"Why are you doing this?" Betty screeched, still struggling to get free.

"Because of the Bad Time."

"What?" A whimper. A sagging of the body.

"Getting tired, are we? Good." Martine inhaled a deep breath. "The Bad Time. When you left the fucking cutter guard up and didn't tell my dad it needed to go down."

"Oh God . . ."

"Yeah. He lost his hand, remember? Of course you do. You got a disciplinary for not following the proper rules at work. What was it, you being suspended for three months, when my dad's had the rest of his life to go around one-handed?"

"It was an oversight," Betty gasped out. "I didn't *mean* it. I was stressed, had so many people to teach."

"Can't you take responsibility? No, your excuses say you can't. Well, now you're paying for it properly, like you should have done years ago. The moon, Betty. Look at it." Martine yanked the head back a bit more. Giggled at how it must be a strain on the old bag's neck and throat.

"Please." Betty sounded demonic, her voice low, the word drawn out. "Please, I can't . . . my chest . . ."

"Well, you needn't think you're having a bloody heart attack on me, woman. That's going to the Grim Reaper lightly, that is." Martine pressed the blade harder. Imagined the skin splitting. Blood trickling. "One, two, three . . . and go."

She drew the knife across, keeping hold of the head so the blood gushed forward and into the dry ground. Betty gurgled then went silent, limp. Martine sat there for a while, waiting for as much blood to drain as possible. While the heart had stopped beating, the fluid still had to go somewhere until it coagulated. She'd Googled that. You could find loads out if you searched for it.

When her fingers cramped from holding the hair so tightly, she got off Betty and, still holding the head, walked round to the front so she could crouch away from the blood to look at her face. "Yes, definitely dead. No light in those eyes of yours." She cocked her head. Stared. "I'll leave you there for fifteen minutes until the blood stops."

She set a timer on her watch then walked over to her tool bag to place the knife in the plastic compartment. Paced. Waved with both arms over her head to Dad, letting him know the deed was done, but she'd bet his stump knew all about it already. Hot as a bloody flame, she reckoned.

She took her phone out of her pocket and did a Google search: *Song. Meet again.* The first result was a YouTube video.

It was by someone called Vera Lynn. Martine clicked on it and bent to put the speaker of the phone to Betty's ear.

"One last time," she said. "Because I bet they don't play this where you're going."

While Vera sang her heart out, Martine thought about the next victim. It was possibly dodgy, going after them, especially if their shift changed. She'd only been following that one for a week, but next week could be a different story. Waiting until the shift switched back again would stall things. Martine wanted this over and done with so she could move forward, live a normal life.

The song ended.

Martine spent another few minutes walking up and down, took some pictures of the body for Dad. If she'd thought this through properly, she could have sat a metre or so away, paid Baby Smith's and Nan's remains a visit, but she hadn't bought any flowers. Those that had been there before, dried out from the sun, she'd taken away earlier.

Her watch alarm bleeped.

Martine switched it off. Kicked Betty over onto her back. Clicked on her phone torch app and shone the beam at the dead, wrinkly bitch.

"That's a nice gaping slit you've got there, Betty. I'll soon have it closed up again. After a fashion."

Martine pocketed her phone and dragged Betty farther away from the blood on the ground, positioning her right above Baby Smith's and Nan's graves. She stepped across to her bag. From one of the compartments, she took out a packet of wet wipes and washed the blood spatter from her hand and arm so she didn't transfer it onto the next thing she needed, although that was daft, as that would get blood on it anyway. Still, wet wipes dumped in the plastic side of the tool bag, she took out a roll of clingfilm and straddled Betty again, this time sitting on her belly. She wound layer after layer of film around the neck to stop any blood from seeping.

"There, that's brilliant."

She scooped up her clothes and the tool bag, and ran across the moor to the cottage. In the back garden, she collected the wheelchair she'd got from a charity shop (a fiver) and pushed it back to the kill site. Thankful she was fit and healthy, Martine lifted Betty and sat her in the chair.

"Aww, don't you look precious?"

She gathered Betty's bag and pushed the hag home, parking her on the rear patio. Dad stood at the back door, his sights on Betty, not his daughter's nakedness. That would be weird if he did the latter, wouldn't it? In the light coming from the living room, Martine grabbed the hose with the showerhead attachment and switched the outside tap on. While the water filtered through, she sprayed Betty with carpet cleaner that she'd left sitting by the drain, then directed the hose's hard stream at the body and smiled at all the bubbles frothing.

"All traces, Dad," she said, "just like you taught me."

"Aye, all traces. Did she accept the blame?"

"No."

"Didn't think she would."

"She made excuses."

"Batty whore. I've laid the tarpaulin out for you, look. Did it when you were on your way over."

"Thanks."

He didn't struggle with just the one hand anymore. Amazing what a person could adapt to. If he had one of those special hands they made these days, life would be so much easier, but he'd refused. Said he liked wafting his ugly stump under Mam's nose whenever the fancy took him.

With the front of Betty clean, Martine put gloves on then carried her to the middle of the tarpaulin, placing her face down. She sprayed her with carpet solution again and repeated the washing process on her head, her back, her thighs. She'd spotted this ace squeegee in one of the bargain shops the other day. It had a long handle, and she swept the soapy water off the tarpaulin. It crept along the patio slabs, falling into the cracks where the cement had long given up the ghost. Martine turned the tap off. Wound the hose onto its holder. Smirked at Sue and Gary having the same one.

She wrapped Betty up, using bungee cords to keep the shroud secure.

"I'd best get dressed and take her away," she said. "I'll leave you to burn Betty's bag and clothes. Don't forget to put the knife in the dishwasher and set it on a hot wash."

"Rightio." Dad lumbered over.

Martine unzipped Betty's bag. Peered in. Clothes. A purse. Nothing witchy. "She's got ID, not that we need it." Martine reached inside, the purse squeaking against the gloves. "I can leave that for the coppers anyroad, extra proof, like."

Dad nodded. "I'll give the wheelchair a blast with the hose, too. We don't want to be putting your mother into a dirty seat when you take her out for fresh air, do we?"

"No."

Martine lifted Betty and hung her in a fireman's carry. Dad scratched at his stump.

"Itching, is it?" she asked.

"Like the devil."

They laughed and laughed.

* * *

Paws Veterinary Surgery

Martine had driven to the vet's between Scudderton and Mollengate, a mile up the road from Smithy's Cottage, parking around the back of the building. She'd been here on numerous occasions to see what was what — no CCTV, no one working until all hours, no nearby houses. The place was set back a bit from the verge, and formerly it had been some farmhouse or other, owned by a man called Braithwaite. Betty, who had seventeen cats and a vociferous parrot who said "fuck off" a lot, had told Martine the vet didn't sleep in the flat upstairs anymore but lived in Scudderton since he'd got married. Funnily enough, he lived in the same street as one of the other victims she had yet to kill. Life was full of wonderful coincidences. There were no emergency appointments to be had here, Mr Animal Doctor only worked nine till five. If pets needed checking overnight, an assistant came out between 2 and 3 a.m., so Martine had plenty of time.

Betty had been obsessed with the vet, always talking about him, admitting to having a little crush, even though he was young enough to be her son. She'd made a crass remark about the shape of his willy being visible through his trousers — "A right long one, he's got. I wouldn't mind that sausage going in my bun!" — and Martine had held back a heave. Sometimes, that woman really had acted gross.

She took Betty out of the boot and lay the package on the patio. Removed the bungee cords and unrolled her. Left her lying on her back, gazing at a moon she'd never see again. Mr Animal Doctor would recognise her, seeing as one of her cats was always here for some ailment or other — Betty's way of seeing him often, although apparently, the parrot was as healthy as anything — but Martine placed the purse on Betty's belly regardless. A little leg-up for the police.

She was nice sometimes.

Tarpaulin folded, bungee cords coiled, ready to be burned at home, Martine glared down at Betty. "I suspect you can see me from Heaven — or are you looking up from Hell? Either way, I bet you're giving me daggers. Well, you old stinky mare, I don't give a toss." She sniffed the balmy air. Caught a hint of the lavender the vet had planted to encourage the bees.

"All gone now. Betty is dead."

Martine drove home, whistling a merry tune. She'd check Dad had burned Betty's things properly, add the tarpaulin and cords to the fire, then lock up and tell Mam all about it. Mam would be disgusted, and if she could get up and storm out, revolted by the story, she would.

But she couldn't, so she'd have to sit there and put up with it, wouldn't she?

Stupid bitch.

CHAPTER ELEVEN

Paws Veterinary Surgery — Sunday

What the fuck? Was that *clingfilm* around the neck? It reminded Carol of the time she'd swaddled a turkey carcass in it one Christmas so the smell didn't seep out into her flat.

If this woman hadn't been spotted today and had been left out in the summer heat until Monday, her smell would have invaded the air, except out in the countryside, there would be no one around to notice it. Carol had been told by a uniform that this place wasn't open at the weekends, but until the owner said otherwise, she wouldn't believe it. It sounded a tad odd to her, especially as he'd been the one to find the body on a Sunday.

Maybe he lives upstairs and spotted her from his bedroom window when he opened the curtains. That must have been a shock.

Today was yet another hot one. Bees buzzed around a cluster of lavender planted at the edge of the patio. She imagined the vet and his employees used this space to let dogs have a wee when they stayed here. It was nice, calming, with a field stretching out then meeting the moors farther back.

Last night, she'd slept fitfully, tossing and turning, the Cuttersby case filling her mind in the small hours to the sound of the traffic rumbling by. She'd ended up losing the battle and rising around seven. Made breakfast — crumpets, coffee and a poached egg — then sat on her living room windowsill at the front, watching the street, mulling over how Gary must be feeling, waking up for the first time without Sue in his life. At least he had a better view. The sea, a blue sky, maybe a few boats bobbing along. All Carol had were houses, a slice of green beside the last one, then the row of shops, The Lord, the Chinese.

When her phone had gone off, she'd known. Hadn't had to look at the screen to confirm it was Joy on the line.

"Another murder for you," the desk sergeant had said. "Some old lady at the vet's on Murdoch Lane. Dumped out the back. Naked."

"Bloody hell. Okay, we'll be there shortly."

Dave hadn't been pleased to answer his door and see her standing there, a to-go flask of coffee for him in her raised hand and two crumpets on a plate in the other.

"Fucking hell," he'd said. "Just . . . fucking hell."

Now, she stepped inside a tent for the second time this weekend and stared at a body, once again in a back garden. Okay, it was a garden for the vet's practice, but nevertheless, it may well be significant. Rib had already informed her the dead woman was called Betty Tavers, ID in a purse left on her stomach, and it being Betty was bloody interesting as the name had cropped up in the Cuttersby case. So were the locations some form of "thing" if this was the same killer? Did the gardens mean something?

And were there more bodies to come?

What was the connection? Sue and Betty — had they had an altercation with someone else at the factory? Carol didn't really want to go and question everyone there, it was time-consuming and generated a lot of paperwork, but if something didn't light the way today to steer them from that route, she'd have to visit the factory tomorrow with a few uniforms, plus Dave, maybe Michael, leaving Katherine to man the incident room.

Sadly, she'd had to call Michael in this morning to do a background check and whatever on Betty. They needed a next of kin.

Dave sighed behind his mask. "I bet she's got marks on her neck or something."

Carol nodded. "Why would the killer want to hide them, though, under clingfilm of all things? They didn't hide Sue's injuries."

Rib sat back on his haunches. "So you're linking the cases, then, even though it isn't the same MO?"

"For now, until I prove they're separate incidents," Carol said. "Betty's name came up yesterday with Sue's murder, see."

"Ah." Rib cocked his head at Betty. "I'll remove that clingfilm once I've taken her in, but going by the colour beneath, the darkness, I'd say she's been sliced. Seems our killer doesn't mind a bit of blood, so they're not squeamish, although why they covered it up, I don't know. Probably doesn't help you, but still. I can't tell whether the killer is right- or left-handed either until I set eyes on the wound, if there is one. For all we know, that darkness could be something else entirely. Bruising, for example."

Frustrated at having no real idea of what had gone on, only a suspicion, murder by injury to the neck, Carol asked, "Estimated time of death at least?"

Rib stood. "Again, rigor is present. Going by the rigidity, I'm guessing between midnight and three a.m. this time. The stiffness is advanced."

"Hmm." Carol thought about that. As Sue's estimate started at midnight, too, were they dealing with someone who perhaps worked shifts? Or was that just their preferred time to kill? Did they wait for their family to go to bed, then nip out, do the business and get home again before anyone woke up? That's if they even had a family. They could be a loner. In that case, maybe they chose that time so no neighbours spotted them coming and going, because for Betty, they'd have needed a vehicle to bring her here, and someone might have heard it starting up or arriving home.

Did that rule out the woman in the bush?

No. She could have parked around the corner by Sue's. Such a pisser there's no CCTV around there to check.

Nor was there any here.

"What I *can* tell you," Rib said, "is that it's unlikely she was killed here. There's no blood anywhere, and she smells of some kind of cleaner. Whoever did this murdered her elsewhere, washed her, then brought her here. If you look at her hair, you can tell it's been wet and dried naturally."

"Right, thanks. I'll have a quick word with the vet, then we'll be off." She left the tent, punching the air that Rib hadn't called her Bird today. She glanced around and, seeing no one but SOCO and a uniform with the log, peered through the patio doors.

A man sat in what appeared to be a waiting room, Pitson lingering close by.

Dave came to stand by Carol's side. "Got to be rough, getting up for work and seeing that."

"Like we do all the time, you mean?" She pulled her mask down and let it dangle beneath her chin. "Poor fucker. Come on, let's nip round the front and go in, get this bit over and done with."

She walked to the edge of the building, signed the outside log and changed out of her protectives around the corner. At the front door, she put on fresh booties, signed with a uniform to enter the practice and wandered down the hallway and into . . . yes, it was a waiting room.

"Mr . . . ?" She glanced from the man to Pitson.

"Thomas Lines," Pitson informed her.

"Thomas, I'm so sorry you had to go through that first thing, or at any time, I might add." Carol approached the man and held her hand out.

Early forties, jet-black hair, clear skin, he rose and shook her hand. "I fully expect to see dead animals dumped here, but a human being? No."

Shocked, Carol frowned. "People leave dead animals in the garden?"

He sat again. "Yes. Probably so they don't have to pay for cremation et cetera. And it isn't just in the garden. Sometimes they leave them on the doorstep, even on the driveway, not even in a box or blanket."

"That's horrible."

"Better than that corpse out there," he said and retook his seat. "I can deal with animals, but people? Not my bag."

Carol sank onto a chair a couple down from Thomas. Dave moved over to the corkboard on the wall, which displayed leaflets about fleas and such, and got his notebook and pen ready.

Carol cleared her throat. "I should think you've already been through this with PC Pitson, so I apologise for asking you to repeat yourself, but I need information so we can move forward. What time did you see the body this morning?"

"Well, I arrived here about six, so—"

"Arrived here? So you don't live in the flat upstairs?"

"No. I used to, keep meaning to rent it out to someone, but I'm wary of that, seeing as we have animals staying overnight at times. I wouldn't want just anyone here. I did offer it to my assistant, but like she said, she'd have felt obliged to keep checking on the animals more than the usual once a night, and that isn't fair when she's off the clock. Plus she likes where she already is — very adamant she can't move from there."

"So you live where?"

"Scudderton. The new-builds on Skimmers Lane. I left home about twenty to six. The wife was still snoring." He laughed, and it sounded unsteady, as though he felt guilty for revealing one of his wife's secrets. "Not her fault. Adenoids. She's having them out next month, thank goodness."

Carol assumed he waffled through nerves. She thought about the current time. Ten or so. Four hours had passed since his arrival. "Did you not see the body straight off, then?"

"Obviously not, no, otherwise you lot would have been here sooner."

She couldn't work out whether he was being deliberately obtuse or if this was just his way. "What then?"

"I made a cuppa in the staff area, then went to check on the animals who'd stayed overnight. Only two — a bulldog and a canary. My assistant had checked them during the night, and she—"

"An assistant was here? Sorry to interrupt. When would that have been?"

He pulled a mobile from his pocket and brought up a screen. Showed it to her. "You'll see where she texted me to tell me all was well. She gets paid triple time for coming out. Lives up the road in Mollengate, so not too far for her to come."

Carol glanced at the phone and said for the benefit of Dave's notes, "Three minutes past two." *Fuck going to bed then getting up a few hours later to come out here.* Then she read out the phone number. "So we can only guess that she hadn't seen the body, otherwise she'd have told you, yes?"

Thomas put his phone away. "There'd be no reason for her to go out the back unless the dog wanted a wee, and it seems he didn't, because yes, she'd have definitely told me if a naked old lady was on the grass."

Do I detect a bucketload of sarcasm there? "Sorry to sound like I'm suggesting obvious things and draining your patience, it's clearly annoying you, but in our line of work, you'd be surprised how many people either forget or just don't tell us certain information. We have to check everything. Can you give Dave her address, please, as we'll need to speak to her."

Thomas's eyes widened. "It wouldn't have been her who did it. Did that. Killed the woman."

"No, I don't think she did, but I still need to talk to her."

"Right." He looked at Dave. "It's Tanya Bedford, sixty-two French Avenue, Mollengate."

Dave scribbled that down.

Carol needed to move things along. If Michael found Betty's next of kin quickly, they'd have to leave here, deliver the bad news, then go and see this Tanya woman. "So, you made a cuppa, nipped in to see the animals. What happened then?"

"I checked their vitals then fed them — both had had an operation Friday afternoon. Once they'd eaten and I'd ensured they weren't having any adverse effects, I did a bit of paperwork, sent a few invoices out electronically for those who have *yet* to pay." He rolled his eyes. "They promise they'll settle, then they leave it for weeks, expecting me to live on thin air. Anyroad, I went into reception to deal with any messages left on the answerphone overnight. Two people had called to book appointments for next week, and I was about to write down their details ready for Susan tomorrow — that's the receptionist — so she could book them in, but the dog barked, so I went to see what the matter was."

"You won't be open for business, I'm afraid. Might be an idea to let everyone else know they can't come in."

"It's fine, there was only those two, from the answerphone. We don't open on the weekend."

"Don't animals get ill on Saturdays and Sundays, then?" she said.

"Of course they do, but I'm on my own apart from Tanya. I can't see to everyone all the time. I have weekends off, bar coming in to check on the animals, like I did today. There's an emergency vet in Scudderton if needed."

Prickly pear. "So the dog barked and . . . ?"

"I went in to him. This was around quarter to nine. He needed to go outside, so I put a lead on him and went out the front so he could wee on the patch of grass there. But he tugged me round the side, and I followed in case he wanted a bit of a walk — there's a field out the back, the farmer lets us use it, providing we pick up any poo. Then I saw her . . ."

"Did you approach the body?"

"Not at first. I tied the lead to a drainpipe so the dog stayed put, then went up to the body and . . . it was obvious she was dead, and with that bloody hideous clingfilm around her neck, I couldn't check for a pulse there, so I did it on her wrist and . . . Rigor." He shuddered.

"And that was the only part of her you touched?"

"Yes, I backed away. Couldn't move fast enough, to be honest. Like I said earlier, I deal with dead animals fine, but people? No. I untied the dog, took him back inside, and phoned nine-nine-nine. Told them who it was. Betty came here often because she has so many cats."

"What did you do then?"

"Remained inside with the door locked. I had no clue whether someone was lurking about. As you can see, I'm in the middle of bloody nowhere, not many cars going by. Anything could have happened to me."

"Sensible," she said. "So then the police arrived?"

Thomas gestured to Pitson. "Yeah, and I was told to come in here and wait."

"When are your patients due to be collected?"

"Tomorrow. I'm not a heartless bastard. If pets have ops on Fridays, they board here for the weekend without charge. I don't expect people to pay for boarding if it's my decision not to be open at the weekend."

Carol winced at what she'd have to tell him now. "Depending on what's going on here, as we'll have to check inside the building as well, just in case, you may have to deliver the pets yourself and cancel the Monday appointments."

"Bloody hell," he muttered.

"Sorry for the inconvenience." *I'm sure Betty would say sorry, too, if she could.*

"Doesn't matter. I could do with some time off anyroad."

Oh my God. "Then Betty's death has done you a favour." She stood so nothing else popped out of her wayward mouth. "Thanks for your time. You'll have to repeat everything again when you give a formal statement, but I'll send a uniform round for that, to your house rather than here, or you can pop to the station. Up to you."

"I'll go to the station later."

"Fine. Again, thanks for your time." She made a move to walk out, then stopped. "One more thing. Do you have any idea why her body would be left here?"

"Not a clue."

"Do you know much about her?"

"That's two things, and no, not if you mean family and such. All I know is she has lots of cats which she brings in with so-called ailments, only for me to discover there's nowt wrong with them. Susan thinks Betty has a soft spot for me, but I think she just likes getting the attention a so-called ill pet receives. She paid her bills on time, so if she wanted to waste it by paying me for pointless consultations . . . I could hardly say no, in case one of the animals *was* really ill."

"No, that would be unethical." *And it swells your coffers, replacing the money you miss out on with the pets boarding at weekends.* "Okay, bye for now."

Carol left, Dave following, and she stood on the doorstep to sign out of the building. What was the real reason why Betty had brought her cats here so much? Paranoia that they were ill? For company? Didn't she get enough at work, or did everyone avoid her because of the naked dancing thing?

She stripped her booties off and popped them in a bag by the door, waiting for Dave to do the same. In the car, she stuck the air-conditioning on to dry her armpits and sighed as Dave climbed into the passenger seat.

"Was it a full moon last night?" she asked.

"No idea. I didn't look up on the way to the Chinese."

"I'm wondering if Betty was dancing, seeing as she's naked. Someone said yesterday that she did that when it was a full moon. Any thoughts?"

"Only that for an old woman to shell out for numerous vet bills when she doesn't have to is crackers. She must have had more money than sense."

"Or she was particularly attentive to her pets. They could have been her babies and she overly worried about them. Which is a problem we need to solve. Those animals will need taking away — either by any family members or the rescue centre. But back to the dancing. If Betty has no family, it's looking likely that someone at the factory will know where she does the naked business."

"So it could be a *worker* who killed Sue and Betty?"

"Hmm." She phoned Michael. "Got owt yet?"

"I was just about to get hold of you. As far as I can see, Betty never married, didn't have kids and only has a niece, a fifty-year-old woman who lives in Mollengate."

"Oh fuck. I hope I don't know her."

"I suspect you might. Liz Bath, the manager of the Co-op."

"Shite. Okay, can't be helped. We'll go out to see her now. After that, we'll be off to see the vet assistant, Tanya Bedford."

"Okay. As for social media, Betty wasn't on it. She didn't have a mobile phone, so . . . Anyroad, I'll get on."

"Cheers — also, I'll need you to grab someone to look at CCTV on the roads leading to the vet's, say from eleven p.m. until three a.m., to see if anyone from Scudderton went that way. I realise there are no cameras on the actual road from Scudderton to Mollengate, but if we can find any going in that direction, it might help."

"Gotcha."

"Catch up with you in a bit." She ended the call and turned to Dave. "You'll never guess who we have to go and see now."

"Who?"

"Liz from our Co-op."

"Shit."

"Indeed." She started the engine and prepared herself for what was to come, dreading it, because Liz was . . . an acquired taste.

CHAPTER TWELVE

Smithy's Cottage

Mam wasn't being very receptive to the latest news. *Of course she isn't. Never is these days.* She stared ahead, looking straight through Martine, ignoring everything she said.

"I didn't expect you to answer, you never do." Martine paced in front of Mam's armchair. "I think you need to go outside for a bit."

She untied her, lifted her into the wheelchair and pushed her into the garden. Parked her by a flowering bush facing the moors. Martine dragged a plastic patio chair over and sat a metre or so away. She didn't want to accidentally brush Mam's arm or anything. That would bring back memories of better days, when Martine had loved Mam touching her — she used to stroke her hair back as she fell asleep. Martine missed that and sometimes did it to herself, pretending it was her mother.

"Over there, that's where I did it. Sliced her fucking throat." Martine pointed into the distance. "I swear the man in the moon smiled, same as he did that night when me and you had words and you understood how it was going to be from then onwards."

She remembered that episode so well, the argument, the laying down of the law. Mam's skin had changed since then, but Martine wasn't about to put moisturiser on her or do anything nice like that. The only time she touched her was to heft her from the armchair into the wheelchair and vice versa, or when she took her upstairs to the bathroom. It was a routine she'd stuck to ever since they'd had cross words, and at lunchtime, Martine nipped home from work to sit her on the toilet so Dad didn't have to do it. Carrying her brought on his bouts of coughing. Martine hated it, the routine, it was pointless, but Dad had insisted they had to have some semblance of normality going on, and if that meant carrying Mam about, then so be it.

"What did it feel like when you found out your lover was coming here that night, Mam? I know you shit yourself, I could see it written on your face, but like I just said, what did it *feel* like?" Martine chuckled at how she'd texted him from Mam's phone, making out she was her, telling him the husband and kid were away for the weekend, so come on over and stay for two nights. What had she called it? *Unbridled, dress-up passion.*

"Okay, don't answer me, then. Honestly, I don't know why I bother. Talking to you is a ridiculous waste of time."

The shuffle of footsteps alerted her to Dad coming round the side of the house. He planted a hand on one hip, his stump on the other, and shook his head at Mam. "Still being obstinate, I see."

"She always will be."

"I've got Guest coming round in five minutes, so put your mother in the garage out of the way."

Martine stood. "Okay, but if Guest gives me any grief, just be aware I might lump them one. I'm tired of being told how to do things. *You* make the plans, I carry them out. *They* have nowt to do with it."

"I said that on the phone when they rang."

"God, what did they want?"

"To tell me off because it was Sue not Gary."

"Oh, fuck off."

"That's what I thought." He patted his brow using his stump. "Bloody hot out here."

"It is. The weatherman reckons there's rain in a couple of days, Tuesday he said, so I'll get the other two sorted before then. I don't want to be leaving any footprints behind." She hadn't told him what she'd done in Sue's garden, pressing her boot into the grass.

"Good lass. Nowt on the news so far about Betty. That's pissed me off, that has."

"Why are you miffed? I left her at the back of the vet's. Doubt anyone will find her until Monday, so of course she wouldn't be on the telly. That was the plan."

"I know, but I still hoped."

"Has Sue been on, then?"

Dad nodded. "A short segment on the local breakfast telly this morning."

"It's probably for the best it was short and that Betty's death hasn't made the telly yet. Means people won't be looking for owt strange going on, worrying there's a serial killer running around."

"True." He glanced at Mam. "Come on, she needs moving. I don't want her being seen."

"I doubt Guest would say owt anyroad. We have too much on them."

Martine wheeled Mam around the side, across the drive to the double garage, which had a wall between the two doors. She chose the soundproofed one and opened the up-and-over door — Mam's car was housed in the other side. She pushed the silent woman past boxes of junk to the back and left her beside another chair. "You two can chat all you like while I'm gone, but don't be too loud, got it?" She laughed at that. Sobered and looked at the person strapped to the second chair. Gave them the middle finger. "Stare all you like, it won't bother me."

She flounced out and returned to the garden.

Dad sat at the patio table. "Stick the kettle on, duck."

110

"Yep. Are you keeping Guest outside? It really bugs me that they insist on being called that, like it's their name, for God's sake."

"Yeah, outside is best."

"Fine."

She walked inside, made tea in a pot, and by the time she'd loaded it all onto a tray with three cups and took it outside, the rumble of a car engine announced Guest had arrived. Martine sucked in a long breath, gave Dad a look of warning to watch what he said in case things turned sour, then indicated her sock and the flick knife sticking out of it.

"Just in case they start owt funny, like," she said.

"That's my bad girl."

They laughed until the visitor popped their head around the corner, their hilarity fading at the look on Guest's face. Someone wasn't happy.

"There you are. I thought you'd gone out to avoid me." They came over and sat opposite Dad. "I'll have you know, I'm that livid about what you've done. Bloody livid. Today was supposed to be so different. I was meant to be giving advice to Sue, but instead, here I am, still avoiding Gary because I can't bear the man. Just in case you want to do the job *properly*, he's down at the Cove house."

Martine cottoned on to what Guest had said. "Hang on, I *did* do the job properly, you cheeky prat. Do you want tea?"

"Please. And no, you didn't. Gary was the target, not Sue."

"In your mind." Martine poured milk into the three cups from Nan's flower-patterned jug then added tea. She pushed a cup to Guest. "Put your own sugar in."

"I usually have sweeteners," Guest said.

"We haven't got any," Martine snapped, "so either put up or shut up."

"You really are rude, Martine. There's no need for it." Guest spooned sugar into their cup. Stirred. Sipped. "That's a good cuppa."

"Martine's the best at brewing," Dad said. "So, what can we do for you?"

111

"I want you to do what should have been done Friday night. Kill Gary." Guest sipped again, eyeing Martine over the rim.

Martine glanced at Dad.

He gazed back. Blinked.

"Oh dear." Martine sighed. "I really didn't want to have to do extra work."

Guest bristled, their eyes red-rimmed from crying. "You wouldn't have to if you'd followed my instructions properly."

"Not Gary, *you*." Martine whipped the knife from her sock and flashed the blade out. "Honestly, the things we have to do to get a bit of peace around here."

CHAPTER THIRTEEN

Co-op

The shop smelled of fresh-baked bread and cakes. Carol sniffed it in, reminding herself to buy them something to nibble on for when they got back to Scudderton. The manager, Liz — skinny, her nose a thin, hooked beak, her cheeks hollow beneath prominent cheekbones, hair a grey bob — stood behind the only checkout, chatting to Stanley, the eighteen-year-old spot-ridden blond lad who worked weekends, supposedly so Liz didn't have to. Yet here she was . . .

Reminds me of us. Can't get a weekend off for love nor money most of the time.

A couple of others stacked goods, one on biscuits, the other on personal care, the shelving opposite one another, so the pair of them chattered among themselves. Carol caught part of the conversation, and it seemed, after she and Dave had left The Lord last night, that someone had punched Carol's lover in the face — he'd jumped in to stop a pair of men fighting and got clipped himself. She supposed, if she were any other woman, she ought to go round there and see if he was okay, but she *wasn't* any other woman — if she showed up, he'd think she cared in the way he wanted her to, and she definitely didn't fancy giving him that impression.

She switched her attention to Liz and gauged her mood. Going by her expression, it was difficult to tell, although the reddened cheeks and narrowed eyes leaned more towards her bad side. She was either acerbic or your best mate, no in between on that one. Today's mood may well have been elevated to pissed-off status because she'd clearly been called in to work.

"If he asks you to do it again, tell me," Liz said to Stanley. "I'll chop his knackers off and feed them to Brathwaite's pigs up in Turnaround Field, the fucking bastard."

Acerbic, then. Shit.

"Ah," Liz said, "if it isn't our resident coppers. I was just telling Stanley here that I'll be chopping off Mr Watson's bollocks if he cons him out of scratch cards again — just so you know, like, when the crime's reported. Hands up, it will be me, officers." She laughed darkly and raised said hands, then dropped them to her sides at the lack of a response. "No sense of humour, you lot. He comes in here, that Watson, making out to Stanley he's got a tab. Now, you know I don't do tabs, and even if I did on the quiet, I wouldn't offer him one because he's a bloody conman, convincing our Stanley to go against the rules. As of this morning, he owes fifty-five bleedin' quid. You'd think he'd have paid some back out of his winnings yesterday, but oh no, he waltzed off with it. *One hundred and twenty quid.* Cheeky shit. Come to think of it, I'll go round there in a minute and tell him to pay up, say I've got the police on it — detectives, no less."

"That's not really our department," Dave said.

"Well, it should be. Any lawbreaking, and that's your area of expertise. If you want to prevent a crime, me going there with my knife, then stick around until I've marched him back here so you can say he's committed fraud, which is what it amounts to." She smoothed her palms down the sides of her bob. "Anyroad, what can I do for you?"

Carol cringed inside. With Liz in this sort of state, who knew how she'd take the news. "Can we have a word out the back?"

"Certainly." Liz puffed up with importance and nudged Stanley in the ribs. "You mind the shop, there's a good lad." She led the way through a door marked "Staff Only" and trotted down a corridor, past the bakery with its plastic flappy doors, and into another room with office on a plaque beside it.

Carol stepped inside. A desk with the usual on top, a few boxes to one side with manufacturer labels on them, and a mahogany coat stand with a lonely black-and-white checked scarf hanging on one of the prongs, its tassels matted.

"I'd say take a seat, but there's only one and it belongs to my arse." Liz flumped down on it and leaned back, spinning it round to face them, the seat squeaking. One of the castors was bent, the plastic about ready to crack. It'd put the cherry on top of Liz's so-far crappy day cake if it broke. "Close the door there, duck."

Dave did as he was told and propped his back on it, his notebook out. Carol sat on the corner of the desk beside Liz, mindful she didn't knock over a stack of invoices.

"Now then, what's this all about?" Liz nodded at Dave. "Him with his little book over there, got to be something official. 'Ere, I'm not in the shit about those scratch cards, am I? Did head office send you, because this isn't the first time Watson has swindled us. I've only just found out about this weekend's scam, as you know, so there's no need for this."

Carol took a deep breath. "It's about Betty, Liz."

"What, my aunt who only speaks to me when she wants something?"

"Yes. Betty Tavers."

"What's she gone and done, tripped over in her old age or something? Needs me to watch all those fucking cats? Not to mention that creepy parrot. It swears all the time. *Fuck this, fuck that.* Even called me the C word once, and it wouldn't have been Betty who taught him that. No, what's-his-name, that fella with the mangy ear, he sold it to her, said he was allergic to the feathers or something."

"Liz."

"What?"

"Can you hold fire for just a minute?"

Liz snorted and folded her arms. "That doesn't sound too good."

"It isn't. I'm sorry to have to inform you, but Betty was found dead this morning."

Liz's face whitened, and she slapped a hand over her mouth. Then she lowered it and wrung an imaginary cloth in her lap. "Oh. Oh, well, I wasn't expecting that. What did she do, take a tumble like I said?" She paused, looked at the ceiling. Something dawned on her. "It was a bloody full moon last night. She'd have been dancing on the moor. I *told* her it was dangerous, that anyone could come by, that she could trip and bang her head on one of those bloody stones out there, but would she listen? No. She shut the front door in my face, actually."

"She might well have gone dancing, love, we've got officers poking into that, but she didn't trip and fall." Carol placed a hand on Liz's shoulder. "She was murdered."

"*What?*"

"Someone left her naked body at the vet's on Murdoch Lane."

"Braithwaite's old place?"

"I don't know who owned it before the vet. But she may have had her throat cut."

"May? Either she did or she didn't. That's easily seen, for goodness sake, no 'may' about it." Liz closed her eyes and gulped. "Oh God, that's . . . Poor woman." She opened them again. Tears fell. "How can you not tell for sure?"

"Someone wrapped clingfilm around the neck. We won't be revealing that to the public, so please keep it to yourself."

"Clingfilm, like she's a ruddy cut of meat?" Liz covered her face with her hands and sobbed.

Carol let her cry it out and glanced at Dave. He shrugged, seemingly at a loss on what to do, but he shook his head: *I don't think it's her, do you?*

Carol shook hers, too. "Liz, I know you're upset, but we have a few questions we need you to answer. It'll be hard, considering what you've just been told, but we need information about Betty to help us with our enquiries."

Liz dropped her hands to her thighs and clutched them, digging her fingertips in. "I don't know what I can tell you, because she never wanted me to visit, said it upset those bloody cats of hers. She has seventeen, did you know that? *Seventeen.* Plus that swearing parrot. Jesus Christ, I can't have them, my landlord won't allow pets. The minute I took them in, someone would see and tell him. You know what village life is like. You fart and everyone smells it. What will happen to them?"

"We'll arrange for them to be rehomed, don't worry yourself about that now." Carol patted Liz's shoulder then tightened her grip for reassurance. "I know you didn't see her much, but do you know her routine?"

"We barely spoke since my mam died ten years ago. I only nipped there when she phoned me to drop pet food off, stuff like that, and she didn't let me in. She went to work at that factory still, wouldn't retire because she said she couldn't afford the vet bills on her pension."

"The vet said she went there often with her animals."

"I don't know why, she'd have kept them all healthy. Obsessed with them, she was. I have no idea what else she would have got up to apart from work and that full-moon dancing she'd taken up. Word gets round, people in the shop laughing about it. Said something about Betty being a witch. I don't believe that for a second. She's more spiritual. Elements, I do remember her going on about those. Elements, vibrations, and she's always had a thing about the universe helping you in life."

"Do you know of anyone who'd want to kill her?"

"Well, if she was naked, I'd say someone went to the moors and got to her, wouldn't you? Then dropped her at the vet's."

"It seems odd that someone would have driven there specifically, don't you think?"

"I don't know *what* to think. Them moors, they stretch for miles. She could have been past Braithwaite's field out the back, he still owns that, and someone sliced her throat, then Betty staggered to the vet's. I don't know, I really don't know."

"It's unlikely she died where she was found. She'd been cleaned, love. Washed."

"Oh my life! That's creepy, someone doing that. Lord. Despite her being an oddball, she was a good sort. Bought me sweets when I was a kid, always gave me a pound note at Christmas."

"If owt comes to mind, you will let us know, won't you?"

"Of course I bloody will." Liz sniffed. Held a finger up. "I've got a spare set of her keys at home — sometimes she rings to ask me to put some shopping in the front porch. Do you want them? For sorting the cats and whatever, you know."

"That would be helpful, yes. Thank you. We'll need a formal identification, even though the vet recognised her, and ID in her purse left at the scene let us know who she was, but someone will ring you about that. She'll have to have a post-mortem first, so I'd say you have a couple of days to process it all."

"God, she'd hate being cut up."

"We can't avoid it, I'm afraid."

"No, no, I understand. Would it have hurt, having her throat sliced?"

"Momentarily. It would have been fairly quick after that, her dying." *Although those minutes would have felt like hours.*

"Good. Good. That's something."

A softening of the heart prodded Carol. "We've got to go round to see someone else in Mollengate regarding Betty's case — not a suspect, just someone who may have seen something — but afterwards, we'll nip to Mr Watson's and remind him he owes that money and not to ask for things on tick again, all right?"

118

"Would you? I'll be in trouble if the takings are down, and with Betty and everything, that's the last thing I need."

"If you can give Dave his address then . . ."

Liz did that, then they went with her to collect Betty's keys, Carol giving her a receipt. Liz only lived down the road in the house beside the little green, and in no time, they were giving their condolences then leaving the woman to her grief.

Sometimes, this job really punched Carol in the gut. Liz might come off as brash, but she'd clearly cared for the old woman, evident by her wailing sobs as they walked away towards the car, Liz asking the sky, "Why? Why her? What has she ever done to deserve that?"

That's what I intend to find out, love.

CHAPTER FOURTEEN

Smithy's Cottage

Getting Guest in the garage hadn't been difficult. They'd gone in somewhat willingly, albeit glancing over their shoulder every so often, the knife thrust in their direction so they realised they had no choice, Martine chivvying them along and loving the fear she inspired. What Guest hadn't expected was to see Mam and her companion, something that had been hidden from them until now. Dad had told Guest a while back that Mam had run off with her lover, and they'd accepted that as the truth.

Why wouldn't they? If someone told you something plausible, you believed it, didn't you?

It was a good job Martine had shut the door before switching on the light, else Guest's bellow of alarm might have alerted the dog walker who usually came past around this time, that old fella with the Doberman who trotted from his cottage half a mile down the road to go into Mollengate. He usually reappeared an hour or so later, a Co-op bag swinging in his hand beside him.

The unexpected change in plans annoyed Martine. Like she didn't have enough to do as it was. Dad blinking at her, one of their little codes, telling her to sort Guest out, have a word . . . Not what she needed on a Sunday morning. She'd planned to have a nice relaxing soak in the bath, come in here to tell Mam the rules yet again, then wheel her into the house and park her up in the corner. She'd had an afternoon of reading on the cards while a roast cooked. As for Mam's companion, this was where he lived, the garage, sitting in the dark in his own filth, no more than he deserved.

He wasn't welcome inside the cottage.

Guest pressed themselves against the left-hand wall, wedged beside a stack of cardboard boxes containing all Mam's things. The visitor pointed to Mam and *him*. "What the hell are *they* doing there? That's foul, keeping them tied up like that. What the hell has happened to them? It's . . . Fucking hell, I can't even describe it. I thought they'd left . . ."

Martine glanced at Mam. "Are you going to tell Guest why you're here?"

"How can she?" Guest said. "Her mouth . . ."

Martine shrugged and glared at Guest. "Don't concern yourself with those two. They're shit beneath our shoes. Filthy pair, they are. And Mam's a cow for what she did, what she planned to do, running away with *him*, but I soon put a stop to it."

"I can see that. You're mad. Seriously mad." Guest splayed their hands on the breeze-block wall. Behind it was the sound-proofing. They glanced at the door with all the egg cartons stuck to it. "What's that for?"

"None of your business." Martine wasn't about to tell Guest the attempt at soundproofing was so no one would hear the slightly dampened sounds of those two *back then*, maybe a driver coming past with their car window open, picking up the screaming. Plus she could scream herself in here. Get out her frustrations at her situation, how she wasn't the master of her own destiny (which had irked her some-thing chronic since she'd woken up today), Dad pulling her strings more than she wanted him to. If he heard her, he'd say she was a liability. He'd worry she didn't have it in her to see this shit through until the end.

He might hear me anyway. The edges of the garage door aren't flush to the frame. There's a gap all the way round.

Why didn't I see that before?

I'll have to fix it in case . . . in case I don't stop doing this sort of thing.

Guest eyed Martine. "What are you going to do to me?" They glanced at Mam and *him* again, probably freaking out she'd do the same to Guest.

Martine sighed and glowered at the visitor, one she'd never felt comfortable having around. "Nowt if you just do as you're told. Listen, you're getting too big for your boots, dishing out orders. You came here to visit Dad the first time, asking how he was, saying you hadn't seen him around for years since his accident, then you got chatting, kept coming back, asking where Mam was. How you had the bollocks to bring up killing Gary I don't know, but you're in this up to your eyeballs as much as we are, so if you think you can waltz into our garden this morning and tell us what to do, you're mistaken."

"I realise that now." Guest flicked their gaze to the egg cartons again. Had they seen the gap and contemplated calling out? "I'll forget what I've seen here, forget what you did to Sue, to those two, I won't tell anyone, but please, please reconsider Gary. I can't stand the thought of him still breathing. It affects *my* breathing. Can't you just, you know, go to the Cove house tonight and do him over?"

"I've got somewhere else to be. Why don't *you* do it?"

Guest laughed unsteadily. "What?"

"You heard me. If it bothers you that much, you could kill him yourself. You've said enough times how much you've imagined getting rid of him. Now's your chance. With Sue dead, the police will think the killer came back for another shot."

"I wouldn't know the first place to start."

Martine stalked over to Guest and gripped their top in a fist, the movement dragging it down. She placed the point of her knife to their throat. "You need to *think* of a place to start then, because we're not doing your dirty work. Sue's dead because Gary needs to suffer, because Dad wanted it that way, not because you happened to want him dead. This isn't about *you*, it's about my dad." *And me getting my life back once this crap is all over.*

"How will your dad even know he's suffering? For all we know, Gary could be pleased his wife's snuffed it. It'd leave him free to maul women without worrying about being caught."

"I can keep tabs at work, report back, let Dad know how broken the boss is. And so he should be. He was *there*, feeling up someone's tits in the corner when Dad's hand got sliced off, couldn't have cared less about owt at the time other than getting his dick wet."

Guest had blinked at the word "tits" as if they were stunned that Martine knew about it.

Martine laughed. "I'll be letting him know why his wife is dead, that it's his fault — just not yet, not until Dad says I can. If you kill him before that, no skin off my nose. But listen to me, and listen good. If you ever come here bossing us about again, this knife," she pressed it a little harder into their skin, "will go right through your throat and come out the other side. Do you understand?"

"Yes, yes, I get it. Sorry."

"You will be. No more phone calls either. Dad doesn't need the hassle."

"Right. Okay. Okay."

Martine took the knife away and stepped back. "One word about those two . . ." She jabbed the knife in Mam's direction. "And I'll kill you. Now fuck off."

Guest darted for the door, fumbling to open it. Eventually, they lifted it, then shot out into the hazy heat of the summer day, legging it up the drive to their car. They reversed, tyres squealing, and Martine wondered why Dad hadn't blinked *and* nodded, which meant she'd have had to kill Guest. That would have been the better choice, seeing as they knew so much.

But he trusts them. Said they're all right and if they haven't blabbed by now they never will.

Possibly because they know we can blame it all on them.

Martine cracked up. Dad had recorded a segment of conversation with Guest on his old one-tape Binatone cassette player. Martine had Googled the company, and two brothers had founded it, naming it after their sister, Bina. Yep, she'd learned a hell of a lot on that computer — and also that Dad's bad boy was a cunning little shit, seeing as he hadn't said anything incriminating in that recording, so if they needed to send the tape to the police, it would sound like Guest was discussing a hit on Gary and Dad was incredulous over it.

Martine sighed. Reckoned she'd read Mam the riot act now, take her indoors, stick the joint of pork in the oven, *then* have that bath. She glared at her mother. "You saw nowt. You heard nowt. You'll say nowt. You'll continue to sit in either that chair or the one in the living room, and you'll do as you're told, like you've done ever since we had our first chat about how life was going to be. Personally, I think it's time to let you and *him* go, but Dad's not ready. One day, though, you'll be out of our hair for good, and I can't wait. You've been nowt but a deaf and dumb burden."

Martine thought about what she'd done to Mam that night, how brilliant it had felt, her all-powerful, *them* reduced to tied-up wallies. God, it had been so liberating to let rip, allowing the bad girl inside to roam free — and there was nothing they could have done about it. Then Dad had instructed her on what to do next — the library had been her friend then, her going in to read a specific book he'd given her the title of — and he'd declared she'd done a bang-up job, just like he had with Nan before he'd lost his hand.

As for the other part, he'd done that by himself.

What would she do when this was all over? When she had no one left to kill? Could she return to how she'd been before she'd attacked her mother and *him*? Just *think* about killing instead of actually doing it, like she'd done before she'd offed Baby Smith? Or should she collect some animals ready for when the urge took her?

"I don't know, Mam, I just don't know. It's a case of wait and see. Not one of us knows how things are going to turn out in the end, do we? I mean, look at you. I bet when you were my age you didn't think you'd be in your situation. I doubt anyone would, to be fair."

She wheeled her mother out of the garage, shut *him* inside and strode into the back garden. Dad still sat at the table, pouring himself another cuppa from the pot, the flab on his good arm flapping.

"Guest left, then?" he said.

"With a flea in their ear."

"Good."

"Why are we keeping them alive? Isn't that dangerous? Especially now they know Mam and her fella are here, not off somewhere living their best life."

Dad shrugged. "I'll have a think on it. I doubt they'll say owt. I've been talking to them for three years, remember. I know stuff about *them*, too. Confessions and the like. They won't want their secrets blabbed."

"Thank God, because I have a bad feeling about them. They know too much, and once they see it on the news about Betty . . . Guest only thinks we were after hurting Gary. With the old gal gone, they'll put two and two together. What if they twig why the people are connected and warn the other two on the list?"

"You've gone into panic mode."

Martine took a deep breath. "Sorry."

"Think about it logically. They won't be sure whether there even *is* another two. Remember, I've never told Guest about getting rid of everyone involved, although I'll admit to telling them the story a few times, so the players' names might ring a bell, but still, they'll be up shit creek if I produce that cassette recording." He placed the teapot down and stared mournfully at his stump.

125

Martine nodded. "You're right. I got twisted up in worry."

"Don't. A worrier makes mistakes, and you can't afford to do that."

Martine couldn't argue with that. It was *her* freedom on the line, not Dad's. If she got caught in the act or leaving a scene, *she'd* be the one going to prison, not him.

He wouldn't last five minutes in a cell.

* * *

Mam, strapped to a dining chair with several bungee cords, stared at Martine. "What are you doing? Get these things off me right now."

Mam couldn't do it, she had her hands tied behind her back, and Martine wasn't about to set the silly cow free, not after what she'd done and said.

They'd had a conversation about how Mam would never leave again, to go to the Bode Hotel and shag that man of hers. Things were going to be different now. Mam had begged, pleaded, but Martine hadn't listened. Dad's plan would be followed whether Mam said she'd behave herself from now on or not. If she hadn't gone off in search of another fella, none of this would be happening.

Mam only had herself to blame. She'd shied away from the stump, and that had been the start of everything unravelling. It confused Martine how Mam had stayed with Dad despite not liking it at Smithy's Cottage, getting on with things, seemingly not resenting him for wanting to stay here, but a month or so after he'd lost his hand, when the bandages had come off for good, she'd gone weird. Their marriage must have been something Mam wanted to remain in before that, considering she'd stuck around. Even years later she'd still been there, albeit mucking about with that other fella, but she hadn't left them.

Why had a stump changed things? Why had she remained here?

Or had his depression and weight gain during his recuperation been the final nail in the coffin and she'd sought comfort elsewhere?

Martine could remember it well enough, the change in her mother, her mood souring along with Dad's, the snappy sentences, the jolting movements. Martine hadn't been immune, hadn't been spared it because she was an innocent child — had Mam sensed the bad girl inside her daughter? Had some inner sense told her something was wrong and that was why she'd become distant with Martine, no more cuddles, no more laughter?

It didn't matter anymore. Those things had happened and had to be paid for.

Martine, strong and wiry, held up one of Dad's awls that he used to make divots in leather when he'd done all that sewing on the Singer, ages ago now. It had a nice shiny handle, the end rounded, the wood smooth, and the point on the end of the metal spike was sharp — Martine knew, she'd tested it by pressing it to her fingertip.

Dad had told her what to do, explained why he needed her to do it. Mam wasn't allowed to see anymore, hear anymore, wasn't allowed to speak. Martine had the job of ensuring things went to plan.

"I can't help you," she said to Mam. "I've had my instructions, and even if I hadn't, I'd still be doing this. You were no mother once Dad lost his hand, not the proper kind anyroad. Flighty, Dad says, and I see it now. Never satisfied with your lot. This cottage. Most people would kill to live here, in the peace and quiet, but you? No, you wanted a big place in Scudderton, and how ungrateful is that when Dad went to all that trouble, killing Nan so we could live here."

"What?" Mam's face blanched. "He killed her?"

"You believed the story that she'd just walked away, didn't you? Went off with someone called Bert — who doesn't even exist. Stupid cow. You're so gullible."

"Jesus Christ . . . That poor woman. What . . . what did he do with her?"

"Her remains are on the moors. Buried."

"When the hell did he do this?"

Martine shrugged. "Don't know."

Mam narrowed her eyes. "What instructions were you talking about? What did you mean by that?"

"To tie you up, sit you there. Do stuff."

"Stuff?"

"Shut up. Someone's coming round in a bit. On that motorbike of his."

Mam's face paled even further. "No . . ."

"I can't believe you didn't you think we knew. Like I told you earlier, I've been following you for ages. The Bode Hotel, cheap — that just about sums you up."

"This is between me and your father. You don't need to know about this."

"Already do. Dad's told me everything. How you can't stand his stump. How you suddenly started putting lipstick on and going out of a night. Bingo, you said. A book club, you said. Whatever excuse you could think of, you used it. Except, unless you play bingo at the hotel or meet people there to discuss books, something you've never been interested in, then I'd say you're a liar." Martine smirked. "Bit silly of you to keep his number in your phone, don't you think?"

"Martine, I swear, if you don't untie me . . ."

"What. What will you do?" She laughed. "Nowt. You can't, you're tied up."

"Where's your father? Get him in here so we can talk."

"He's around, and don't order me about. I don't like it. Never did. Never liked you either."

Mam's face crumpled. "Never?"

"Nope, not since I was about five. You aren't the same as us."

Mam wailed in frustration. "What are you talking about?"

A shaft of light speared through the living room window, the rumble of the motorbike engine loud in the night.

Martine grinned. "He's here."

"Don't let him in. This isn't his fault. I won't see him again, I promise," Mam said.

"That's lies, and you know it." Martine shoved a rag in Mam's mouth and walked out, into the blackened hallway. Reached back into the lounge and clicked the light off.

Dad sat on the stairs in the shadows. He'd been listening, like he'd said he would. He stood and went over to the kitchen doorway, standing there, hiding from view so their visitor didn't spot him in the gloom. Whispered, "Stump's itching. Let him in, bad girl."

Martine smiled, clutched the awl in her hot hand and approached the front door. She stood behind it. Opened it up. Waited for him to step inside.

He did, laughing. "What are you playing at, sexy?" He turned to look at who he thought was Mam — and he would think it was her. They were the same build, same height, and with no lights on, he wouldn't be able to distinguish one from the other.

Martine pushed the door shut. Said in a childish voice, "Go into the living room to your left."

"Josie? You sound different . . . Ah, I get it. This is one of your games? Who are you tonight, a young girl? Got a uniform on, have you?" He chortled. "Okay, okay, I'll go into the living room. But what am I? The headmaster or a naughty schoolboy?"

"A naughty boy, that's what you are."

He laughed again, and his shadow-shape disappeared through the doorway.

Martine snuck a peek at Dad, a figure now with lit edges where the moonlight came in through the kitchen window. A cloud must have shifted away from the moon. She entered the living room, sensed Dad at her back, following, and she smiled at the click where he'd closed the door. The curtains blocked out the moonlight at the patio doors, so Mam wasn't really visible sitting in the chair at the opposite end, although the chair itself presented as a dark structure, only her head showing above the back.

Martine placed the awl on the sofa and picked up a silk scarf she'd put there. Walked behind Mam's lover. Took hold of one wrist, then the other, and positioned them at the small of his back, adept at it even in the dark.

"Oh, it's like that, is it, you saucy bugger?" he said. "Fine, I'm game."

Martine had practised tying wrists, Dad as her willing guinea pig, although sometimes the scarf slipped off his stump, but she'd got the general idea of how to do it quickly. She glanced over at him. He stood by the door. Was the lover thick? Why hadn't he seen his figure there?

Too caught up in the idea of a sex game, most likely.

Martine knotted the scarf and bit back a retch at the thought of her mother with this man, like that. They must have got up to all sorts of weird things at the Bode Hotel. Was Dad thinking the same thing? Probably. Those thoughts had tormented him already, he'd told Martine as much. Kept him awake at night while his lying bitch of a wife slept beside him, her conscience seemingly clear.

"Close your eyes," she chimed in her little girl tones.

"Okay . . ."

Martine placed her hands on his high shoulders and steered him towards the other chair beside Mam's. "Sit." She waited for him to turn and gingerly lower himself to the seat. She reached over to the sofa for the bungee cords and, while he chuckled, she secured him to the chair.

"Now we can begin," she said.

Mam whimpered, the stupid cow.

"Josie? Is someone else in here?" he asked.

"Of course there is," Martine said in her normal voice, right by his ear. "There's me, you, my mother and my father."

"Fuck. Shit. Josie, J-Josie, you said they'd gone away for the weekend."

Martine cracked up and moved to stand in front of this pair of adulterers — he was married, too, the filthy bastard. "No she didn't. That was me. Now shut up, Tim Dougan. Yes, I know your name, fornicator." She paused. "Dad, lights."

The room flooded with brightness. Tim blinked, shaking his head slightly. He was forty-one, so Dad had informed her. Black hair, strong jaw, bright-blue eyes, all the makings of a heartthrob. Kept himself fit. He struggled to get free, but like Mam, with his hands behind his back, he was shit out of luck.

Tim looked at Martine, his face paling. "You're the daughter?"

"Hmm. And that's my father, Josie's husband, the man you two have been fooling. I wonder what your wife, Sally, will think when you don't come home tonight. Will your kids miss you? Jessica and Polly, isn't it?"

"Don't you dare. Don't you dare hurt my kids." Tim kicked out at her, the toe of his shiny black shoe missing her by a whisker.

"I'm not into hurting kids, not like I'm going to hurt you any-road. But they will be hurt emotionally when they realise Daddy's gone missing. Still, they're only three and five, they'll get over it. Forget you. As for your wife . . . she'll be taking extra shifts at the factory to cover your missing wages. Unless you've got life insurance, and even then, she can't claim it until you've been missing for yonks, presumed dead years down the line. She's got a tough road ahead."

For the first time, he gave Mam his proper attention, turning to stare at her. "Josie, please, get this stopped."

Mam's eyes bulged at Martine collecting the awl. Her garbled words behind the rag in her mouth meant sod all.

130

Tim focused on Dad. "Look, I'm sorry, pal, she said the marriage was over, you were basically separated but living in the same house. I don't want any part of . . . this, whatever it is. Fucking hell, you're insane if you think you can get away with tying me up." He kicked again, bucked in an attempt to tip the chair, although what he thought that would achieve was a mystery.

Dad didn't give him the time of day. "Do what we discussed, bad girl."

Adrenaline surged through Martine. She thought of Baby Smith, how easy it had been to kill the budgie. How satisfying. She swept her gaze from Mam to Tim and back again several times.

"You'll see nowt. You'll hear nowt. You'll say nowt." She smiled.

The metal of the awl entering Tim's eyeball was a breeze. His scream a symphony. Mam's muffled screech a pleasure. Martine had only gone in enough for the point to go through to the other side of the eyeball, and she wrenched that fucker out, ripping the stringy membranes, holding it up to the light, admiring the blood, the gooey substance hanging off it. Loving Tim's silent wail of pain. His agony. His terror.

"Three more eyes to go, then I'll ram this fucker inside your ears." Martine giggled. "Now, then, I must get on. Dad still hasn't had his supper. A hungry man is an unpleasant one, and you don't want to deal with him in a grump, do you?"

Blood streamed down Tim's cheek.

Martine leaned forward. Licked it.

"Tastes just like pennies." She raised the awl again.

Later, Dad said, "Stump's burning."

* * *

That was why Martine thought talking to Mam and expecting an answer was ridiculous. What was the point of that charade when the woman couldn't hear her? Couldn't speak? Martine had sliced their tongues off, cooked them up for Dad in the frying pan, nice thin slices that she'd sprinkled with pepper and placed on top of his mountain of bolognese. He'd asked her to do it, cook them.

"I want their lies inside me so I can hear them," he'd said.

It was daft, because that would never happen. Digesting a couple of tongues didn't mean he'd know things, but he had his quirks, and she'd done whatever he'd said. What she *wouldn't* be doing for much longer was taking Mam out the back for fresh air or to the bathroom. That was too much, and once this was all over, she'd sit Dad down and explain to him how silly it all was, how they should get rid of Mam and Tim, forget all about them, and move on to a better life until his lung condition took him away from her.

She'd have to see what his mood was like before she suggested anything, though. Like Martine had a bad girl, Dad had a bad boy, killing animals in his teens, raping that woman on his twenty-first birthday, then hiding his darkness away once he'd met Mam. He'd said he'd recognised the badness in Martine right from when she'd been about five, and their secret chat sessions had begun, him putting tentative feelers out, checking how she felt about certain things, moulding her to become who she was today.

His "doer", someone who did everything he couldn't.

But one day soon, it would all be just memories she dredged up to pick over. He'd die from his condition, and she'd be left to fend for herself in the cottage that had once belonged to his mother. There might be questions. How he'd come to "own" the place. Where his mother was, as no record of her death existed. If Martine didn't remove Mam and Tim from their lives before Dad passed away, there'd be them to explain, too.

No, Dad had to face up to things. He was ill, and when he died, most likely at his computer while staring at the photos she'd taken, she'd have to phone someone to come and collect the body.

Unless she buried him with his mother's remains and Baby Smith. Buried Mam and Tim there, too. Erased the lot of them, kept herself under the radar, and if anyone asked where Dad was, she'd say he'd moved to Cornwall or something.

Martine needed his money, though, the monthly cash sent to him by Gary, plus his disability payments. Her wages from the factory weren't enough for what she had in mind. Holidays abroad where she'd have fun, laughter, pretending to be normal, all the while hiding her darkness. Hiding the bad girl.

She glanced at Dad, who sunned his face in the garden, tilting it to the sky. He coughed, whipped out a tissue to cover his mouth. Gawped down at the blood on it and quickly stuffed the offending item into his pocket.

It was time to say something. Force him to acknowledge what was going on. They couldn't live in cloud cuckoo land forever.

"You'll need to switch your bank account into my name," she said.

"I know." He coughed again. "I'll set it in motion later. Go online, put in a request, but there might be questions. The DWP might need telling the account name has changed — unless, because it's put in there automatically, it just goes on the account number. Let me do it, see if the money still goes in as usual, and if it does, we don't need to say owt to them."

"What's going to happen about her?" She pointed at Mam in the wheelchair in front of her. "And *him*? What's the best way to go?" She wouldn't say what she wanted to happen. Not yet.

"Once the other two bastards are dealt with, we'll talk about it." He sighed. "I wasn't supposed to get ill, Mart."

"No." *At least he's admitted it now, that he's sick.*

"It wasn't meant to be like this at all. I stuffed it away, the bad boy, and tried, tried so bloody hard to be normal. Then you came along, and I saw it, that we were the same, and . . ."

"It's okay. I'm glad we had the talks. Because of them, I knew I wasn't alone. Knew you understood. We're like *Dexter* and his dad. Adoptive dad, whatever, you know what I mean."

"We are. What will you do after I'm gone?"

"The same as you tried to do. Stuff the bad girl away. I think that's for the best, don't you?"

"But what if she doesn't want to go? Mine didn't. He came out again when I killed your nan, and again when the

Bad Time happened, making me think about killing everyone involved."

"No, you didn't think that sort of thing until the Mam and Tim business three years ago because Guest started coming round after that. Guest wanted Gary gone, so *they* put the seeds in your head, not the bad boy. But I'll deal with whatever happens — what else can I do?"

"You'll need to be careful if you carry on."

"Yep, I know."

"I can't stand to think of you getting caught, not having my guidance."

She pushed the wheelchair to the patio doors, turned her back to the cottage and tugged Mam up the ramp she'd made out of wooden slats. "Don't worry about that now, Dad. Everything will be all right."

She parked Mam in her usual corner in the living room, couldn't be arsed to heft her out of the wheelchair and into the leather one. "Don't look at me like that, you fucking bitch!"

Mam's replacement glass eyes stared straight ahead.

"I really don't like you, creepy cow," Martine said. "Still, if I have my way you'll be gone soon. I think we'll have a tea party once you and your fella aren't here. Sausage rolls, triangle sandwiches. I might even make a trifle." She sighed at the thought of it. "It'll be the best day of my life."

CHAPTER FIFTEEN

62 French Avenue

Carol and Dave had taken a little breather for half an hour after they'd left Liz. Carol had been intent on moving on to Tanya Bedford straightaway, but lethargy had overtaken her in a sudden rush, and she'd grabbed a couple of to-go coffees from The Lord. They'd sat in the car outside, sipping, thinking, sipping again.

Now, they were back at work, Carol's head in the game.

Tanya's house, a pretty, ivy-covered stone building on the outside, an immaculate palace inside, triggered Carol's envy gene. She'd love to live in a chocolate-box place like this instead of her poky, somewhat dingy flat, which had about all the life and soul of a party for one. Maybe she could look into it, moving, finding somewhere that didn't cost an arm and a leg. One day.

Scrap that. With Dave living in her block, she kind of liked the fact he was close by. For security. The knowledge that if someone tried to break in, he'd be there in a flash.

This living room, done out with a beige theme much like Charlotte Majors', spoke of someone who liked order and cleaned a lot — the scent of disinfectant was overpowering to the point Carol's nose itched inside, a sneeze threatening. She swore grey was the "in" colour these days, on the walls at least, and fluffy silver rugs on near-black laminate, but the beige was nice. Calming.

Sunlight speared in through French doors at the bottom, casting multiple squares of illumination on the walls, resembling cream picture frames with no images inside. The doors opened out onto a decent-sized garden, paved, plants spilling over the edges of terracotta pots, flowers static, no breeze helping to bob their heads.

I wonder if anyone will bother to water Sue's garden now.
Flora might do it.

Dave walked over to the double doors and stood by the threshold, hands on hips. "Lovely view. You can see the moors from here. Ever spotted anyone out there, dancing?"

Tanya, early thirties, blonde hair in a high bun and as skinny as a rake in her Lycra outfit, the top with a polo neck, glanced at Carol, who stood by the sofa. "Um, should I have?"

Carol smiled. "Let me explain. We're here because of a case we're working on. An elderly lady, who liked dancing naked, has been found dead."

"Not Betty Tavers?" Tanya raised a hand to her chest and sat with an abrupt thump on an armchair, the seat cushion sighing at her weight, which wasn't much — she must only be about nine stone. Her elbow nudged a bottle of nail varnish off the table beside it. Red. That quick-dry gel stuff.

"Yes. I suspect you know her from the vet's." Carol, holding the can of Coke Tanya had offered them upon their arrival, popped the tab and sipped. Wished she'd taken the diet version as the syrup in this one was a tad too much. The bubbles popping on her throat were nice, though. Nothing better on a hot day. "I'll start from the beginning then ask you some questions. Thomas, your boss, found her on the patio at the vet's this morning. She'd been murdered. The reason we're here is that you could have crucial information."

"Me?" Tanya shrieked. "Why would you think that?"

"You might have seen or heard something that you dismissed when you went to check the animals during the night, but now, in light of what's happened, you might recall a significant clue."

"Oh. Yes." Tanya slumped back. "Murdered? Bloody hell . . ." She absently rubbed a fingertip down her throat, perhaps to ease a lump of fear that had gathered there.

I feel for her. Carol took news of a death in her stride these days. Not that she wasn't bothered or it didn't affect her, that was far from the truth, it was more that it had become part of her job, like an accountant using a calculator — par for the course. As a civvy, Tanya may need some time to process what she'd heard.

Carol smiled in sympathy. "Talk me through your movements from when you left here to visit the animals, to being there, then coming home."

Tanya launched into a list of what she'd done, talking in bullet points. Once she'd related what she could remember, she said, "There was nowt, nowt out of the ordinary. It was as silent as usual. Not many cars or whatever come by in the middle of the night."

Lucky you. Outside my gaff's like Grand Central. "Was it just the extra wages that prompted you to take up the job of doing the night visits? Thomas said it's triple time."

"Yes, that and I'd be awake anyroad, worrying about the animals. Thomas used to live above the practice, so he nipped down to see to them then — he had a baby monitor so heard them if they howled or whatever. When he moved out, I found myself waking a lot more than usual, thinking about them."

"A lot more?"

"I haven't slept solidly for years. Insomnia, you know."

"Maybe you could move into the flat? It'd save you going out into the night like this."

Tanya's body went stiff. "No. No, I like it here. I have to stay here."

"Okay. What I will say, then, is that until we've caught whoever this is, consider varying your times when you visit the vet's during the night. If someone has been watching, they'll know you go there at the same time . . ."

Tanya shuddered. "Oh God, do you think they've been spying on me?"

Carol needed the woman to do as she'd asked, so she nodded. "It's possible. Many people scope places out prior to committing a crime, especially those who make meticulous plans. Others, opportunists, grab the chance to kill when it's presented to them, but this person, I believe they've worked out exactly what they're going to do and when."

"How do you know that?" Tanya frowned.

Carol thought it was worth taking a punt here. "Do you know Gary and Sue Cuttersby at all? Cuttersby Clothing?"

Tanya stared at the floor, biting her bottom lip. "I heard their names on the news after I got back, twenty minutes or so before you arrived."

"Where did you go?"

"Just out. Are the cases linked or something? Sue and Betty?"

"I think so, but we're not certain of that yet."

"Shit, this is so awful. I can't . . . I mean, this is a lot to take in."

"I understand. So you didn't know of the Cuttersby couple until you heard it on the news, is that right?"

Tanya continued eyeing the floor, obviously dazed by what she'd been told.

Carol quietly sighed at the lack of response. *Cut her some slack. This is a difficult thing to handle.* "Let's get to Betty, then. Did she ever tell you, when she brought her cats in, that she danced on the moors?"

"I'd heard something about it from the receptionist, but whenever I saw Betty, she was too busy fawning over Thomas."

"Fawning?"

"Hmm. In a creepy way. Like she fancied him. At her age!"

"Okay . . . Explain her behaviour."

"She batted her eyelashes, touched his arm a lot, laughed at everything he said, even if it wasn't funny. Seemed annoyed when he told her the cats were fine."

"How often did she bring one in?"

"It had to be once a fortnight at least."

"And what did she suspect was wrong with them?"

"Bladder infections, ulcers, tumours, the list goes on. To be honest, I thought she had that syndrome, the one where people make up ailments and get off on their kids being ill, except with her it was cats. Munch something or other."

"It's now called fictitious or induced illness, but it sounds to me like she just wanted to see Thomas and used her pets to do that." *A mental disorder. Something to look into?* "Okay, moving on. Did you know Betty well?"

Tanya shrugged. "Not really."

"So you wouldn't have a clue who'd want to kill her, then?"

"No." Tanya got up and walked to the front-facing window. Hugged herself. "I'm sorry, but can you go now? This is all a bit much."

"Of course. If you think of owt . . . I'll leave a card on the coffee table." Carol placed it down. "We'll leave you to your day, and thanks for the Coke."

Outside by the car, Carol sipped from the can then said to Dave, "Bloody waste of time, that was."

"Yep, and we're about to waste some more by going to see Mr Watson."

They dealt with him, Carol giving him a stern warning and the instruction to go to the Co-op and pay for the scratch cards immediately, and if he didn't they'd be back to arrest him for coercion and theft, then she popped back into the shop to tell Stanley the money should be arriving soon. She bought a few of the fresh-baked pastries, asked for them to be put into three paper bags, then drove to Scudderton.

* * *

Incident Room

Michael was busy at work, his head bent, writing on a large pad.

"Got owt?" Carol handed him a bag of goodies then placed hers on Katherine's desk and Dave's on his. "I'll make a brew, shall I?"

Michael peeped into the bag. "Danish." He smiled at Carol. "I bloody love you."

"I should sodding well hope so. I fed you Greggs yesterday as well — I happen to feel guilty about you giving up your weekend, so don't expect a treat every day of the week from now on. Only special occasions." She walked over to the drinks area in the corner — something she'd set up herself so cuppas were close by, saving time going to the staff kitchen when they were up against the clock — and flicked the kettle on. "So I take it you've got bugger all, seeing as you haven't answered me."

Michael paused his chewing, a flake of pastry clinging to the side of his mouth. "Sorry, no, nowt much to report — whatever I've got is on the board — but I phoned Whitney. She's still with Gary, so I asked her to question him about Betty, see how well he knows her, but not to mention that she's dead. I thought you'd like to see his facial expression when you inform him of that. He said he has some stories he could tell, so you might want to go down there."

"We will, after we've had a scoff." She made the drinks, dished them out, then sat at Katherine's desk to enjoy her sugary lunch, planning to eat between talking.

Dave, feet propped on his desk, a Danish in one hand, tea in the other, stared at the ceiling in thought. "So what reason are we going with for these deaths? A row with a third party? Someone at the factory?"

Carol nodded. "It's looking that way — and let's face it, we don't have owt else. Whoever it is knew Sue enough to know she waters her plants at night — okay, I'm supposing there, we don't know her being in the garden had owt to do with it, but as it's a regular thing, we can afford to assume. And with Betty, they knew of the vet connection. Otherwise, why bother leaving her there?"

"Want to know what I think?" Dave said. "Because Betty lives alone, it's unlikely she'd be found for days, maybe weeks, and so they chose the vet."

"That contradicts my thoughts," Michael said. "What do you think about the fact they might not have wanted her found until Monday — so like, they *did* want her found, just not yet. The vet is closed at the weekends."

Carol could see his point. "The killer might not have known that, though."

Michael took out another cake. Eyed it. One of the fat raisins plopped off onto his notepad. "But if we go back to the woman in the bush, which suggests the Cuttersbys were being watched, wouldn't the killer do the same with Betty? Watch her, watch the vet's place, spot the opening times online?"

Carol nodded. "I just said similar to Tanya Bedford, the vet's assistant, warned her to switch the times she visits the animals at night, just in case the place was under surveillance."

"Where from, though?" Dave asked. "I mean, it's in the sticks. No trees close by to hide behind — well, there are, but they're a good two miles away, closer to Scudderton. They'd need some bloody good binoculars or a telescope. If they came along in a car, they'd have to park it somewhere. Even if they left it down the road and walked to the vet's, someone driving by would have seen them and the abandoned car. Too risky."

Carol was in agreement. "It could be like Michael said. They looked at it online. Google Maps. Street View. All done in the comfort of their own home, and if they did go there to scope it out in a car, maybe they just got lucky. Uniforms have been out to two cottages along that stretch, a father and daughter, and an old man, and none of them saw or heard owt."

Michael swallowed a mouthful of tea then picked up the raisin and popped it in his mouth. "So, the connection. What we think might be a row. What about that?"

Carol swept pastry bits off her trousers. "Both snippets of info could have been spoken about, in the canteen, say. Our killer overheard. Used it later to their advantage after what we think might have been a barny. It's difficult to tell without speaking to the factory lot and seeing if there was any tension going on, and you can imagine the time it'd take us to get through them all."

"Surely Gary would know, save us going down that route," Michael said.

Carol barked out a laugh. "From what we've gathered, I'd say Sue basically ran things while he got busy touching up the female staff, so would he necessarily be thinking with the head on his shoulders enough to pick up on spats at work? Also, I'm tempted to go to the factory and ask those women if his advances were welcome. We could have historical sexual harassment claims in our future if they admit he didn't like the word 'no' — I'll make damn sure of it."

"He sounds a right wanker," Michael griped, "and where's the bloody HR at the factory? Didn't anyone think to use it to report the harassment? Unless, of course, they liked him groping them."

"Whether he messed about behind Sue's back or not, there's something about him that says he isn't bad through and through." Had Carol been sucked in by him like all the other women? Could he charm any bird out of any tree if he wanted to, including her?

Not Flora. She held in a snort. *Flora detests him.*

"But yes," she agreed, "he *is* a wanker for behaving like that, and going anywhere near him in the love department is dangerous. We've only got to look at his reaction regarding Charlotte's pregnancy to know that."

Dave piped up. "I wonder if he'll pack it in now. You know, having it away with others might not be so tempting if his wife's not around. Some people get off on the thrill of doing something naughty behind their backs." He sighed. "Like my wife."

Carol's eyebrows shot up. Dave hadn't told Michael or Katherine why he'd moved out, only that he was having problems in his marriage and they were separating.

Michael whipped his head round. "She *never did*."

"She did. She is." Dave shrugged.

"Fucking hell, pal." Michael gaped in sympathy. "I'm sorry. No wonder you moved out."

Dave didn't seem bothered anymore, although if he'd mentioned it, he must be. Or maybe he'd wanted to let Michael know what had really happened, and this way, during a briefing, it didn't seem so bad — plus Michael could tell Katherine, saving Dave the job. "Her life. I'm just glad to be out of it."

After their chat last night eating Chinese, Carol honestly thought he *was* over it. For the most part anyway. Promising himself to move on. Who wanted to stay with someone who'd cheated on them?

She scrunched her pastry bag into a ball. "Suppose we ought to go and see Gary, but I'll just have a look at the board first." She got up, threw her rubbish in the bin and took her tea to the whiteboard.

Michael had added Betty's name and a few things underneath: date of birth, address, the location she'd been found, where she'd worked, the fact she had no mobile but did have a landline. A credit card debt — probably all those payments to the vet — to the tune of four thousand and something. The alleged moor dancing, the nakedness. Carol jotted the info about the universe, elements and vibrations that Liz had told them.

"Can you look into these three things while we're gone," she asked Michael, and tapped the board with the end of the marker pen, explaining to him what they meant. "See if she belonged to some sort of group, spiritualists or whatever these would come under."

He nodded. "Will do. By the way, nowt on CCTV close to Murdoch Lane. I had a quick squiz on fast-forward, and no cars went in that direction during the timeframe."

"Bollocks."

"Shall I give Rib a poke about Sue's post-mortem?"

Carol shook her head. "No, leave him. He's likely to drag his feet for longer if he knows we're desperate for info, the sadistic fucker, plus he was called out to Betty earlier so might not even have had the chance to see to Sue. It's the weekend, and murder inquiry or not, he may have chosen to pop them in the fridge until tomorrow."

"Probably." Michael sipped his tea.

Carol drank half of hers, dumped the cup in the little sink, then waved at Dave. "Come on. Let's get down to Cove and see what stories Gary has to tell us about Betty. What with the naked dancing, I dread to think . . ."

* * *

Seashore Heights

Gary hadn't slept too well. His mind had been on Charlotte, of all people, his brain focusing on the hot topic of whether she really planned to ensure his sons knew what their father had been getting up to. He had a month's grace to dwell on it, think about how he could tell the boys without upsetting them more than they already were, although it was bound to crush them. On the other hand, meeting a little sister might be just what they needed to take their mind off things.

Who am I kidding? They're going to hate me. Feel sorry for Sue and give me the cold shoulder. Can't say I blame them. I hate myself for what I've done. And I might have to tell them sooner. A month walking on eggshells, waiting to speak to Charlotte . . . could send me batty.

All of his self-hate was too late. When Sue had been alive, his main focus had been hiding everything from her. He'd been prepared to lie until his last breath, even going so far as to imagine moving his family away so Charlotte didn't know where he was. He'd forfeit looking after Starbell, which would be a shame as he could admit to being fond of her lately, but with the risk of the girl growing into an adult who turned up on his doorstep . . . well, he'd pondered on whether it was best to cut ties while she wouldn't remember him.

Yes, too late to feel bad now — and *why* did he feel bad just because his wife was dead?

Because now Charlotte knows about Jack and Joseph, and the decisions will be taken out of my hands.

If Gary refused to allow a meeting, Charlotte was the type to find out which school the boys went to and wait outside, springing the surprise of their sister on them, and there wouldn't be a damn thing he could do about it.

For now, he'd try to put Charlotte and the baby out of his head and concentrate on being there for his sons. There was no point him getting coiled up about something that hadn't happened yet. He'd face what he had to minute by minute, hour by hour, until some sense of being able to cope better came along — cope with the reality that he had a funeral to arrange, a body to bury once the police finally release her.

Jack and Joseph had gone to see Flora, although she'd said she'd leave the spare key beneath the flowerpot in the back garden as she had an errand to run. Why the fuck she'd want to run an errand when her child had been killed Gary didn't know. But he *did* know really, he knew Flora from old. It was more likely she'd gone into town, hoping to catch the eye of people she knew so she could siphon all their sympathy out of them, be the tearful star of the show, and tell each and every one of them that Gary should be the one in a morgue fridge, not Sue. Instead of being chilled and awaiting the scalpel, he was stuck in a state of suspension. His mind was on constant churn, and he wished he could stop it.

Gary supposed the walk to her house might go some way to clearing the death-soaked cobwebs in the twins' minds. Or maybe they wanted to be near their home, the one they'd grown up in. In truth, they probably wanted to get away from him. They'd hardly said two words, preferring to chat to Whitney. According to her, SOCO should be finished by this evening.

Gary imagined the gossip flooding social media. Whitney had said there was a discussion on the Scudderton Facebook page about Sue, advising him not to look at it. He'd asked why, and she'd been honest.

"Some people are saying you did it."

"Fucking hell . . . It wasn't me, I'd never have harmed her."

"Just stay away. It isn't worth the aggro. You know the truth of the matter, so don't worry about armchair coppers. There are so many amateur sleuths cropping up I had to check all their surnames weren't Holmes."

He'd appreciated her trying to lighten the mood, but he'd tormented himself, seeing all the comments in his head, scrolling through his mind like they would on the screen.

The husband did it, stands to reason. Always the partner.
I bet he was having it away with someone else — dirty bastard.
Or him and his bit on the side planned it.
Yeah, wouldn't surprise me. He always was a pervert.
Could never keep his hands to himself.

"Shit," he muttered. "I can't handle this."

Earlier, Whitney had received a call from the station, and while whoever it was had stayed on the other end of the line, she'd asked Gary about Betty Tavers. Why, he didn't have the foggiest and had no energy to ask, the lethargy of grief pulling him down. No one told you your body seemed to weigh more when you had stuff like this to deal with. How every step you took was the equivalent of wading through treacle. Was that where the saying came from, having the weight of the world on your shoulders? It bloody felt like he did. But he'd answered Whitney, saying he had some stories to tell but could it wait until he'd had some fresh air?

Now, he stood out on the cliff and stared at the sea doing its thing, bobbing despite the stillness of this summer day. A few people were out on paddleboards, their life jackets yellow or orange specks on the blue vastness. A red buoy marked where it was safe to swim out to, and beyond it, dolphins broke the surface, three of them, performing a diving arc then disappearing back beneath the depths.

Sue would have loved seeing them. It was her favourite thing to do here, seeing if she could spot them, sitting on the ground, her feet bare, grass poking between her toes. If he had the energy, he'd take a picture of the dolphins, get it blown up for a frame. Put in on the wall in her memory. But there was no energy to be had.

He swiped tears that burned his eyes — it was *all* too little too late. He should have done those things when she was alive. Sat beside her out here, spent some time to listen to her instead of chasing every bit of skirt he could. Anger at this unfairness, at how he'd behaved, swamped him, telling him in a taunting voice that he'd had to have his cake and eat it, couldn't just stick with Sue, when all along, she'd been everything any man could need. He didn't understand why he was a womaniser, no more than he could understand why she was dead. Who would want to *do* that to her?

He pulled his sunglasses down from the top of his head to cover his gritty eyes. Cast his gaze to the sky. Heaven. Was she there with his father? And there was the visit to his mother he had to get through, telling her about Sue, Mam not knowing who the fuck he was talking about, her memories of his wife soaked up by a dementia sponge, forever held inside the honeycomb holes, never to be released. Mam would probably stare at him like she always did these days, either scared at having a "stranger" in her room, screaming for the nurse to come and get him out, or on the other end of the scale, being indifferent to his presence, telling him about the son she had who was too busy to go and see her, when he was there, *right there* in front of her, wishing she knew it was him.

He sniffed, emotions getting the better of him, a new one coming along in the form of despair. Then Carol Wren's car appeared, and she parked close by. What did *she* want? Had they caught the killer?

Gary didn't turn to face her as she and Dave approached. He remained staring out at the sea, wishing he had the balls to wait for the tide to come in, jump over the cliff edge later, let the salty water carry him away, then under, into a cold death, one he deserved after how he'd treated Sue. But he wouldn't do it. He had Jack and Joseph to think of. Couldn't leave them to Flora. She'd have Gary's memory tainted inside a second.

But despite telling himself that, the urge was still there.

Carol came to stand on his left, Dave on his right. It felt as though they were flanking him as a menacing duo who'd come to arrest him, and he shivered.

"How are you bearing up?" Carol sounded kind and genuinely concerned, like she actually gave a shit.

Gary shrugged. "Beating myself up. Wishing I'd been a better husband."

"Regrets. They're cruel, but we learn from them. Going forward, maybe you'll keep your hands to yourself."

Ouch. He should have been angry at her for being so in his face with that comment, so blunt, but he deserved it. He nodded. "I will. It was just a thing I did, no harm in it if Sue didn't know, and the women, they were up for it. I'm not some deviant."

"That's good to know, but I've made the decision we're going to be asking them just the same."

"Dotting the i's."

"Something like that."

"No news, then?"

"No, not about Sue, although we have something we think might be linked."

Linked? "What's that, then?"

A gull swooped. Squawked. He envied it its freedom. He'd like to fly away, leave everything behind, but that was ridiculous because his problems would follow him. He'd still have a dead wife, a baby he'd never wanted and sons who'd hate him once they knew about her. Talk about making a hash of things. And there he'd been, king of his world, thinking nothing could stop him doing whatever he wanted, then someone had come along and killed his wife, and all the worms he'd held inside a tight-lidded can were spilling out.

Carol sighed. "Betty Tavers. What can you tell us?"

Gary sighed, too. "Whitney asked about her. Betty's been on the books from day dot. Started in sewing, learned cutting, pressing, basically a dab hand at everything now. I know if someone's off sick, I can get her to fill their place for the day. She's a bit . . . off the wall these days, but she's just an old woman learning new things."

"Like what?"

"Embracing energy, something along those lines. Dancing naked. Full moon. Some reckon she's funny in the head, getting old, but I see her as a woman finding herself after so long of conforming to what society thinks she should be. Sue, on the other hand, she thought Betty . . . well, she told me she's mad, weird, a witch. Which is odd, because Sue didn't usually say mean things. Maybe Betty unnerved her, got under her skin a bit too much."

"Did Sue like Betty?"

Gary stuffed his hands in his shorts pockets. The tissue he'd blown his nose on earlier tickled his fingers. "There wasn't a bad word between them, if that's what you mean. Sue, she had her ideas about her, and from a work perspective, she thought it was high time Betty retired. The gossiping to the other employees was getting annoying, disrupting the flow. Betty thinks nowt of wandering around from department to department, waffling on. I turn a blind eye because . . ." His voice wobbled. "Because my mother's about the same age, and she's stuck in that bloody care home, unable to do owt. I suppose I want Betty to do whatever she wants because she still can. It sounds silly. I can't explain it."

"I understand."

"Sue planned to ask her to tone it down or retire." He recalled their last conversation, where he hadn't particularly been listening, Sue babbling on about Betty, getting quite irate if he recalled it right. He told Carol that now, then apologised if he'd repeated himself, as he couldn't remember whether they'd already spoken about this yesterday. "I can't see Betty killing my wife, though, and anyroad, Sue died before she had the chance to have a word with her. Unless she phoned her after I went to bed Friday night."

"I've had some info back from digi forensics, and if she'd phoned Betty, I'd know about it."

Gary supposed he'd better ask, see why there was so much interest in the old woman. "Why all the questions about her? Betty, I mean."

The gull headed their way, dipped low as if ready to come and peck their eyes out, then crested, going up, up, up, wings wide. Then it shot closer again, darted down a few metres, and let out a shriek that sounded suspiciously like laughter. Like it mocked him.

Gary shuddered. "Fucking things. Size of cats, some of them."

"The gulls? Hmm. As for Betty, we're here because she's dead."

He looked at Carol then, snapping his head round, his mouth opening in shock. She appeared brown-tinged, him viewing her from behind his sunglasses. "*Dead?*"

"Murdered."

Gary's heart rate thundered. What the *hell* was going on? First Sue, now Betty? Carol had mentioned a link when she'd first arrived. Did she mean the factory? Was the killer one of his *employees*, for God's sake?

"I . . . my head's all over the place, I can't take it in," he said. "Betty's *dead?*"

"Yes. Her body was found at the vet's on Murdoch Lane this morning. Do you have any pets? I don't recall seeing one at your other house."

"No, Sue didn't like the idea of all the hairs. What's that got to do with owt?"

"I wanted to see if there was a connection with Sue and the vet's, that's all."

"No, nowt, not that I know of." He looked out to sea again. A thought popped into his head, one that seemed to shrivel his brain cells with spite and the malicious intent to upset him, get him imagining Sue with someone else, a torment much like she might have gone through when she'd found the hotel receipts. Karma. "Does Thomas still run the place?"

"Thomas Lines? Yes . . ."

"Sue used to go out with him, before we got together."

"A tenuous link but one all the same. Thanks for that. Were they serious?"

"No. Teenagers. Lasted about a month."

One of the paddleboarders fell off, crashing into the water. Normally, Gary would worry, wait for them to surface, be safe, but he found he didn't give a shit. His mind was too busy showing him Sue on a bed with Thomas, and his jealous streak spread through him. How odd that it bothered him now, yet when she'd been alive, the idea of her going off with someone else had been ludicrous.

Did she cry when she knew I'd been staying at Betterway? God, that poor woman . . .

He asked, "How was Betty killed? The same as Sue?"

"No. I don't think you need that kind of information at this time. You're going through enough. So, to reiterate, you don't know of any reason as to why someone would kill Sue and Betty?"

A lump formed in his throat. The paddler was okay, back on the board, and it was so unfair. Why couldn't Sue have got up? Why couldn't she climb back on *her* board? Why couldn't she still be here so he could change, treat her better, make up for all the times he'd played away? The idea that she'd known about it before her death crippled him. How long had she been aware? She'd never acted any differently towards him. Any other woman would have confronted him after finding the hotel receipts and ripped his eyes out.

"No," he said. "No idea at all."

"Whitney said you have some stories to tell about Betty. Care to share?"

"Not really. They wouldn't be relevant. Just stupid things she got up to at work over the years."

"Stupid? Like what? And I'll be the judge of whether they're relevant or not."

"Fine. She forgot things sometimes." Gary winced. Thought about the worst thing she'd done. "Like not putting the guard down on the cutter. It sliced a man's hand off at the wrist."

"Bloody hell . . ."

"Hmm. Dad put an early retirement plan in place for him, then Dad felt so guilty about the accident he turned to drink. I still pay the bloke a wage to this day. More of a pension, really."

"Who is that?" Carol asked.

"Smith. Harry. Lives in one of the cottages out Mollengate way. Murdoch Lane."

"The road the vet's is on. Betty must have felt awful, but clearly, she didn't lose her job."

"No, she was suspended for a while, pending an enquiry, but it was ruled as an accident."

"Did Mr Smith accept that?"

Gary nodded. "Yes, as well as the monthly payments."

"I see. When did this happen?"

"Oh, years ago now. Can't remember exactly when, but I can sort the info out for you when I go into work tomorrow." *But I do remember I was in the corner with some young woman when it happened. Fuck, I've been such a bastard. If I hadn't been messing around, I'd have seen the cutter guard was up.*

Funny how Harry had never told anyone Gary and the woman were there. They'd gone in after Betty had walked out. Why hadn't Harry said something? Or hadn't he noticed them? He'd been distracted, Gary knew that much. Probably running Betty's instructions through his head. Got flustered. Used the cutter and . . .

Carol linked her hands and pushed them outwards, stretching her muscles. "So too long ago for Mr Smith to want to get even years later? With Betty?"

"I'd say so. Nice fella. Placid. I can't see him doing owt like that."

Carol dropped her hands to her sides. "Was Sue around during that time?"

"She worked at the factory, yes, but she was in my office when the accident happened." *I made sure of it. Gave her a job to do to keep her out of the way.*

"So she had nowt to do with the incident?"

"No."

"Did you?"

"No, but I was in the room when it occurred."

Carol kicked at a tuft of grass. "Must have been nasty."

"It was."

"We'll look into it, just in case. I like to cover all angles."

Gary's stomach turned over. Harry hadn't said anything before, but that was then. Would he say something now, that Gary had been there, been negligent? Would Carol then reopen that enquiry, meaning Gary got into trouble after all?

He swallowed tightly. The worst had already happened to him, his wife was dead, so whatever went on now, well, he'd just have to deal with it. Same as he would when Charlotte came knocking.

The appeal of jumping off the cliff had just grown stronger.

CHAPTER SIXTEEN

The Bushes

Behind the bushes on a patch of grass between Gary's house and the one next door, Guest spied on him and the coppers, conscious it was daylight and they could be spotted, especially as the neighbouring house had a side window at what must be the top of the stairs. What were the police doing here? Previous to their arrival, Gary had come out to stand and stare at the sea, probably secretly chuffed Sue was dead, bastard that he was. He was free to do whatever he wanted now, mucking about with other women, and Guest's whole body had stiffened with anger about that, hands clenched into fists, teeth gritted.

Gary shouldn't be over there, living, breathing. *He* should be the dead one. How had the Smiths got it so wrong, killing Sue instead? Martine had been scary earlier, putting the knife to Guest's neck, acting threatening. Why had the father-and-daughter duo gone with their own plan instead of Guest's? It made sense on all their parts to kill Gary — he'd been there when Mr Smith's hand had been chopped off, and Guest wanted Gary removed from this planet because of—

No. Concentrate on doing it yourself like Martine said.

The problem with that was, Guest had no clear way to get Gary on his own. That other copper was there, hanging around indoors like a bad smell. Guest had gone as close to the open window at the side of his house as they'd dared earlier, listening to the conversation inside. Whitney, that was the copper's name. She'd asked Gary about Betty, and that had chilled Guest's bones.

I heard about what happened to Betty.

It had to be the Smiths who'd done that. Guest recalled Harry talking about Betty being the one at fault regarding his missing hand. He must have ordered Martine to kill the old woman because of it. Gary had been targeted for being there and not seeing the cutter guard was still up, so it made sense Betty had also been killed.

Guest shrank lower behind the bush — the two coppers out on the cliff were leaving.

I can't stay here. I'll come back later when they're asleep. Break in. Kill him.

Only then would Guest rest easy.

CHAPTER SEVENTEEN

Smithy's Cottage

Harry's stump itched. Something was afoot, although he didn't know what. Martine was having a bath, and the smell of the roasting joint filled the air. He'd said it was daft to have the oven on when it was such a hot day, they could have a ham salad instead with some nice new potatoes, but his daughter had insisted, reminding him he liked routine, adding, "A bit too much and for no reason sometimes." He knew what she was getting at but chose to ignore the jibe.

He stood in the living room and stared at his wife, loving the sight of Josie like that, strapped to the wheelchair, unable to ever leave him for a moment again. Martine hadn't transferred her to the armchair earlier, but not to worry, this bitch here could sit anywhere he chose. He was in charge of her now.

Josie had got exactly what she deserved, her freedom taken away from her, like his had been. Yes, he could admit he was well able to go back out into the world, live as he had before, minus going to work, but he was afraid of his bad boy coming back, pushing him to rampage around Scudderton, maybe even Mollengate, a gun in hand, killing everyone in sight like those mad shooters did, then killing himself. He'd entertained that far too many times to count, hating the fact that they could all go on, oblivious to his pain, their worlds undisturbed by a set of tragic events that had brought him to the here and now.

If he stayed home, the bad boy couldn't hurt anyone.

But he still does, through Martine's bad girl.

They were a right old pair, weren't they?

As a child brought up by a single parent, he'd always known he wasn't right. Hadn't ever fitted in. Had always been on the chubby side until he'd changed his ways. Just before then, he'd raped that woman. Couldn't get it from anyone else, could he? Girls didn't like a fatty, so he'd been told. He'd enjoyed himself with that sexual encounter so much he'd told himself to lose weight, get fit, snag a woman of his own — and he had.

Josie had come on to him, not the other way around — Harry didn't have the self-confidence at the time, even though he came off as a muscly man who had his shit together. The outside of a person hid a multitude of insecurities that swirled inside, at least in his case. Looking back on it, he should have realised she was a slag by the way she'd behaved. She'd been overly keen to take him home from the pub, get him into her bed, her parents dead, her owning the house outright. But at the time, he'd been so pleased to have someone notice him, he hadn't given her forwardness another thought. Put her eagerness down to how he looked, toned and fit.

They'd married, and he'd hated living at her place in Scudderton. Too busy there, too noisy, and as he'd been brought up in Smithy's Cottage, in the peace and quiet, the country air tinged with the tang of salt from the sea, he'd made the decision to kill his mother. Convinced Josie to move to the cottage and rent her house out to that nice young couple with the little boy. For a year or so she'd been fine, probably the novelty of being alone with him in a place no one could disturb them, but then Martine had been born, and she'd harped on about selling her house and the cottage, putting the money together to buy a big place in Scudderton.

No, no and no. How could he sell the cottage when he didn't have legal proof it was his?

He'd got his own way. Josie had sold her house, the money ploughed into doing the cottage up, just as he'd envisaged. They'd trundled along for a few years. His weight returned after the Bad Time; he ate to comfort himself, stopped exercising. Depression had draped itself over him, growing worse when Josie had so cruelly said she didn't want his stump touching her. They'd continued for a few more years, Harry pretending he didn't notice the change in his wife, too concerned with having his talks with Martine, teaching her bad girl the ways, but when Josie had taken to going out with lipstick on, at night — well, he couldn't have that. Martine had not long passed her driving test, and she'd followed her mother in an ancient Capri he no longer owned, gathered intel, and the rest, as they say, is history.

He perked up at the sound of a car engine. It wasn't unusual, people drove by either towards Mollengate or back the other way to Scudderton instead of using the noisy Robottom Street with all those lorries, but the pitch was wrong, as if a vehicle was slowing down, same as it did whenever Guest came to visit — and when those two uniforms had come by to see if he'd heard anything unusual during the night. He'd said no because that had been the truth. What had happened with Betty was *usual*, what he'd planned.

He returned his thoughts to the car noise. Maybe Braithwaite's grandson was out on one of the horses again and the driver was following the rules, going at a snail's pace so the animal wasn't spooked.

Harry strained his ears to catch the sound of the clip-clops of hooves on tarmac, but there was nothing other than that car and his wheezing chest. He moved closer to the front window and peered through the nets to the left. A car indeed slowed, coming from Scudderton, then turned onto *his drive-way*. Shit, shit, shit, who was that? He panicked, his heart throbbing, his poor lungs constricting, bringing on spearing pain.

Don't cough now. Don't get yourself in a state like you did earlier with the plods.

He rushed to the bottom of the stairs. "Mart! Mart! Someone's here again!"

"Hang on!" came her muffled voice, followed by a slosh of water where she'd undoubtedly sat up in the bath.

He pelted as much as he was able into the living room, coughing, his inner thighs chafing, and went to grab the wheelchair handles with both hands, forgetting he only had one. It fooled him into thinking it was still there, his missing hand, and he gritted his teeth to stop tears forming. Angry at the memory lapse, he gripped one handle and pushed his wife to the patio doors and down the wooden ramp, parking her against the house beneath the kitchen window. Back inside, he snatched a throw off the sofa and went back out, covering her from head to toe, muttering, "You're a fucking pest. Maybe it's time you left us for good."

Sweating, he ambled back inside just as the doorbell chimed. He used his stumpy forearm to wipe his wet brow, took a deep breath in an attempt to still the panic racing around inside him, then walked to the bottom of the stairs.

"Mart!" he whisper-shouted.

"I'm *drying* myself, Dad!"

He drew on his reserves, hid the bad boy deep down inside and pulled out the dopey version of himself, the one who wouldn't hurt a fly. Thick as mince, some had called him. He latched on to the man his cheating wife had fallen in love with, except now he was covered in multiple layers of fat and his lungs were giving out on him.

Harry opened the door, lifting his eyebrows on purpose, feigning surprise at having visitors. He said to the man and woman, "Oh, hello there. This is a treat. We don't get many people stopping this way. Had two coppers earlier, and now you pair. Are you from the church?" *You know they're not. You know exactly who they are.* "Only, someone came last Sunday an' all, Catholics, and I don't want to be rude, but we're really not interested. You have your beliefs, I have mine. Let's keep it that way, eh?"

The woman held up some ID. "No, we're from the police station, Mr Smith. It *is* Harry Smith, isn't it?"

Fuck me. Come on, Mart, help me out here. "It is."

"I'm DI Carol Wren, and this is DS Dave Waite. Could we pick your brains for a few minutes?"

Picking his brains didn't sound too bad. Didn't sound ominous or scary. People said that sort of thing when they wanted a bit of help, didn't they? There was nothing to worry about here.

Relieved this wasn't anything sinister, he relaxed. "Of course, come in. I suppose you're here about something going off down the Lane; those policemen earlier asked me about it. My daughter's just getting out of the bath, so don't mind her if she appears, looking like a drowned rat." He led the way into the living room, panting, suddenly angry he hadn't had the chance to check the room properly before he'd opened the door. Josie's slippers must have fallen off when he'd hastily wheeled her outside, and her handbag was on the coffee table, same as it always was, exactly where she'd left it the night Martine had solved their issues.

It's okay, they'll assume they're Mart's.

"Would you like a drink?" He held his stump up. "I might be minus a hand, but I can still make tea." He laughed to put them at ease, to show them he was a happy-go-lucky chap who didn't mind having no hand, when really, he hated it. Detested it with a passion.

He tamped down the rage threatening to boil.

"No, thank you." Carol smiled. "We won't take up much of your time. Just a few questions." She moved to the corner and stood beside Josie's armchair.

Her partner remained beside the doorway, a notebook and pen in hand.

"Take a seat if you like." Harry sat on one of the sofas, annoyed his chest rattled.

Carol smiled again. "No, you're all right. Like I said, we'll not be here long."

That's something, then. "Fire away. What can I help you with? Although I doubt it's much, because since this happened, I've been a recluse." He waved his stump around. "It gets a bit wearing, people staring at you. Well, my arm."

"Yes, that must be difficult. I'm sorry to dredge up the past, but I wanted to ask you about your accident, actually."

Harry smiled through his fear. "That was a long time ago now, I'm well past it, happy with the outcome. I got a pension out of it, plus disability. And that's what it was — you know, an accident. I'm to blame, too. The cutter guard was up, yes, and I don't recall being told to make sure it was down, but I should have realised. Common sense, isn't it?"

"So you don't blame Betty Tavers for it? Harbour a grudge?"

You have no idea . . . "Good God, no. Why would I? I've had years to come to terms with it, and I can still sew one-handed. Got a Singer, I have. The only thing bad to happen afterwards was my wife buggering off a few years later, but I've come to terms with that an' all. Got together with some fella called Tim, so she said. Couldn't hack my depression when I first lost my hand. I couldn't hack myself during that time, so it stands to reason she couldn't either. Shit happens, but we make the best of it, don't we?"

"So she left your daughter behind?"

"Martine, that's my girl, she wanted to stay with me, so . . ."

"Have you seen Betty Tavers recently?" Carol asked.

"Not for years. I don't leave the house anymore. Martine does everything I can't." *Doesn't she just.* "Last I saw Betty in the flesh was the day of the accident." *Liar. I've seen photos. Know she hasn't aged well. Know what she looked like when she was dead. I saw her flesh then, all right.*

"Years, then."

"Yep. Martine will have seen her, though. She works at the factory, Cuttersby Clothing. Ask her when she comes down. Are you sure you don't want a drink? A glass of pop or something? I've got ice cubes. It's so bloody hot, isn't it?"

"This summer has been a bugger, I'll give you that, but no, honestly, we're fine. Thanks, though." Carol smiled then shifted her focus to the doorway.

Martine had appeared beside Dave, her hair long and wet, cheeks rosy. She looked at Harry, the picture of a daughter worried about her father. "Everything okay, Dad?"

He nodded. "Police again, love. Asking about the Bad Time, you know, my hand."

"Oh, has the enquiry been reopened or something, then? I thought it was an accident?"

Carol linked her hands in front of her and went to the window, her back to it. "We've had to come and check your father's feelings on it, that's all. We're investigating another case — Betty Tavers is involved. Someone mentioned the accident, and we're chasing all leads. Your dad said you'll have seen Betty recently. At work."

Martine nodded. "Yes, I'm sometimes in the same area as her. What's up?"

The skin beside Carol's eye twitched. "How would you describe Betty, Martine?"

"A bit batty, if I'm honest. She went all weird the last few years. Got into that spirituality thing, kept talking about vibrations from the earth, being at one with the elements, nature, that sort of rubbish."

"What else have you heard?" Carol asked.

She doesn't sound like she's interrogating her, more as if she's going through the motions. We're safe, aren't we?

Martine rolled her eyes. "Apparently, she dances naked when it's a full moon. On the moors. Which is just daft. I can't see an old lady doing that myself, but she swears she does. Never seen her out the back, though, have we, Dad, so God knows where she does it. Maybe nearer to Scudderton — I'm sure she said she lives in a bungalow there. Anyroad, I know her mind's on the turn because she's one of them cat ladies. I heard her telling someone she's got seventeen of them, plus this parrot that swears. I feel sorry for her. She's obviously lonely."

"So she's always been okay with you?"

Martine frowned. "Why wouldn't she be?"

"Because of what happened with your dad. She might have shied away from you out of guilt."

"Nope, she's as chatty as ever."

Carol focused on Harry. "I know you said you don't leave the house anymore, but as a matter of procedure, I have to ask. Where were you in the early hours of Friday, from midnight until six, and the early hours of this morning, from midnight until around three?"

It's okay, she said it's just procedure. "In my bed, why?"

Carol turned to Martine. "And you?"

"Same. Has something happened?" Martine glanced from Dave to Carol.

"You might have heard it on the news, but saying that, if you're asking, you probably don't know. You'll find out at work tomorrow, no doubt. Sue Cuttersby was murdered, as was Betty Tavers."

"What?" Martine grabbed the sides of her hair.

Oh, she's good, my girl.

"Take a seat." Carol gestured to the sofa. "This has obviously come as a shock to you."

"Who'd want to kill *them*?" Martine sank down next to Harry, doing a good impression of someone shaking from that shock Carol had mentioned.

Harry patted her arm. "There, there, duck. I know how much you liked those two."

Martine sobbed. "God, this is awful. What about Gary? Is he okay?"

Carol nodded. "He's . . . well, you can imagine."

"Poor fella," Harry said, holding back laughter.

"Okay, I'm satisfied with what you've told us, so we'll leave you be." Carol sniffed. "Something smells nice."

Harry chuckled then realised he probably shouldn't have done that, given the circumstances. "Martine's cooking us a roast."

"Lovely. Well, enjoy the rest of your day, and I'm sorry to have been the bearer of such bad news."

A sniffling Martine showed the coppers out, and Harry's rictus smile slipped. Jesus Christ, that was a close call. He'd seen on the news they'd found Sue, and he knew they'd also found Betty. He'd browsed social media earlier with his fake account — BadBoy2022 — and some wanker had mentioned Harry might have a grudge against her because of her part in things. Someone else had shot them down, saying it had been years ago, water under the bridge. Harry *did* have a beef, only he hadn't acted on it until now because *one*, he'd had to wait for Martine to be old enough to do what was needed, *two*, he'd tried to keep his bad boy quiet, and *three*, Guest coming for visits had pushed him towards making plans and finally putting things right.

He'd thought years between the Bad Time and the murders meant no one would tie things together, but he'd been wrong. As well as that fella on social media bleating about it, those coppers had come, and he should have known the elephants of this area would have long memories. As for it being Wren on the case . . .

I should have known it would be her an' all.

Who had suggested Harry having a grudge?

You know who it was. The name churned your stomach.

Yes, he knew. Why had that person put Harry's name out there? What had Harry ever done to them? Well, maybe it was time to kill them. Martine knew about the commenter, and she wouldn't care if she had to do them over.

Martine came back in and stood by the window, watching the car drive away, her eyes dry of crocodile tears now. "It'll have been Gary who told them about your accident."

"You might be right there."

"I told Guest to go ahead and kill him if they weren't happy that we'd done Sue over. I know it means I won't

164

be able to spy on him at work and tell you how much he's suffering, but I imagine he's suffered quite a bit already. Will that be enough for you?"

Harry thought about it. Nodded. "It'll have to be, because he needs shutting up now if he's blabbing to the police. Fuck Guest's motives, we'll change our plans. Add Gary to the list. There's the third one to do tonight as well. Sort Gary after."

"But I haven't ever spied on the Cove house, and coppers might be sniffing around."

"True. As always, let me think on it."

Martine turned from the window. "Where's Mam?"

"In the garden, baking under a blanket." He swallowed. Coughed. Tasted blood on the back of his tongue. "I'll get the ball rolling on that bank account now." He pushed himself off the sofa and waddled over to the desk. Sat and switched the computer on. Worried about dying, leaving Martine, unable to help her if Carol Wren got to the bottom of things.

Don't. A worrier makes mistakes, and you can't afford to do that.

He'd heed his own words, ones he'd so recently said to Martine. If he did that, everything would turn out fine.

He coughed again, and the large blood spots on his tissue told him otherwise.

It wasn't going to be fine at all.

* * *

In the Car

Carol parked in a lay-by on Murdoch Lane and mulled over what the Smiths had said, frustrated the lead had turned to dust. The father and daughter had been nice, not the type to wreak vengeance at all, even though they must have had a rough ride since Harry lost his hand. An accident, that's what he thought it was, so if it hadn't been him who'd killed Sue and Betty, who was it?

Besides, going by his weight and size, he'd soon be out of breath if he had to lug Betty from the kill site to the vet's.

He'd wheezed a lot just by walking across the room and sitting, and if she was any judge, he wasn't a well man. His skin had a funny pallor to it, a hint of green around the gills. No one in his condition, whatever was wrong with him, could murder someone. As for Martine, she was whip-thin, and the other person on their radar, the bush woman, was around ten clothes sizes bigger than her.

"This is doing my nut in." She smacked the steering wheel and accidentally honked the horn.

Birds scattered up from the field to the left, buggering off into the clear blue sky. Guilt hounded her at disturbing them.

"It's certainly throwing us curveballs," Dave said. "On the way here, I'd convinced myself Smith was our man with a grudge. Thought we had someone we could arrest."

"Same here. Look, let's have a break. I'll phone Thomas Lines about his relationship with Sue, then call Michael, tell him to get himself off home, and I'll treat you to a roast at The Lord. Smelling that meat at the Smiths' cottage has made me hungry. Then we'll go back to Scudderton to Betty's, see if those cats are okay while we wait for someone to collect them. I forgot to phone the rescue place, so I'll do that now and arrange to be there in two hours. Deal?"

"Yep. I'm not turning down a free meal."

"Didn't think so."

She made the calls. Michael was relieved to be going home. Thomas stated he hadn't thought about Sue in that way for years, and he hadn't seen her around either. Carol took it that the vet connection didn't exist — just because Sue had been out with Thomas back in the day wasn't a reason to dump Betty there. The animal sanctuary man agreed to meet them later.

She stuffed her phone away. "I'm beginning to think getting money from Gary means you can live in the lap of luxury. Did you see the nice stuff in the Smith cottage?"

"I did. That furniture would have cost a fortune, and the computer at the back of the room was a top-of-the-range one."

"Ah well. Jealousy will get us nowhere."

She turned around and headed for Mollengate. They approached the cottage they'd so recently been discussing, and Carol glanced over. Martine was going inside one half of a double garage. The door closed behind her, and Carol swore she picked up a scream.

"Did you hear that?" she asked, her heart thudding in shock.

Dave nodded. Pointed ahead. "It's those bloody seagulls."

"Hmm." She drove on, her mind now on roast beef and Yorkshire pudding, her belly thanking her for remembering it needed to be filled. A Danish pastry or two just didn't cut it.

* * *

Betty's Bungalow

The place stank of cat shit, cat food and freshly dried piss, although it was spotlessly tidy. With an overfull belly, queasy from the stench, Carol stood in the living room, a protective suit on, and avoided a lump of brown on the floor beside a curio cabinet containing at least one hundred crystal ornaments. Were they indoor cats, or did Betty let them out? If there was crap on the carpet, maybe they were used to using the garden. Cats wandered around yowling or lounged on the furniture and the windowsill, and one tabby beast sat in the doorway as if daring her to try to get past it.

"Nowt looks off," Dave called, his footsteps thumping down the hallway, "although there are wet patches where the cats have had a tinkle. With the place shut up in this heat, it bloody stinks."

Carol walked towards the tabby that acted as a bouncer. It stared at her then lost its nerve and scarpered, disappearing into the kitchen.

"*Fuck off!*" a voice shouted.

Carol glanced at Dave.

"The parrot," he said. "Chunky bastard an' all."

"I don't like being close to birds." Carol shuddered.

"It's in a cage. Come and see."

They trooped down the hallway and entered the kitchen. A large cage spanned the right-hand wall, taking up any space a dining table and chairs would have, big enough for the bird to fly back and forth. The tabby glared over at the parrot from its seat on the worktop. The bird was indeed chunky, overfed by the look of it. The grey feathers appeared dusty, and a plume of red jutted out as a tail.

Perched on a branch, it parted its hooked black beak and sussed them out using one orange eye, the fluffy feathers around it white. It kind of resembled a pigeon but not. "*Fuck you, and fuck you, too. Out! Get out of my house!*"

Carol gaped. "How the *hell* do they speak? It's weird. Doesn't seem right hearing an animal talking."

Dave took his phone out and prodded a gloved finger at his screen. "Looks like this is an African grey. Even creepier, they apparently understand what they're saying, like humans."

"Pack it in," Carol said. "That's like imagining cats with hands. It isn't right."

"*Cats with hands!*" the bird said.

"Oh, and they can copy you after hearing words only once or twice," Dave informed her.

"Put that bloody phone away. That kind of trivia is giving me the willies." She switched her attention to the rest of the cage; the parrot's stare unnerved her. Betty had filled it with tree branches, giving it quite the fancy habitat. White food bowls had been clipped to the wire mesh, and she peered over to see if it had enough to eat. A few seeds and whatever coated the bottom, although there wasn't anything in the other one, and she suspected it had contained water which had either been drunk or evaporated in the heat.

The house was stifling.

"I don't think we need a big team of SOCO," she said, "just three officers to give the place the once-over. It doesn't look like owt's happened here. No blood or signs of a struggle, but best to be on the safe side. The killer could have cleaned up."

"Which tells me if the death occurred here, Betty must have let them in, because there's no sign of forced entry."

"True. And can you imagine a killer dodging all this cat shit on the floor?" She turned to face the hallway at a knock on the front door.

"*Who's that* now?" the parrot asked.

Carol walked down to open it and stepped outside, closing the door so no cats escaped. She smiled at John Walters, the rescue fella. "I'm going to have to ask you to put booties and gloves on. SOCO need to come in."

"Fine by me."

She took some from the boot of her car and waited for John to sort himself out.

"Seventeen cats, eh?" he said.

"And a parrot that's just told us to get out."

He laughed. "Sounds like an African grey. They speak as well as humans."

"Hmm, so Dave said. Right, come on, let's get you inside so those poor cats can be seen to. They'll be hungry as their owner was killed in the early hours."

"Poor buggers." John grabbed a large animal carry case that he'd placed by the door. "This'll hold about four at a time. I'll have to keep going in and out to put them in the bigger cage in the van. I've got a smaller one in there for the parrot, and I've put a blanket between them so the cats don't start any trouble. Cats and birds, you know."

"Well, I hope you don't mind its colourful language."

They entered the house and joined Dave in the kitchen.

"*Piss off, you nasty piece of work!*" the parrot shouted at John.

"I'll deal with him first," he said, laughing, "although it'd be amusing to see what else he has to say while I gather all the cats."

Carol shook her head. "Your call. We'll be outside if you need us."

169

"*Go, then!*" the parrot screeched.

Carol and Dave beat a hasty retreat. In the front garden, Carol phoned for SOCO to come, cringing because one team were probably still at Gary's Wexford house, the other at the vet's, and some poor bastards would be called in on their Sunday off to deal with Betty's place.

Can't be helped.

John came out with the parrot in the carry case.

Carol sighed, rubbing her belly. "Shouldn't have had that apple crumble and custard."

"Me neither," Dave said.

"*Greedy,*" the parrot told them. "*Greedy little pigs.*"

Carol shuddered at how true that was. They *were* pigs — police — and that bird was far too clever for its own good.

"A coincidence," Dave said.

Carol wasn't so sure and smoothed over the goose bumps on her arms. "Hang on, John."

He placed the case in the back of the van.

Carol crouched to peer through the wire at the bird. "Where's Betty?"

"*Gone dancing,*" the Grey said. "*Dancing in the moonlight.*"

Carol rose and looked at Dave. "D'you reckon we can trust this bird?"

He shrugged. "Who knows, but if SOCO don't find owt here, then we can take it the bloody thing's telling the truth."

Carol nodded. Sighed again. "Okay, we'll wait for the team, then we'll call it a day. Tomorrow, we're going to have to speak to that lot at the factory now Harry Smith isn't anyone to worry about. Someone there must know why Sue and Betty are connected."

And if they didn't? Another dead end. But Carol was tenacious. Once she got her teeth into something, she didn't let go. Whoever had killed Sue and Betty, she was coming for them.

No matter how long it took.

CHAPTER EIGHTEEN

Betty's Street

Night had come, and Martine, the padded suit covering her body, stood in Betty's dark road, away from the street-lamp so no coppers could get a proper look at her if they happened to glance outside. The shadows were her friends. The police were in Betty's bungalow, although a neighbour, also watching the comings and goings, had said the coppers would be gone just after midnight — he'd asked, they'd told him. Vince, he'd said his name was, the name grating on her sensitive nerves, but lots of old men were called that, and she was just being shitty. He was a nice enough old boy but a nuisance just the same, a presence she tolerated. After all, telling him to fuck off would only give him the green light to study her harder, imprint her features in his mind, although she'd put a lot of makeup on for this, in lieu of having no face-like mask to hide her identity, and with her hair twisted into a high and tight bun instead of a low ponytail, she could pass as someone else. Once she'd discussed killing Gary with Dad and she'd returned to him after getting changed, he'd said he wouldn't have recognised her if he didn't know who she was, so if Vince *did* memorise her, it'd be a wasted task.

She felt better for reassuring herself. Less prickly. Less inclined to punch the old man's face in. Watch him fall to the pavement. Stamp on his head until it split open, just because he shared a name with someone who'd hurt Dad. Not a good thing to do with the pigs so close by. She was running a risk as it was, standing there, tempting fate.

She'd come to break in, collect a cat or two, and the infamous parrot, so she could kill them in the garage, show *him* she was still of a murderous mind. He'd watch her from his chair with his glass eyes, her describing what she was doing, getting satisfaction from snuffing the life out of the animals.

But that had to go out of the window now.

"Someone came earlier and took all the cats and the bird," Vince had said a few minutes ago. "It's terrible, what's happened."

Martine had yet to answer him, lost inside her head, and she reckoned it'd be weird if she did it now after a period of silence had passed.

"That Wren copper," Vince said as if they hadn't had a break in conversation. "The one who was in the news a lot. She came with that fella she works with, then the animal sanctuary van turned up."

"Hmm." *So Liz hasn't taken the pets on, then. Calls herself a niece, does she? Selfish cow, more like. Betty was right when she told me it was best to stay away from her.*

Vince sniffed. "What are you doing here so late anyroad? Young woman like you, out in the dark. It's dangerous, that is."

"On my way home. Saw all the police cars, wondered what had happened to Betty. I'm a bit nosy so decided to stick around, have a gander."

"Same. You learn a lot when you watch. I'm on my own now. Wife died. Cancer got her good and proper. Find myself at a loose end most days. No kids who'd want to come and see me. Got nowt else to do, so I tend to look out of the window a fair bit."

Martine stiffened. Had he seen her here before when she'd come to stand in Betty's back garden?

"I've seen you around here," he went on, confirming her fears, funnelling panic into her bones, not to mention annoyance. "Going round the back to Betty's. Know her well, did you? I saw it on the news about lunchtime. They said she's dead. I suspect them coppers have gone in to see if she died in her place, although the local Facebook page said she'd been found at the vet's. A bit odd, that. I put my opinion forward and left a comment saying it's to do with that man who lost his hand."

Martine's guts churned. Dad had mentioned that, told her the name of the commenter. Vincent Marsh. Vince? Blimey, talk about a stroke of luck. This saved her doing all the legwork in finding him and shutting him up. She had a score to settle with him anyway, one of her own. "Yeah, I knew her. Used to come and have a cuppa with her. Keep her company, that sort of thing." She paused. Danced from foot to foot. "Can I borrow your loo? I'm bursting. Mr . . . ?" Best to double-check.

"Marsh. Of course, lass. Come on, I'll show you where it is."

Inside with the front door closed, she stood on the mat, the kind that had bristles, ones that dug in like pins if you had bare feet. Vince ambled along the hallway, paused halfway down and glanced over his shoulder.

"Come on," he said. "It's just off the kitchen."

Martine clutched her throat and mimicked choking.

"What's the matter, lass?" Vince turned and came towards her, his face wreathed in concern.

She kicked him in the bollocks. He bent over, winded, crying out in pain, so while he was incapacitated, she shoved him against the wall, punched him in the face and threw him to the floor. The sound of a bone cracking got her smiling, sizzled on all of her pleasure senses, and she let out a giggle of euphoria.

On his back, he stared up at her, fear showing in the whites of his eyes. "What . . . what on earth did you do *that* for? Think I was a pervert, did you? Were you defending yourself? I'm no pervert, duck. Help me up, will you?"

She sat on him. Wondered if he was confused by her apparent size not matching her weight. Decided she didn't give a monkey's chuff.

"Get off me!" he wheezed. "God, I think my heart's going to give out. I've got a pain . . ."

"This is for saying stuff about my dad."

She curled her hands around his neck, her gloves stretching over her stiff fingers. Vince gurgled something or other, but she didn't care to work out what it was. Whatever he was saying didn't belong inside her ears. He drummed his heels on the floor behind her, and while she squeezed and squeezed, she thought about what he'd said. Dead wife. No kids who'd want to visit.

What a load of crap.

He seemed too "with it" to have a carer coming in. How long would it be before someone found him? How many days would pass until someone scented death in the air, the stench of a rotting body, and knocked on his door, bending to peer through the letterbox, the sight of him revealed, dried fluids on the floor? *Oh, fuck me, he's dead!*

Martine squeezed on. Looked forward to telling Dad about this quirk of fate.

One last thrum of his heels, and Vince stilled. He stared up at her, and she'd say confusion lived in his eyes, but who cared, she had to get out of there and follow the rest of the plan. This detour hadn't been on the cards for tonight, although it was a welcome surprise.

"All gone now. Vincent is dead."

She tittered and left the bungalow, walking around the corner where she'd parked Mam's car, head down, smirking that coppers, mere feet away, had no idea a murder had taken place in the vicinity, almost right under their piggy noses.

* * *

Scudderton Royal Infirmary

Nabruah Panjib hurried out of the hospital and headed towards his spacious ground-floor flat in a new-build block two streets away. Skimmers Lane the road was called, catering to folks with money who preferred to surround themselves with those of like mind, although Nab didn't share their ideals nor their reason for living there. He'd chosen it because of the location, so close to the hospital, and shied away from interacting with his neighbours, who all seemed to preen whenever they got into their expensive cars or oversaw their gardeners toiling in the flowerbeds. He'd said hello to a few if they'd said it to him first, but as much as possible, he minded his own business. The only persistent person was the vet's wife — Mrs Lines, she'd said her name was. She was always desperate to engage Nab in conversation.

Although an affluent surgeon earning roughly seventy-five thousand per year, Nab didn't hold with the sort of system where everyone looked down on others who were less fortunate — he'd lived that life in India growing up, his childhood a mixture of happiness in abundance at home but a confusing mire outside it. The life of a castoff, someone to be pitied or held in disregard. He'd felt the stares, the malice coming from the rich as he'd walked home from school, his bare feet dusty from the road.

He'd been born into a family full of love, but they'd been penniless, and he'd vowed to change his life, his family's, as soon as he could. That's why he worked for the NHS and hadn't gone into the private sector — he preferred the "same treatment for all" mantra, no one turned away because of their status. Anyway, seventy-five thousand a year was a huge amount to a man living by himself, and if he did overtime, he obviously earned more. He'd dedicated his life to saving others, shying away from marriage and children, his calling tending to people, not to his emotional needs and material wants. He didn't want the distraction of outside influences and had come over from India thirty years ago to study, become who he was today.

He liked England — loved it, in fact — but went home every year at Christmas to see his mātā, his sister and his niece. His father had died years ago, and he missed him. Nab always sent the family money, and they lived well because of him, and those he saved here in Scudderton and the surrounding areas also lived well once he'd mended them, or that was his intention. A few had slipped through the net of life and entered the dark waters of death while on his operating table, or in recovery, or afterwards, but he'd tried his best to patch them up, hours in the theatre, his mind solely on fixing them so they could continue on their destined path.

He'd been called in on emergency duty tonight — he was always the first port of call as he had nothing at home to keep him there other than falling into his bed to sleep. Him going in meant other surgeons could spend quality time with their loved ones, another service Nab was happy to provide.

This evening, a road traffic accident had brought in a woman with bones poking through the skin of her shin, and he'd swept in and put metal plates in place, hoping that would be enough to ensure she could walk without too much of a limp. She'd have one, though; he'd had to cut the jagged bone, losing about an inch. She'd be in pain, it would be weeks before she could attempt to stand on her feet again, but he'd left her in the recovery room, awake if somewhat groggy, smiling sleepily when he'd told her, "I have fixed you, madam. You will be okay."

The words he loved saying.

The warmth of the evening curled around him, its questing fingers sticky, and he nipped into the small Tesco at the end of his street, glad of the air-conditioning that dried his sweat and gave him a chance to breathe properly. The heat of the town in India was oppressive but not to the point where he wanted to claw his skin off.

England's sun wasn't his friend.

He collected a sandwich (cheese) and chose a packet of crisps (Quavers) and a drink to go with the meal deal, a nice cold bottle of orange juice. He'd eat the snack for his supper, hungry after missing out on a proper dinner earlier when he'd been called back in after his usual shift to deal with the RTA. He'd only managed a hastily made sandwich then, too, so needed topping up. Maybe tomorrow he'd get to eat the lentil stew he'd left in the slow cooker all day. He didn't fancy it now.

Nab paid for his purchases, preferring the self-service checkout, then braced himself to go back out into the cloying air, a carrier bag in hand. It was like walking into a furnace, and immediately, sweat popped out of his pores. If he got a move on instead of dawdling and grumbling, he'd be home much quicker, so he upped his pace. On his wages, he could afford the new-build flat with its fancy air-conditioning, and it was with much relief that he slid his key in the lock and pushed open his front door, eager to switch the unit on.

A smack to the back of his head had him crying out, and he dropped the carrier bag, his other hand automatically going up to the affected area. He pressed his palm to it, eyes watering, his senses shot. His skull throbbed with pain, and he staggered forward, losing his balance from blurry eyesight, falling onto his hands and knees on his patterned Indian rug, sent over by his mātā.

His heart kicked into overdrive as his thoughts cleared. *Someone hit me. They're at my front door.*

He peered around. Caught sight of a pair of ankle-high men's boots. Black leggings over chubby legs. A long black T-shirt stretched across a bulbous belly with several folds. A face, lots of makeup. Hair in a top bun.

It's a woman?

"All right, Nab?" She stepped inside and closed the door.

How did she know his name and he didn't know hers? He saw so many patients but prided himself on remembering them all. Was she a neighbour? Had she introduced herself when he'd come home from a long shift and he'd been too tired to file her name away in his overworked brain?

He scrabbled forward, at the same time trying to get to his feet, but his head swam and he collapsed back down, his body refusing to function properly. With much effort, he managed to turn over onto his back and planted his palms behind him, his arms keeping his top half upright. God, his head hurt so much, throbbing with pain. What had she hit him with? A rock from the communal front garden? What had she done with it, tossed it aside?

He thought of his mātā, getting ready for their weekly video call, his eyes burning because she might not get to see him again. His sister, sitting beside her, his niece bobbing about in the background, unable to keep still for long. Would they think he was still at work and cut the connection? Would they leave it for a week before videoing him again? Mātā had given up texting him as he rarely had time to answer right away.

He had a terrible feeling, a sense of doom so vast his heart hurt from it. What if this woman killed him? How long would his body lie undetected? People from work would notice his absence, that no permission had been given for him to have time off, but as his schedule was so busy, perhaps someone would phone to ask where he was, and then, getting no answer, they'd come here to see if he was okay.

And find out he wasn't.

And his tender heart panged at the idea of a colleague finding him, seeing him dead, a terrible shock to their system, the image of him indelibly etched into their minds forever. He didn't want anyone to have to go through that because of him.

Because of her.

"Who are you?" he croaked, the word coming out on a gasp.

"I'm here for my dad," the woman said, "I'd have thought you'd gather that."

She seemed offended he didn't know who she was.

Should I?

Nab racked his befuddled brain, but no, his mind might be jumbled, but he really didn't recognise her, didn't think he'd ever seen her in his life. "Who's that?"

"Harry Smith. Bloke without a hand, thanks to you."

Nab's skin chilled all over, despite his house being warm from the relentless heat of the day. He remembered Harry Smith, how could he not? The operation had been a failure

— the hand that had been brought in was a mangled mess, and there was nothing Nab or the other surgeons could have done to save it. The cutter had sliced it clean off at the wrist then dragged it inside the machine, chomping away at the skin, the nerves, the everything. Someone had removed it, packed it in ice bought swiftly from the shop around the corner from the factory, but no amount of ice would have helped.

Two days after his operation, where a plastic surgeon had grafted skin from Harry's backside to create a cover for the stump, Harry had gone for Nab at the hospital with a fork that he'd swiped after dinner that day. Accused him of being useless because he hadn't been able to save the hand, sew it back on. But it had been too damaged, and if Nab or a colleague had attempted to reattach it, it would have died, turning grey, going bad, killing him with gangrene.

It had been one of the most frightening times of his working life, seeing that fork coming for his eye, seeing the intent look of hatred on Harry's face. One of the nurses had said she'd call the police — they had a zero-tolerance policy at the hospital regarding staff being treated badly — but Nab had said no, no, please, just give him a sedative to calm him down.

"I won't forget," Harry had said as two nurses led him away. "I'll *never* forget. You didn't do your job. Call yourself a surgeon?"

Nab stared at Harry's daughter, who held a knife in her hand.

"Please, I can explain. It wasn't my fault," he said — and he knew, without a shadow of a doubt, that no nurse would come to guide this young woman away, giving *her* a sedative, making everything okay again.

This was it, the end, he was sure of it.

"It was your fault, Nab. Why can't you just admit it?" She shrugged. "That's unlikely after all this time, but it doesn't matter anyroad. Dad's had a fair old while to think about it, and it's time for you to go."

* * *

Martine had parked up and hauled Nab out of the boot of Mam's car. He was a light fella, slim, so she'd managed it perfectly well, conscious that the people next door were up as their lights were on. She propped him against the wall outside Gary's house, beneath a side window, and went down on her haunches to whisper, "All gone now. Nab is dead."

She chuckled quietly. His head drooped to one side, a blood smear on the wall showing its path. His hands rested on the grass, and she giggled at the thought of the police finding not only Gary but Nab, too, scratching their heads to work out how their deaths were related. She stood, ready to have a nose at the place, see where she could break in.

She'd come to end Gary. The bad girl was here to stay for the time being.

"Martine!"

She spun, freaked out someone was even here at this time, that they knew her *name*, and a peer towards some bushes between the properties showed her a head hovering above them. Was that what she'd looked like while standing outside the Cuttersby house in Wexford Close?

"Who's there?" she said quietly and moved forward, step by step, her bloodied knife out in front of her.

"It's me. What are you doing here?"

Guest? Oh, for fuck's sake . . .

* * *

Guest couldn't believe it. Martine had come, and she'd put a *body* against the house. Who *was* that? Why had she brought it here? Did she want to frame Gary for a murder? And why was Martine overweight? She'd piled on the pounds since this morning — that wasn't even possible — and lumbered over, her head odd and small in relation to the larger body.

Martine came behind the bush and crouched, tugging Guest down with her, whispering, "I didn't think you'd actually do as I said and come here."

"I didn't think you'd go back on your word and come here either."

"Change of plan. Dad's decided Gary being alive could fuck things up. Shall we do it together?"

Guest shook their head. "No way. If you're here, you do it. And why do you look like . . . that?"

"D'you dig it? It's a padded suit. People will think I'm fat."

"That word isn't nice."

"Nope, but whatever."

Guest peered through the leaves in the bush. "Who's that?"

"Never you mind."

"Why is he dead?"

"Again, never you mind." Martine nudged Guest. "Bog off, then. If you're not going to be of any use, I can't be doing with you hanging around."

Guest sighed. Crab-walked away. Stood, running along the road, the sound of the shushing sea turning into whispers: *Go home. Quickly. And never come back.*

Once Guest had entered the housing estate behind Gary's, sure no one had seen them, they slowed and got into their car. Hands shaking, they drove away, conscious that even at this time of night, someone could be awake, glance out of the window. But Guest had to be grateful. They hadn't had to kill Gary, although they wondered whether Martine and Harry would now have a greater hold over them. It had gone beyond just talking, planning a crime. Guest supposed they'd see it as a favour, getting rid of that man, an "extra" they hadn't planned. All the time Guest had been visiting Harry, planting the seed to go after Gary fucking Cuttersby, Harry had known Martine wouldn't do what Guest wanted. All along, he'd played Guest for a fool, as had Martine.

But at least I'll get what I wanted in the end.

Martine was there now, about to do the deed, and Guest drooped in relief, so much so that they lost concentration and almost drove into the kerb.

Pay attention. Act normally, for God's sake.

Because if they didn't, things could come tumbling down.

CHAPTER NINETEEN

Betty's Street

Carol was getting a bit pissed off with dead bodies. Not that the deceased could help it, but for goodness sake, it meant a killer was out there, someone she couldn't find. Every dead body was more heartbreak for those left behind.

She'd been called out at 1 a.m., direct by SOCO — a door had been left open across the road from Betty's, and an officer had spotted someone on the floor in the hallway when he'd gone to the van. She'd phoned it in, actioned for uniform to come out, left Dave to his sleep and now stood on the path in her protective suit, looking inside at an old fella wondering whether it was connected to the current case.

A livid bruise on his face. Marks around his neck. He lay on his back, arms by his sides, fists indicating posturing — something that happened when someone was either throttled or hanged, the clench occurring at the point the brain died.

Carol had a flashback to finding her father dead. Admitting to Dave that she'd experienced relief at seeing his body had brought on a sense of shame and guilt, then a rush of peace had overcome her, that she'd finally let it out, one of her deepest secrets — and it had been *okay*. The world hadn't caved in just because she'd confessed something most people would keep to themselves. It wasn't every day someone said they were happy their parent had died. Did this man in front of her have anyone who'd feel some kind of emotion now that he'd passed away? Did he have children who'd either cry or dance for joy?

The night-time desk sergeant, Alton Sinclair, was getting someone to look into who this man was. It saved hauling Michael out of bed and into work, and if this was what she cringed at calling a "simple" home invasion gone wrong, the main investigating could start in the morning; she could pass it on to someone else. The only reason SOCO had called *her* in particular as well as uniform was the significance of the vicinity, the man living opposite Betty — a possible link? Had Sue been a mistake? She wasn't elderly, yet Betty and this fella were . . .

"Burglary that ended in death?" she asked Sergeant Oliver Havers as he walked up the path behind her and stopped by her left side.

A seasoned officer, like Alan Piston, he preferred uniform life.

"Seems so from here, but inside tells us different." He seemed to notice her *Oh God* reaction. "Sorry. I don't think this is going to be an open-and-shut situation. His telly, laptop and phone are still indoors, so why weren't they nicked? I touched the mouse pad on the lappy — gloves on, yes — the screen came to life, and fuck me, it was a Facebook page, wasn't it? A chat about Betty Tavers, would you believe? The deceased is Vincent Marsh, seventy-two."

"Bugger, I just bothered Alton about finding that information. I didn't realise you'd already been inside — suppose that's what happens when I live in Mollengate. Takes me time to arrive."

"But it separates you from work when you're not on the clock, a plus side in my book. Don't you worry, I'll get hold of him in a sec for you, if you want, like, because that laptop has all the info we need to be going on with for now. I wrote it all in my notebook, actually — wanted it on hand as SOCO will be in there quick as lightning to bag the laptop and phone up. Seems our victim liked keeping a folder with all his personal business in it — bank account numbers, the lot."

"Yep, if you can do that, that'd be great." She thought of all the SOCOs spread thin, all because someone had decided to end these people's lives. At this rate, she'd be calling for help from another division. "Did the Facebook chat show owt?"

"Well, as luck would have it, it did. Vincent had commented a few times. A couple were about the killer being a sandwich short if they thought they'd get away with it, plus that they were cowards for ambushing an old lady, but he also said he reckoned Harry Smith would have a grudge against Betty on account of him losing his hand. Now, I remember that very well — I'm coming up fifty, but my memory hasn't packed up just yet. Terrible business, that hand being cut off, then it was dragged into the machine and mangled." Oliver grimaced. "Just the thought gives me shivers. Anyroad, I don't know what Vincent was on about because there's no way Harry would take revenge years later let alone at the time. Not the sort. I knew him from school. All right, he was younger than me, but back then, we all hung out together on the field at playtime. You get a sense about people, don't you?"

"You do. We went to visit him already. Seems a nice enough man, if clearly unwell."

"Unwell?"

"He was a light shade of green and had trouble breathing. Other than that, he was in good spirits, said what had happened was an accident, nowt more."

"Hmm, so I suspect Vincent's opinion of Harry having a grudge is based on his own feelings — like *he'd* have a beef if it had happened to him, so he thinks everyone would feel the same way."

"Probably. It won't hurt for me and Dave to go and see Harry again tomorrow, I suppose, using the excuse we found him being discussed on Facebook."

She swivelled at the sound of a car — Rib had turned up.

Oliver cleared his throat. "I'll nip off, then, get on the blower to Alton, then get a shift on with finishing the door-to-door palaver." He trotted down the path.

Carol faced the bungalow again and made a mental note that the victim had clothes on, not pyjamas. The SOCO who'd phoned her said he'd spoken to Vincent around 10 p.m. The old boy had been out in the street, alone, and asked when the police would be finished inside Betty's. The officer had told him sometime after midnight or thereabouts, then went back into Betty's until he came out again later and saw Vincent's door open.

Between those two times, Vincent had been killed.

Three SOCOs brushed past her and, one at a time, entered the house and balanced on the wooden threshold to put booties on, murmuring their hellos. Two stood at the bottom of the stairs out of the way while the third took his camera out and got on with his job. Rib remained outside next to Carol, his bag in one hand and an evidence step in the other.

"Wonder what we've got here, then, Bird."

"A murder maybe?" she replied.

"Funny. I see you're in your usual grumpy mood."

"Only in your company." She sighed, the click of the camera burrowing into her ears. Annoying. "It's looking like this might be connected to Sue and Betty."

"How so?"

"Victim is Vincent Marsh. His laptop shows a Facebook thread where he names someone as a possible suspect."

"What, and he was killed because of it?"

"Maybe. But they made an error. If they knew Vincent had written those comments, went to the trouble of finding out who he was, then came here to kill him, wouldn't you think they'd have looked around for a phone or computer so they could delete the comments? His devices are still in the bungalow, specifically the laptop with the conversation open on it."

"What was said?"

"A name was offered up, Harry Smith, but we've already spoken to him, and unless he's superhuman, there's no way he could commit murder in his state. But what I'm interested in is Vincent saying the killer is basically thick in the head and a coward."

"Ouch. That could send some people over the edge."

Carol pointed at the body. "Which it did, although why someone would kill this man here on Harry's behalf is beyond me."

"Well, I can see he was strangled. Struck in the face, too. Poor bastard. Likely didn't stand a chance. I mean, look at him. Skinny as owt. Old. What could he have done to defend himself?"

"I feel sick, to be honest. And angry."

In a rare display of empathy, Rib wedged the evidence step between his legs and patted her elbow. She stared down at his gloved hand, then at his face, which didn't seem so irritating in this instant.

"If you tell anyone about this show of compassion, Bird, I'll deny it." He took his hand away. Held the step again. Stared ahead at the photographer.

"No one would believe me anyroad." She smiled. Watched him from the corner of her eye.

He smiled, too.

* * *

While Rib got on with assessing the body now the photographer had finished, the other two SOCOs doing their thing inside Vincent's bungalow, Carol joined Oliver in the street. No matter the time of night, he'd been doing house-to-house enquiries with two other uniforms, and she wanted to check in with them.

"Have you got owt?" she asked.

Oliver nodded. Consulted his notebook. "I was just gassing to some old dear. Hang on . . ." He ran a finger down the page. "Ah, here we are: Mavis Button, cute as one, too. She's two doors down from Vincent. Said someone was out here with him for around half an hour. Mavis noticed them when she got up to close the lounge curtains. I woke her up by knocking, but needs must an' all that. Anyroad, she said, and I'll give you her non-PC quote: 'A fat girl with a little head. She had a bun, her clothes were black, and she had big boots, the clumpy kind builders put on.'" He raised his eyebrows, the streetlight giving his face an orange tinge. "'Girl?', I said to her. She then said: 'Well, she's a girl to me. You know, the type in their twenties.'"

Could this be the woman in Wexford Close? There had been that squashed print left in the grass. A builder's boot? It was a bloody coincidence if it wasn't. "Interesting. Anyone got CCTV round here?"

"No."

"What a surprise. Has everyone been spoken to?"

"Yes. Everyone else went to bed around nine, being old an' all that. Mavis stayed up as she has a direct line of sight into Betty's and couldn't help keeping an eye on things."

"Did she have any idea who'd want to kill her?"

"She said she didn't know her as such, only to wave to of a morning, so any information there isn't forthcoming. Same with everyone else. Betty didn't integrate much."

So it seems like we're definitely after the plus-sized woman. Who the fuck is she?

Carol sighed. "So Betty kept to herself at home but chattered about her life at work? Maybe she didn't think of herself as old, like her neighbours, so she minded her own business. It's handy to know someone else saw our main suspect, though. She was seen in the Cuttersby street as well, possibly standing in their bushes out the front."

"Weird."

"Not to her if she was watching them, it'd be an absolutely normal thing to do, but I get what you mean. It *is* weird behaviour, yet she didn't hide in a bush here, and there are a few."

"Maybe she couldn't, else Vincent would have spotted it. If he was out in the street, asking an officer how long they'd likely be, he must have been a nosy sort. The woman must have come back, as some of them do — to the scene of the crime, so to speak, although a SOCO said Betty's bungalow is clear, so it isn't technically a scene."

"Getting her jollies seeing the mess she's caused."

"Yep. Mavis also said Vincent was out here first, by himself, then the woman came along, stopped to chat. When she shut her curtains, they'd been out here for half an hour."

"Such a shame she didn't nose out after that and see if the woman went into Vincent's bungalow." *Although she probably did.* "Still, no use crying over spilt milk, is there? I'll leave you to it."

Carol walked back to Vincent's, changed her shoe covers at the door, signed the log and entered the hallway. She remained on the mat. Rib knelt on the evidence step beside Vincent, drawing the shape of the victim's position on an A4 sheet attached to his clipboard instead of using the usual form. He shaded in the bruising on the face and around the neck.

"Strangulation, as I said before," he said and tucked his board and pencil into his bag. "Estimated time of death, between eleven and midnight. He was struck by a right-handed punch — if you look closely, you can see the outline of the fist. They have a prominent middle knuckle — I'd say the bone sticks out a lot further than the others, perhaps a slender hand that doesn't have much fat beneath the skin."

"Slender?"

"Yes. Problem?"

"It doesn't match the size of the woman from the Cuttersby case — who may well be the same person seen speaking to Vincent tonight."

"Ooh, the plot resembles thick soup. Which reminds me, have you tried those soup packs you can get? Fresh veg chopped up ready with a sachet of herbs and whatever so you can make it yourself. Saves a lot of time, that."

"I'm not into soup, and if I was, I'd use a tin."

"It's bloody lovely. He still had his own teeth, didn't bite his tongue. No defensive wounds or an attempt to remove the hand from around his neck, so his arms were undoubtedly pinned. Killer sat on him, I'd guess. Gravy — have you ever tried the ready-made stuff in pouches? My nan calls it 'lazy gravy', but I call it beautiful. This killer — now you know I like to get into it and imagine how they felt — they wanted it done quickly."

"There's no way you can tell that, surely?"

"Going by the punch to the face, as well as another indication — subdue, do the business. And your thoughts on the gravy?"

"Fucking hell. Bisto. Beef. Hot water. A jug. Put in on your dinner. Eat it."

"I bet you didn't even know they did pouches, did you?"

"It isn't on my priority list to check, no."

Rib laughed. "D'you know what, Bird?"

"What?"

"I actually like you."

Stunned, she said, "Could have fooled me."

He grew serious. "I had a quick look for other injuries while you were gone. Seems he was kicked or kneed in the nuts."

"Ouch."

"One side is slightly swollen, a bruise forming, so quite the strike."

"Hence why you feel the death had to be quick. Kick, punch, strangle, leave."

Rib looked at her, eyebrows raised. "Makes you wonder if they had somewhere else they had to be, doesn't it?"

CHAPTER TWENTY

Smithy's Cottage

Harry couldn't hold the bad boy back. Josie had enraged him earlier, going on and on about him not bringing much to the table compared to her. His soul diminished by her ranting, he'd had to force himself not to hit her. His inner voice of old had started up, telling him to think of ways he could show her he was worth something, someone she could be proud of. He didn't want to lose her. She had to stay by his side forever.

The bad boy had told him to give her the cottage, and he'd agreed, because you couldn't argue with a whole building, could you? Presented with that, she'd know then that he was a man who had something behind him, just like she did. If his mother gave him Smithy's Cottage, he'd be on the same level as Josie with her house — and he'd had it rammed down his throat enough times that it was her house, not his.

If he were honest, he'd missed the cottage, the solitude, the birdsong, the scents of the countryside, and had soon realised living in Scudderton wasn't something he could handle for the rest of his days, not to mention he had more chance of bumping into a certain person if he remained. The neighbours either side were a noisy lot — how was he supposed to think, for Pete's sake? — and there was always someone out and about, passing the living room window, nosing in like they had the right. A goldfish bowl, that's what it was, and he was sick of it.

At his mother's, he left his car on the drive. If he had his way, he'd build a double garage on it, do the place up so it was fancy, the interior nice and posh compared to what it was now — Josie wouldn't want to leave then, ever. His mother, if she didn't hand the deeds over, would soon see how her "creepy-eyed son" could be even creepier.

She'd never liked his eyes, and right from his earliest memory he recalled her acting afraid of him. He'd known the bad boy had the upper hand, and she did whatever he said in case he turned on her, which he had on a few occasions. More than a few. She'd been glad when he'd married Josie then moved in with her. He'd spotted the way her shoulders had slumped with relief, her eyes shining with the glint that freedom and a lack of pressure brought.

Well, it was all about to change.

He went round the back and opened the door to the kitchen — she never locked it until she went to bed. When he had this place, he'd put patio doors in the living room, block the kitchen one up, and that big larder had to go. It was a room, shelves lining each wall, his mother's silly jars on them containing flour and whatnot, her weird scrawl on the front of each in blue felt tip: Oats, Pearl Barley, Lentils. *Yep, that room could go, and he'd think of something to put in its place. Maybe a new bathroom? The one upstairs was too small for a growing family.*

"Mother?" he called out.

"I thought I heard a car . . ."

He followed her voice into the living room. She sat on her tatty wingback armchair, the one that had always been in the corner by the window, cigarette smoke curling from the rollie wedged between her fingers. A glass of her usual gin sat on the little side table, the standard lamp on behind it, the shade beige from so much tar.

"What do you want?" she said.

"The cottage."

She stared at him in shock. "Beg your pardon?"

"I can't live in Scudderton anymore. It's wreaking havoc with my head. I need this place for me and Josie."

"But it's my home, been in my family for generations. The day you get it is over my dead body."

His bad boy had already told him that could be arranged, and that was why Harry was here, after all. He'd known she'd cast his request aside as if it didn't matter — as if he didn't matter — and he was sick of being treated like some strange entity she couldn't bear to be near.

"I'm not leaving until it's mine," he said.

She stubbed her rollie out. "Then you'll be standing there for a long time."

He didn't intend to stand there for more than two minutes. "It's mine anyroad after you've gone."

"Yes, but until then . . ." She gave him a snide smile, something she rarely did in case he reared up on her. "Why don't you ask your father for help instead of keep coming to me?"

That was the lowest blow she'd ever dealt.

He gritted his teeth. "Because I can't just turn up on his doorstep, can I?"

"Why not? I'm sure he'd be pleased to know how his son has turned out."

"He wouldn't, you said he didn't want owt to do with me. And his wife won't be happy."

"No, especially as she can't have kids. Vincent Marsh is nowt but a piece of shit."

He waited for her to add: just like you.

She didn't.

She went into one then, as usual, lamenting the fact Vincent hadn't wanted her around once she'd got up the duff. How she was all right for a fling behind his wife's back, but the minute he'd had to take responsibility, he'd cast her aside and told her to keep it to herself. She'd gone to show him baby Harry after he'd been born, told him his name, how much he weighed, but Vincent had given her a backhander and told her to fuck off out of it.

She had kept it to herself, though, only telling Harry who his dad was when he'd forced her to a couple of years ago. Harry had found him, watched him and decided he wasn't his cup of tea. Too "man about town", all loud chatter in the pub, his beady-eyed gaze all over the place, probably in search of his next bit of skirt. Harry had listened, and Vincent liked women, plenty of them, while his wife sat at home oblivious.

"I don't want to hear about him," he told his mother. "Stop talking."

"No. I'm telling you now, all the bad things in you come from him. He's a selfish, horrible man, and you are, too, expecting to live here. *What did you want me to do, go into the spare room? No, not on your nelly."*

He stabbed her in the stomach with the poker, no recollection of picking it up. He stared at her wide mouth, blood coating her tongue then seeping onto her chin, her bulging eyes, her hand at the entry site, the poker between two splayed fingers. He wrenched the tool out then rammed it in again, in her heart, and the bad boy grumped because Harry had damaged the skin — skin Harry was supposed to keep pristine.

That night, he phoned Josie to say he wouldn't be home as Mam wasn't well. In the garden shed, he did what he needed to do, the procedure learned from a library book, and he'd fucked it up a bit, but for his first time on a human, he hadn't done too badly. Hours had passed, but he'd managed it. As the sun would be coming up soon on this Saturday morning, he left his mother in the shed and spent the day removing all of her personal belongings and placing them in the loft. It always had a padlock on the hatch, so Josie wouldn't think anything of it being there. For the remainder of the day, he cleaned the place from top to bottom, even the lampshades, waiting for night-time to come again.

Once it did, with no moon to show his silhouette, he spent four hours digging a shallow grave on the moors out the back, the ground soft in the autumn. Having dug three or four feet down, he called it a job well done and walked back to collect her remains, which he'd wrapped in a tarpaulin sheet that had spent years on a shelf in the shed. A few spiders had scuttled out, but he'd squashed them under his boot and told them good riddance.

It had been cathartic, placing her in that muddy hole then covering her over, knowing she was gone, he'd never hear her voice again. No more stories about Vincent Marsh. He'd have to make up a story of his own in a week or two — Mam had gone off with a man, the name Bert would do — and she'd left him the cottage. Then he'd tell Josie that was it, they were moving in, and life would be so much better.

Before that, he'd come back a few times to do what had to be done, then lock his little secret in the loft. Only he'd know it was there, above the master bedroom, and every time he got into bed and stared at the ceiling, he'd look up and know it was directly above him.

His trophy.

* * *

Earlier, Harry's stump had burned fiercely, and he'd known Martine had killed someone. Probably Nab, that shithouse of a surgeon. Tomorrow, it was the turn of the rude physiotherapist at the doctors' surgery who'd tried to get some mobility back into Harry's arm after he hadn't used it for so long. She'd managed it, although her brusque manner and her opinion on him being more careful in future about where he put his remaining hand had incensed him. What had she meant? That he was dumb enough to put it near a blade again? Or had she meant the other type of thing, that hands shouldn't go anywhere near women unless they wanted them to?

Harry hadn't liked that. It reminded him of the rape and how he'd taken what wasn't his because he was a "fatty". It meant he was the same as his father, unable to keep his hands — hand — to himself, and he was *nothing* like him. He remembered the bad boy whispering as she'd explained about some exercise or other: *She needs to pay for saying that.*

She would now.

His stump had cooled, letting him know Martine had finished wherever she was, then burned again, and he'd smiled; she had to be doing Gary.

Harry pondered the similarities between his father and Gary. Both liked women, both were selfish in not wanting to acknowledge a child — oh yes, Martine had found out about little Starbell when Gary had come outside one night to talk on his phone.

When the Bad Time had happened, Harry hadn't been in any fit state to know who was in the cutting room with him. To begin with, his head had been full of Betty's instructions and ensuring he didn't get them wrong. Then she'd walked out, and he'd been in all that pain, had fainted and whacked his head, so when he'd been questioned, he had blanks in his memory. But on one of their visits, Guest had let him know what Gary had been getting up to in the corner and who with, and Harry's bad boy had rumbled inside him. Especially when Guest riled him up, telling him Gary needed to die, not only because of the Bad Time but Guest's gripe, too.

The visits had become frequent, and each time, Guest had planted more seeds, letting Harry see how easy it would be to get back at all the people who'd bothered him in life. His mother and Josie had already had their comeuppance, as had Mr Romeo himself, Tim, the "other man". Harry had found himself wondering: *Would it be so bad to get rid of them all?*

He'd spoken to Martine, and she'd said her bad girl was more than happy to do it if it meant her father was settled and at peace. Harry's lungs had started playing up, and he'd known if he didn't set the ball rolling, he'd be dead before all of his targets.

His father could have remained alive if he hadn't said what he had on social media. Vincent knew who Harry was, knew typing his name was a spiteful thing to do. What kind of man was he to try to get Harry in the shit? Why would a bloke want his son to be under suspicion? Well, Vincent had signed his own death warrant now, forcing Harry's hand — he chuckled at his pun — and the father who'd disowned Harry would finally pay for the crime once Martine had found out where he lived.

Funny how life pushed you to do things, made the decisions for you.

So funny he laughed until he cried, then coughed, startled by a clot of blood as big as a golf ball on the tissue.

That had never happened before.

Shit.

CHAPTER TWENTY-ONE

Seaview Heights

Gary woke and remained still, his breathing growing faster. Had a dream shunted him awake? Or had it been something else? He reprimanded himself — any other man would have forgotten his wife was dead and checked she was okay beside him, but with her sometimes sleeping in the spare room he hadn't bothered . . . and he *hadn't* forgotten. He'd never forget.

He sat up slowly, listening, the insidious thought slipping into his mind that they had an intruder, then he told himself he was just being daft. He settled back down, burrowing beneath the quilt. The house had air-conditioning, and he must have forgotten to change the setting when he went to bed. It was a bit cold now.

Maybe he ought to get up and sort it.

He left the bed and grabbed his dressing gown off the hook on the back of the door. Put it on and exited the bedroom, pausing on the landing to listen again. No noise from his boys' rooms, nor the spare where Whitney was staying — she'd offered to remain overnight in case Jack or Joseph woke and needed someone other than their father to talk to.

Something about nightmares coming once the reality had set in.

She couldn't remain indefinitely, but for now, Gary would take all the help he could get. His boys had barely said a word to him since he'd told them their mother was dead, ghosting through the house, apathetic, no signs of wanting to invite him into their world of grief.

A noise.

He held his breath, waiting for the sound again. It came a few seconds later, just as he'd given in and released the air from his lungs. Something touching something else, a *tink*, as if a spoon had come into contact with a china cup.

He moved along the balcony landing from his room at the end to stand in front of Jack's, peering over at the living areas downstairs. Nothing appeared out of place, and the moonlight shone through the glass ceiling, illuminating it enough that he'd spot a person if they were there, a shadow at least.

He relaxed. Maybe Whitney was in the kitchen, making a cuppa.

At the top of the stairs, he steadied his breathing and descended a few steps. The air-conditioning panel was down there, so he crept lightly with a mission to sort that then return to bed. Three quarters of the way down, something clamped on his ankle, and he let out a shout of alarm. He stared at his foot, at the bunched hem of his pyjama bottoms.

At the hand.

"Fuck, fuck, you scared me," he said on a laugh. "Is that you, Jack?"

That particular son had done this before, finding it hilarious, although it had happened in the daytime then. He'd stretched his hand through the thick steel wires that served as balustrades and shrieked with laughter.

"Jack?" Gary whispered.

A tug had his leg plummeting between two wires, his pyjama material travelling up to his thigh, his other foot going out from under him as the hand yanked his foot downwards. Gary was too annoyed to shout — Jack's sense of humour had gone too far. Landing on the stairs on his arse, one leg through the wires up to his crotch, the other pointing towards the front door, Gary winced at the pressure on his bollocks from the base of a wire jabbing into him.

"Pack it in now, Jack, this has gone far enough," he whisper-shouted.

He didn't want Whitney coming out and seeing him like this, nor Joseph, who might not see the funny side of a prank when his mother was dead.

No answer except for a searing pain going up the side of his calf and the sensation that his skin was peeling apart. It hurt so much he lost his breath, his ability to speak, to form a coherent thought. The hot rush of blood seeping in individual trails brought him back to the now, that something wicked was happening, and he tried to figure out why the hell his son had done this.

His ankle released.

The clomp of footsteps.

Gary gripped a wire in one hand and the edge of a step with the other. Tried to push-pull himself up. Failed. He gritted his teeth in annoyance.

Someone appeared at the bottom of the stairs. A large woman all in black, her hair up in a bun. She presented as a sumo wrestler with caked-on clownish makeup and raced up towards him. He tried to get his leg out as his brain computed the fact this wasn't Jack at all but someone else. Oh God, it was *someone else.*

"What the fuck?" he said, the words coming out strangled.

She dived on him, pinned him down, the edges of the stairs at his back digging in. Something cold and hard settled across his throat, and as her hot breath bathed his face, his mind conjured the image of a knife. Instead of using his hands to bat at her, he kept still, too fearful to move, hating himself for the paralysis. While there was moonlight, with her this close, her nose inches from his, she was nothing but a silhouette.

"Please," he said. "Please, do what you want to me, but don't hurt my boys."

He sensed she smiled — the sound of her spit crackling told him that.

"Gary," she whispered, her voice unrecognisable. "Filthy, dirty Gary."

He came to his senses and opened his mouth to shout for Whitney, but what emerged was a croaky, "Who are you?"

"Doesn't matter who I am," she whispered again. "Just what you did. If you scream out, I'll make it a painful death, then I *will* go after your twins."

"Okay, okay, I'll be quiet, all right?"

"Are you suffering with Sue gone? Suffering more now your leg feels like it's on fire?"

"Yes." He grew bolder, slowly moving his hands from his sides. If he could bring them up without her noticing, grab her upper arms, he might have enough strength to push her up and off so she'd fall down the stairs, giving him time to free his leg and . . .

"Good. You were supposed to live, but the bad boy changed his mind, and what the bad boy wants, the bad girl gives him."

He still didn't recognise her voice. She wasn't from around here, unless she'd put on an accent from elsewhere — London, that was it.

"What can I do to make this stop?" he muttered, the agony in his leg going up a few notches.

"It won't stop, but say you're sorry, that it's your fault. No one else has admitted their part in it, they didn't have the balls. Do you?"

"My part in what?"

She pressed the knife harder to his neck, and wet warmth dribbled down.

She'd fucking cut him!

"In the Bad Time." She sighed. "You were there. You could have stopped it, but instead, you behaved like my grandad, touching up that woman."

Her grandad? "I don't know what you mean. Tell me. Please . . ."

"Police!" Whitney shouted from above.

The woman got off him so fast it was almost a blur, and she ran down the few steps and rounded them to pelt to the rear of the house.

Whitney rushed downstairs in pursuit, calling, "Okay, Gary? Are you okay?"

"Yes, yes, just go!"

He lay back, staring at the glass ceiling, the moon peering back at him, smiling, as if it were the woman's accomplice, a willing witness to her madness.

Gary let the tears fall along with the blood dripping from his calf and neck.

* * *

Whitney phoned in the distress call on her way through the house, chastising herself for being so out of the loop when it came to this sort of thing. Once done, she stepped into the back garden. The sound of an engine fired up then spluttered and died. It roared again, an over-rev, as though the driver was panicking about their vehicle giving up on them at the wrong time.

She stuffed her phone in her pyjama pocket and raced round the side, opening the gate and flinging it wide, confronted with someone sitting slumped against the house.

What? Shit. Shit. Think what to do next . . .

Everything she'd been taught seemed to disintegrate.

She went to run past, assuming they were unconscious, but the smear on the wall had her stopping at the same time the engine revved harder and tyres scattered gravel on the edge of the road outside these three perfect homes.

She crouched, switched her torch app on, and shone it at an Indian man who was clearly deceased. She shot to her feet and pelted to the front, heading left in the direction of red lights on the back of a car. They were too small, the vehicle too far away, she couldn't read the number plate, and they vanished around a corner.

The waves lapped at the bottom of the cliff as if applauding the intruder's escape.

Adrenaline flooding her system, her mind shot with regards to protocol, she called in the death, returning to the body and evaluating the state of him as Gary appeared at the gate.

"Oh God," he said, clutching one bunched pyjama leg at the top of his thigh.

"Don't come any closer. Shit, is your leg bleeding?"

"She cut me," he said. "It isn't as bad as it looks, and my neck's just been nicked."

"Get back, go inside. You're contaminating the crime scene." *He'll have dripped blood everywhere indoors.* "Did you check the boys? Christ, please tell me you did." *Because doing that went right out of my head.*

"They're asleep." He backed away. "Who the fuck *is* that? What the hell is going *on* here?"

"I don't know, but please, go inside."

He disappeared, and she let out a small breath of relief. Drew on her police training. She hadn't been out in the wild for a long time, preferring being a FLO, so it took her a moment to get her bearings.

Check for a pulse even though signs of life are not present.

She did. Nothing.

Assess the area.

She stood and shone her torch. Wandered to the front of the house to see if the door had been jemmied. It hadn't. She returned to the area between the houses and crept to the bushes. Panned her light over the grass.

It was squashed down in places, as if someone had been hiding.

Her phone rang. Alton, who manned the front desk at night. Her boyfriend.

"Hello?" she said, quiet so her voice didn't alert the neighbours. She didn't need an audience, and neither did the poor dead bastard.

"Status?" he asked.

"They got away." *Because I was stupid and went all TV, shouting, 'Police!'*

"Carol's en route, Dave to follow shortly." He was a consummate professional by sticking to the rules during this call.

She'd never been so relieved to hear his voice. "Thank you."

"Uniforms and an ambulance are also on the way. You okay?"

"Yes. No. I will be."

"Want me to stay on the line?"

What she wanted was to cry for being such an incompetent prat, to have him hug her. "Please." She let out a choked sob, wondering why she ever thought she'd be a good copper. "I'm standing by a dead man, Al. A *dead man*."

"I know. It'll be all right. Everything will be all right."

* * *

Carol pulled up to the sight of an ambulance, a uniform car and SOCO putting the finishing touches to a tent. She'd been about to leave Betty's street when the call had come in.

She'd said to Oliver, "No rest for the wicked. Meet me there as soon as you can."

Rib had told her he'd come as soon as he could, too, as he was almost done with Vincent.

She got out of her car, having phoned Dave to tell him to get his arse down to Seaview Heights — by all accounts, the issue here was much bigger than an old man dead in a hallway and she'd need the extra help.

She put on protectives from her boot and approached the side of the house, annoyed at the necessary halogens that lit the area, trained on a bush where grass had been trampled flat, an evidence marker next to it. A glance up at the side window of next door revealed two people staring down, a man and a woman. While she waited for Dave, Oliver and

Rib, she may as well knock and ask the neighbours if they'd seen anything.

As the area between homes had been cordoned off, she walked along the pavement then down their path, the police tape to her left bowing in the middle, attached to a gatepost and a drainpipe.

It took a minute or so for them to answer the summons, and going by their skewwhiff white dressing gowns, they'd rushed off to put them on prior to coming downstairs. The gowns matched, each with an embroidered letter on the right breast. A blue W and a pink L.

Jesus Christ . . .

Carol held up her ID. "DI Carol Wren. Sorry to trouble you, but as you can see, we have a crime scene to the side of your house. Did you notice owt unusual at all this evening?"

The couple had wedged themselves together on the threshold, like neither could accede the prime spot to the other. The man, in his fifties, bald with greying sideburns and a going-white beard, had a ring in his left nostril and a thicker one in the opposite eyebrow. A small gold medallion with a chunky chain nestled in the puff of hairs inside the V of his gown. The woman, brunette and thin, a large chest and alarming swollen lips, probably Botox, was around twenty-five. Father and daughter? Or was there something in the water older men drank around here which forced them to seek out women much younger than them?

The man nodded. "Might seem like nowt, but I know from the telly that owt we can give you might help. If anyone comes up here, with there only being three houses, it's either a visitor to one of us or they go and stand on the cliff edge." He pointed behind Carol. "Tonight, a woman came by."

Carol perked up. "Right . . . What time was that?"

"I don't rightly know, sorry. We were drinking and playing Cluedo."

"Just you?"

"Yeah." He sniffed. "It was dark, I know that much, and she went past — don't know if you spotted it, but the front of ours is basically all glass, so I saw her clearly. She had black on, her hair up in some kind of do."

"A bun, Willy," his companion supplied.

"Yeah, a bun, and she came from down that way." He pointed to the road that led along the cliff to the estate behind. "Not unusual for people to walk up here, so I didn't take much notice other than to check whether she crossed the road to stand opposite. Got to be careful, see. There's been two suicides up here in the past four months. Watched one of them jump over myself. Anyroad, she didn't go opposite, so I assumed she'd gone past Gary's to stand farther up."

"Did you see her come back again?" Carol asked.

"I did," the brunette said. "After another woman arrived."

Carol's guts went south. "*Another* woman?"

"Yeah, she was in black an' all, *and* she had a bun, too."

Willy frowned. "I was sure you'd got her mixed up with the first lady, wasn't I, Lise?"

Lise laughed. "You were, but no. The first one was thin, the second one wasn't."

Carol's body erupted in goose bumps. "This second woman, how 'not thin' was she?"

"I don't like to be mean . . ." Lise bit her lip.

"I need a description."

"She was big." Lise held her hands out to show width. "And I mean big. How she fitted in that car, I don't know, because—"

"Car?" Carol fussed around inside the protective suit for her notebook. "Did you see the make? Where did she park?"

Lise blinked as though two questions were one to many. "She left it down past the first house. I know because I was up having a wee at the time and went into the bedroom to get my pyjamas on after. We have a balcony." She poked her finger upwards. "And I opened the folding window doors up there to let air in — Willy doesn't like running the air-con all the time. I stood up there for a bit, staring at the sea, trying to work out if Miss Scarlet had done the dirty with the rope."

Carol, caught momentarily off guard until she got the memo they were back to Cluedo, looked up. Yep, a balcony, the doors still open. She estimated Lise would have been able to see right along the street both ways from there. "So she parked away from all these three houses, yes? On which side?"

"Yes, and it was our side."

"Sorry to poke, but the make?"

"Now that I *do* know because it's the same as mine. When she got out, the security light on the side of the first house went on. A Ford Focus, but the old kind."

"What colour was it?"

"Red."

"Did you catch any of the number plate?"

"It had a twenty-one in it, and it made me think: *Oh, same age as me!* I said that, didn't I, Willy?"

"You did, lover."

"What did she do then?" Carol's heart thumped hard, and she wrote the information down.

"She put her chin to her chest, and I went back downstairs. As I was about to press the button that makes the blinds go across and close on the wall window, the one at the front here, she got back in her car and reversed."

"What about after that?"

"I remember the engine stopping, but then I got caught up with Willy because I had a feeling he'd moved the middle envelope on the Cluedo board, like he'd peeked at what was inside, so we ended up having a little spat."

"She went on about it so much we had to start again," Willy said, "but I didn't even cheat."

"So you don't know if the larger woman got out of her car?"

"No," Lise said. "Like I told you, me and Willy had a spat."

"Did you see owt while Lise was upstairs?" Carol asked Willy, her patience wearing thin.

He shook his head. "Nope, as I said to Lise when she accused me of cheating, I was in the kitchen making drinks, using the SodaStream, so how I had time to poke into that murder envelope I have no idea, because Lise likes a cocktail, and they take a while."

Carol scribbled notes, her mind ticking over.

A thin woman arrived and went in the direction of Gary's.

A larger woman arrived, parked, then reversed. To Gary's?

"I heard footsteps," Lise said. "Running."

Carol lifted her head. "And?"

"I got up from resetting the board and parted the blinds — we've got those vertical ones, you know the sort. The thin woman was running down the street. I glanced right and saw the Ford parked on the road between our house and Gary's."

Bold to park there when these two were awake and everyone at Gary's might also have been up. "Do you know if Gary and his lot were in bed? What I mean by that is, were any lights on?"

Lise's eyes widened as though she loved all this. "No, and the reason I know that is because of his glass ceiling. There was no light coming from there. Anyroad, the second woman got in the car and parked it down where she had originally, you know, by the first house, then she got out and walked back past ours. Willy had been to the loo, the one downstairs, and he came back, so I left the window and don't know what she did then."

"What are the names of the people who live in the first house?" Carol asked.

Willy piped up. "Jim and Sonya Knight, but they're not here at the moment. Holiday home, much like Gary's usually is, but we've seen the news and realise why he's here. Err, who's that dead fella in the tent out there?"

"I don't know yet. Did you see or hear owt else?"

Lise nodded. "We'd gone to bed. Again, no idea of the time. We sleep with the balcony doors open in the summer. Like I said, Willy and his air-con rules . . ." She elbowed him in the side. "I heard a car starting, then it died out. Then it started again, and it annoyed me so much I got up to see what was going on because of the over-revving. Well, it was the Ford Focus, and it sped off. The gravel on the edge of the road kicked up. Like in the films, it was. A few seconds later, maybe thirty, I don't know, the lady who's staying with Gary came running out and stared after it. I woke you, didn't I, Willy, and I said, 'Something's going on next door!' Worried, obviously, that the killer was here for Gary, because of Sue, and God, I was that scared."

"We got up," Willy said, "and stood by the side window. Gary was by the gate with blood on his leg, and I'm sure there was some on his throat. We watched the tent going up and everything."

Carol blew out a long breath. She had two women to find now, not just one.

"Thank you so much for your time," she said. "Uniform will come here in the morning to get an official statement, or you can go to the station."

Lise looked at Willy, her eyes lighting up again.

"The station," they both said, laughing.

"It'll be like we're in a drama on the telly, Lise."

"I know, Willy. Well exciting."

CHAPTER TWENTY-TWO

Seaview Heights

Like he'd said to Whitney, Gary's leg wasn't half as bad as he'd thought. All the weird woman had done was score a line down the skin, and yes, it had bled like billyo, but the paramedic fella only had to attach a line of butterfly strips down the seven-inch cut, leaving his neck to heal by itself.

What a mess his life had turned out to be. Here he was, sitting in his back garden with the ambulance crew packing their things away, Whitney standing close by talking to PC Pitson, and SOCOs once again invading his property. The boys had awoken at the commotion, and PC Helen May was upstairs with them in Jack's room — something about that being okay for now as they didn't think the intruder had gone up there, but the house would need a thorough going-over just in case.

SOCO were paying particular attention to the area around the stairs and the rear folding doors, where his assailant had broken in using a lock pick or some kind of tool like that, so he'd gathered from listening to the chatter around him. A row of evidence markers led from the doors to the stairs where Gary had rushed out to help Whitney then went back in as instructed. He'd gone up to find his sons standing at the top of the stairs, their features unreadable in the darkness up there.

As for the tent hiding the body . . .

Who the hell had brought that dead man here? Why? Was it someone he knew? A message to the police? It gave him the creeps to know someone had done that while they'd all slept. It was the Sue situation all over again, someone dying while people close by dreamed the time away.

Carol walked to the garden gate with Dave, and they signed what he now knew was a log at a crime scene and changed their booties for clean ones. Beyond them, a van drew up to the kerb, and Gary recalled it from the Wexford house. The bald pathologist. Fucking hell, everything was so surreal again. His throbbing calf, pinching where the strips held, was a constant reminder that bad things were happening and there was nothing he could do to stop it.

Say you're sorry, that it's your fault.

That's what she'd said, that sumo woman.

Carol came over and smiled down at him, a sad smile, tired. "Sorry you got hurt."

"Me too, but at least I'm alive. She had a bloody knife to my throat."

"Tell me what happened."

He'd already been through it in dribs and drabs with Whitney while they'd waited for everyone else to arrive, but he took a deep breath and repeated it again, ensuring he mentioned that the woman must have entered quietly if Whitney hadn't woken up. He didn't want to get her into trouble. It wasn't her fault she'd been asleep and hadn't heard him shout when his ankle had been grabbed, not hearing anything until the commotion on the stairs had accelerated and alerted her to something being wrong. His throat hurt from so much talking. Carol's eyebrows went up when he said something about the "bad time".

"What bad time?" she asked.

"I don't know. And then when Whitney came, the woman ran off."

"What time did you all go to bed?" Carol asked.

"Ten, somewhere around there."

"And you went straight to sleep?"

"Oddly, I did. I didn't expect to with everything going on inside my head, but I was out like a light until I woke up, thinking I'd had a dream, but it must have been when she broke in. I heard a *tink* noise and thought Whitney was making a cup of tea. My bedroom is directly above that door, so I can only assume the *tink* was the woman." He indicated the folding doors in the kitchen area.

"I've spoken to your neighbours, and they saw two women. One thin, the other matching the description of the lady who may have been standing outside your Wexford house."

Gary's skin pebbled. "*Two* women?"

Carol nodded. "Do you know a Vincent Marsh?"

"Not that I recall, although if he works at the factory, I'll admit I don't know all their names because some people only stay around as an in-between-jobs thing, so I don't get to know them." *Plus I started leaving it all to Sue.* "I've got my laptop here, the one for work that the SOCOs returned to me, so I could look on there, or Paul Gedds will have that information."

Dave walked off, phone out, prodding the screen.

"He'll phone Paul," Carol said. "I don't want to touch your laptop in case the woman went near it."

"Okay." Gary frowned. "Why did you ask about the Victor man?"

"Vincent. He lived opposite Betty Tavers and was murdered."

"Bloody hell . . ." Gary's world had just got that much more jumbled and bizarre.

"I've phoned in information about a red Ford Focus, the old kind. Do you know anyone who has one?"

Gary frowned again. His brain wouldn't work. "I can't . . . can't think."

"I understand. You've been through another horrible ordeal. Things you have in your head will resurface at some point, so if there's owt that pops up about this incident here, or regarding the car, tell me immediately."

"I will. What will we do now? Both of my houses . . ."

"Wexford has been cleared to be used again. SOCO have finished."

"No." A muscle in his jaw ticked. No matter what, he wasn't going back *there*.

"Or there's Flora's."

"Absolutely not." *She'd lord it over me that we had to go to her, cap in hand.* "I'll book a hotel, if we can even get a room because of it being high season."

"Have you heard from her at all?"

"Not a peep, personally, although the boys went there today. Well, that would be yesterday now. They walked over. She was out, said she had something to do, but she left them a key. They were gone when you came to see me. When I stood out the front, you know, the Betty conversation."

"Okay. And were they all right when they got back?"

"Silent, nowt unusual since their mother died. Why do you ask?"

"I noticed Flora might be the sort of woman to put ideas in their heads. Their silence is a concern. Could she have planted seeds about —" Carol glanced around and continued quietly — "Charlotte?"

I wouldn't put it past the bitch. "I can see Joseph keeping that to himself, brooding, but not Jack. He'd come right out and say something, accuse me of being a bastard. Not that he'd say bastard, not to my face anyroad."

"Right. So you were saying?"

"They'd had their tea with Flora. They asked her if they could stay the night, but she said she had to go out so they couldn't, which I thought was odd, because she rarely goes out of an evening."

"Did she say where she was going?"

Gary felt uneasy. "Why . . . ?"

"Because we're after a thin woman now. Flora is thin. She has her hair in a bun, like the people next door mentioned.

She had something to do in the evening. Could she have been here, hiding behind that bush out there? Because someone did."

"Fucking hell . . . She hates me, but you don't think—"

"The large woman could have murdered Sue by mistake — Flora had sent her to kill you, but she found Sue instead. In this instance, the killer took a second shot. Flora could have been behind the bushes to give the other woman instructions, but the larger woman was the one to come into the house."

"Larger woman . . ."

"What's the matter?"

"She didn't feel heavy. Not as heavy as her size indicated anyroad. I've only just realised that. I'd have expected her to wind me, but she didn't. And her head was smaller than her body, which didn't seem right."

"Her head was smaller?"

"Yes."

"Someone else gave the same description earlier regarding the Vincent Marsh incident."

"So it could all be connected?"

"It's leading that way. What about her hands? Did you get a look at them?"

"No, it was dark. Why are the hands significant?"

"The pathologist has a theory about someone having a prominent knuckle. Does that mean owt to you?"

Gary's mind closed down. No matter how hard he tried to pull information free, it held it in a tight fist. "There's something, I just can't think what it is." He ignored Carol's muttered *fuck*. It must be so frustrating for her to deal with him, a man who acted as if he was missing the orange jelly out of his Jaffa Cake. "Sorry."

"As I said, things will come to you. Now, I need to go and see the pathologist about that body in the tent. So sit quietly — have a think, if you can. I'll be just out there if you need me."

Gary nodded. It must be the painkillers the paramedic had given him that were fucking with his brain cells. He rested back on the lounger, his groin aching where the steel wire had pressed against the sensitive area.

Carol walked away, tapped Dave on the shoulder, and together they left the garden. Both changed their paper shoes then entered the tent.

He didn't envy them.

CHAPTER TWENTY-THREE

The Tent

Rib looked up at Carol from his crouch beside the victim, his face alight with happiness. Normal people would be tired from bouncing from body to body, yet here he was, animated. "There's ID, Bird."

His use of that name didn't bother her now. He'd said he liked her, they'd had some kind of truce when he'd touched her elbow at Vincent's, so she smiled kindly. "Thank God for that. Who is it?"

He flapped a laminated card with a silver clip, a lanyard. "Nabruah Panjib, surgeon. Scudderton Infirmary."

A surgeon? Oh, fuck me, no. No . . . "Hang on." She took her phone out, calling Alton on the front desk. "It's me. Carol. Can you find something out for me? Ring the Royal Infirmary. Speak to someone about surgeons and ask them if they have a Nabruah Panjib working there. Also, get his address from the system. I need to know if he did an operation on a Harry Smith, okay? I don't know when that was, but it's going back years."

"That could take them a while . . ."

"It doesn't matter. I need it done. Tell them it's urgent." She cut the call. "He could have been the lead surgeon on Harry Smith's hand."

Dave gawped at her. "What the fuck?"

"I know, and there was me thinking Harry was a nice fella. Could he be mistaken for being the large woman? He's certainly big enough."

"What, and he puts a wig on?" Dave belted out a laugh. "But what about his health? He's as wheezy as a bagpipe."

Carol stamped her foot. "I don't *know*, but this is off, yes? Vincent's comment about Harry being a suspect. Nabruah here trying to save his hand — which I bet is who he is. A large woman and a thin woman. Harry and Martine?"

"We could go there anyroad . . ." Dave said.

Rib held up a hand. "Um, this gentleman wasn't killed here. He's had a whack to the back of the head with what might be a grainy rock — there are particles in his hair. One stab to the carotid. There isn't enough blood here to suggest this is where he was murdered, so you're looking for another crime scene. I suspect there will be a lot of blood there."

"His address," Carol said. Her phone rang, Alton, and she swiped the screen. "What have you got?"

"The hospital lady is going through the files, but I thought you'd want his address as soon as. Twelve Skimmers Lane, Scudderton, the new-builds."

"Skimmers Lane?" She glanced to Dave. "Isn't that where Thomas the vet lives?"

He nodded. "Fucking Nora."

"Thanks, Alton. We'll go there now." She ended the call and said to Dave, "What's that look for? You think we ought to go to Smithy's Cottage first?"

"I'd have thought so, yes. Catch them as soon as we can — if it's even them. You can't be all places at once."

Delegate.

She took a deep breath. Was the father's and daughter's work finished for the night? Were they tucked up in bed?

Could she take the risk? What if they were out still, killing another target?

"Let me think . . . Ah, sod it." She poked her head out of the tent and spied Pitson at the garden gate. "I need you to arrange for officers to go to twelve Skimmers Lane. Give them permission to gain entry, granted on the grounds of a possible threat to life: the man who lives there is the dead man in the tent, and someone he lives with might also be dead in there or in danger. Three uniforms if they can spare them, please — get Alton on it."

Pitson nodded and walked out of the garden towards his patrol car, phone to his ear. Carol cringed at him not changing his booties to go past the tent — *For fuck's sake, I'll have to have a word with him!* — and spun to stare at the poor man inside. He'd lost his life for some reason, and she intended to find out what it was so this madness could be put into some form of order in her head and his relatives could be informed. Shit, she needed Michael.

Phone out again, hands shaking, she rang him, apologetic about waking him up. "I'm so sorry, but I need you at the station. There's too much going on. Write this down. Two deceased men — a Vincent Marsh and a Nabruah Panjib. I need every bit of information on them you can find, mainly next of kin before this shitshow blows up on the news — I want their families informed by us, not the telly. Someone else will have looked into Vincent already, but take over."

"No probs. I'm on my way."

"Also, and I know it's a lot to do, another look into Harry and Martine Smith. I have a horrible feeling it's them."

"Blimey . . . Go. Catch you soon."

She phoned Alton. "Alan Pitson got hold of you, yes?"

"Yep, uniforms are en route."

"Brilliant. I need a couple more to meet us out at Smithy's Cottage — a big ask at this time of night, I know, and I apologise." She gave him precise instructions. "But I need them to park down the road a bit. There's a bend just before the cottage. There. I don't want the residents spooked."

"On it now."

"Thank you." She slid her phone away and, mind spinning, gestured for Dave to go with her. They switched booties. Just as she turned to walk towards her car, Gary called her name. She swivelled round and stared across at him where he stood at the gate.

"What is it?" she said.

"I've remembered. About the car and the knuckle."

She knew what he was going to say. "Go on . . ."

"A woman who works at the factory has the knuckle, I remember seeing it when she was cutting once, and she drives a red Ford Focus — that stands out because there's a glut of rust on one of the wheel arches. I know I said I don't recall many names, but she sticks out in my mind because of her father."

"Martine Smith," she said.

"How did you know?"

"We've got to go. Hang tight." She looked for Pitson and shouted, "Alan, you're with us!"

And she ran, stripping her protectives off at the edge of the grass and placing them in a designated bag, Dave doing the same. They dipped beneath the cordon. Dave got into his vehicle, Pitson in the passenger side, and Carol got into hers.

Then they were off to catch a killer.

Or killers, as the case may be.

* * *

Undisclosed Address

Guest hadn't been able to settle since they'd seen Martine outside Gary's Cove home. Was he dead yet? Had Martine managed to get inside that house and end him? It was all Guest had thought about since Gary had done what he had years ago, a memory that wouldn't leave, repeating over and over until Guest thought they'd go mad.

The idea to kill him had come on a night when insomnia had parked its arse and refused to leave. Guest had got up and paced, thinking of all the ramifications if Gary was murdered — there was Sue to think about, those sons of theirs, not to mention whether the factory would continue without him. Was Sue well-versed enough in the way it worked to continue in his absence? Would she even *want* to if he died?

Guest had been in that factory, knew the layout, and had imagined going there, calling Gary aside then luring him into the material storeroom. There was a small office in the back corner, one Gary was rumoured to take young women into when they'd gone beyond a quick feel-up. How he could do that to his wife Guest didn't know, but the filthy man was always at it.

And that was why Guest had come to the decision to end him, but they didn't want to do it themselves. It would maybe be too obvious, people might look at Guest as a suspect, given the fact they'd made no bones about disliking him, especially after the time Harry had lost his hand.

And there the plan had been born. Harry. A man who surely held a grudge against Gary for the accident. So Guest had gone to Smithy's Cottage on the pretext they wanted to check in as a friend, especially as he hadn't returned to work for so many years. Harry had been a tad slow on the uptake when Guest had mentioned, casually the first time, that they'd love to kill Gary, explaining why they wanted it done: the nightmares he'd given Guest, his actions lingering in their brain so they couldn't rest. The second time they'd said it, Harry had sounded offended, upset she'd asked him to do such a thing.

Eventually, Harry had caught up, and he thought *he'd* devised the plan to end Gary's life, exactly as Guest had intended. They'd talked for ages, three years, and it had been a lengthy old road to get to this point, but so long as Martine had killed Gary tonight, all that cajoling would have been worth it.

When Guest had found out dear Sue had died . . . It wasn't part of the plan, and Guest's mind and body had gone into meltdown for an hour or two. They'd barely been able to function. And they'd cried. A lot. How the hell had this happened? How could Guest live with themselves now? Then there was Jack and Joseph, those poor lads without their mother, Gary still walking around because Harry had felt Gary would suffer more if he had to live a life without his wife in it.

Thank God he'd seen sense in the end.

* * *

Smithy's Cottage

The deal was to knock and speak to Harry and Martine as though they were just there on a routine enquiry regarding Vincent Marsh's online comments, the car, and to check for a prominent knuckle. A late visit, but police work didn't stop just because it was dark.

What would they find here?

Two uniforms, Lloyd and Kenner, were out the back, waiting in case Martine and Harry legged it, although Carol suspected Harry wouldn't get very far. Pitson stood behind her and Dave at the front door. Carol knocked, her heart thumping hard, a sluice of adrenaline invading her body.

It took a while for a light to come on at what she remembered was the top of the stairs. She thought about the sergeant, Oliver, when he'd said, "You get a sense about people, don't you?" She'd agreed with him, but their senses, and Dave's, had fucked off when it came to Harry Smith, as none of them had suspected he'd murder someone.

But Vincent had known. How?

The shape of a slender person advanced towards the mottled glass in the front door. Martine, then. The door opened, and she stood there, hair tousled from sleep, down around her shoulders. Carol glanced at her hands.

A prominent knuckle.

"Hi, Martine, sorry to bother you in the middle of the night, but we need to have a word."

"Can't it wait until the morning?"

"No, otherwise we'd have come in the morning." Carol smiled.

"What's this about?"

"Can you get your father up, please? We need to speak to him, too."

"What's happened? Is it Mam?"

"What about your mam?"

"She left us, went off with this man called Tim. Never contacted us again. Have you come to say she's . . . she's dead?"

Hopefully Michael will drag something up about that. "If we could just come in . . ."

"No. I mean, hang on. Let me get Dad up." She went to close the door.

"It's okay, you can do that while we wait in the living room."

"No!"

Martine went to close the door again, faster, but Dave stuck his foot out then shoved the glass, sending Martine reeling backwards. The young woman was hiding something — otherwise, why attempt to shut them out? Dave went inside, placed her hands behind her back and moved her to the kitchen doorway opposite the living room.

"Look, we just want to talk," he said. "I'm holding your wrists as I feel you're a flight risk and a danger to myself and my colleagues, okay? If I need to cuff you, I will, so please behave calmly."

Martine struggled and kicked back at him. "Get *off* me!"

Dave grasped her wrists one-handed. Pitson entered and passed over his cuffs, Dave clipping them to secure her.

"I've cuffed you because you've displayed actions that leave me worried for our safety." Good old Dave, always explaining everything so nothing could come back to bite them on the arse later. "I'm going to take you into the kitchen and sit you on a chair while PC Pitson goes to wake your father. Do you understand?"

"I said, get off me! What are you here for? You can't just barge in!"

Pitson went upstairs.

Carol sighed and looked at Martine across the square hallway. "We're here in relation to the murders of Sue Cuttersby, Betty Tavers, Vincent Marsh and Nabruah Panjib, and the actual bodily harm of Gary Cuttersby under the Offences Against the Person Act eighteen sixty-one."

"You're off your rocker," Martine said. "That was nowt to do with us, but I know who did it."

Carol, unnerved by the switch of direction in the case, was momentarily lost for words. *But the knuckle. She's in the frame for punching Vincent.* "If you know about an offense before it happens, when it happens or after it happens, you are obliged to inform the police."

"What, and risk them coming here to kill us as well?" Martine laughed. "Not likely."

"Who is it, Martine? You'll be safe, we'll make sure of it."

"I need to speak to my dad first. I won't say owt until I know what that bad boy wants."

Carol blinked. She'd heard the term "bad boy", of course she had, like you could have a bad boy curry or say something like, "Let me have a look at this bad boy!" She was young enough to use that phrase, but for Martine to use that term for her father, wasn't that a little odd?

It didn't sit right.

"Bad boy?" Carol asked.

"Forget I said that." Martine blushed.

"Take her into the kitchen," Carol said.

Dave steered her in there and pressed her down into a chair. Carol snapped on gloves she'd put in her trouser pocket in case she needed them, then found the kitchen light switch and pressed it. Bloody hell, talk about a posh gaff. It must have taken some money to fit this kitchen out, and from where she stood in the doorway, she spotted another area. A wet room? Sensible, given Harry's disability and also because she couldn't imagine he'd want to traipse up and down the stairs to go to the loo in his wheezy condition.

Pitson appeared at the top of the stairs. "Um, can you come here, please?"

Carol went up there, a sense of dread seeping into her. She headed for the room with a double bed, a lamp shining on the white cabinet beside it. Harry lay beneath a blue sheet, his eyes closed, his skin grey. A crumpled tissue with blood clots and grey globs on it rested in his upturned hand — bits of lung? — and blood spatter coated the sheet on his chest.

Carol wanted to scream. "Fuck. Dead?"

Pitson nodded.

"Okay, phone it in for me. Poor Rib's in for a lot of post-mortems this week. Harry was ill, so unless Martine says otherwise, this is probably natural causes — if she even knows he's passed away."

Carol went back downstairs, Pitson following. He went out the front to make the call, and Carol entered the kitchen.

"I'm sorry to have to tell you that your father's dead," she said.

Martine screamed. "I know! I fucking know!"

Which means she likely intended to escape when she said she'd go and wake him up. She's as guilty as sin.

* * *

PC Alan Pitson walked down the side of the cottage past a double garage on the left and found officers Kenner and Lloyd standing on a patio. "You might get lucky and be able to go back on your regular shift, but we need to wait until a body has been assessed."

"Bloody hell . . ." Lloyd said.

Alan shrugged. "He was ill so . . ."

He led the way back to the house to the fresh sound of another screech from Martine. He'd heard all levels of scream, and this one sounded like it came from the deranged bracket, of which there were three distinct types that he'd encountered in his career. Martine's was top of the list; she was an out-and-out lunatic if his instincts were right.

Now there was a potential crime scene, they put on their overshoes and gloves then entered the house, Alan indicating he wanted his uniformed colleagues to follow him into the living room. They'd have a quick nose around, see if there was anything significant, which would save Carol the job. The poor woman must be dead on her feet.

Alan turned on the light to reveal a living room filled with expensive things: two leather sofas, nice sideboards, a large TV, a chrome-and-glass desk with a high-tech computer, a top-of-the-range desk chair he knew cost over seven hundred quid because he'd seen it on Facebook, and a Singer sewing machine in the far corner by the patio doors.

Lloyd and Kenner headed for that end of the room where the patio doors led to the garden, and Alan surveyed the lounge area. Nothing out of the ordinary. Until he moved the door to close it and found a pair of armchairs — one leather to match the sofas, the other that didn't fit with the rest of the décor, an old tattered wingback with a side table that had a glass on it and an ashtray full of dried-out rollies.

And . . . whatever the fuck sat in those chairs weren't human.

"Boss!" he shouted, clamping a hand over his mouth as he registered glass eyes staring straight through him. "Boss, you need to come and look at this."

CHAPTER TWENTY-FOUR

Smithy's Cottage

It was an odd thing, looking at these . . . creatures? Dolls? Carol had never seen anything like it. Tanned leather in the shape of bodies, stuffed with what she assumed was the fluff used to pad out teddy bears. The one in the leather chair had no clothes on, although it did have a wedding and engagement ring on the appropriate finger. And a wig. And glass eyes.

And fluffy earmuffs.

Its lips had been sewn shut, the thick black cotton in a line of neat crosses. Around the neck hung a locket, dipping between two overfilled breasts, and slippers covered the feet — slippers Carol remembered had been on the floor when she'd come here before. Ones she'd assumed belonged to Martine. The mannequin, whatever the hell it was, had been strapped to the chair using bungee cords, as though either Martine or Harry thought their stuffed guest would get up and walk away. A triangle of brown carpet had been stuck on to mimic pubic hair.

The other . . . thing . . . A hole in its stomach and one in the heart area had been sewn up using the same rough cotton, a thick X apiece. The breasts had only been filled at the bases near nipples that pointed towards the crotch, their tops flat to the chest. This leather effigy was more crinkled, to perhaps create the illusion of age, and its cheeks had divots in them, as if poked with a sharp point. The grey curly wig, shorthaired, further bolstered the elderly effect, cobwebs clinging to it. An old-fashioned skirt covered the bottom half, thin pleats in a nylon material with flowers all over it. No slippers for this one, but a pair of fat-heeled black court shoes. No earmuffs. And no glass eyes either. The sockets had been sewn like the other areas, that cotton again. The hand of the older one rested on a side table between a glass and an ashtray, posed, creepy.

Carol's phone rang. She ignored it. Sensed the stares of Pitson, Lloyd and Kenner at her back, their heavy breathing indicating they were as staggered as she was.

"I don't know what the fuck this is, but it's sick," she said. "Pitson, call it in. Tell Alton I said we need more SOCO for this as the couple I had in mind to check Harry's bedroom aren't enough."

Pitson walked out, white as a sheet, and she imagined him outside, gulping in lungfuls of air, wishing he wasn't on duty. Poor bastard.

Carol turned to face the other two, her phone going silent. "Did you have time to check owt else in here?"

"No," Lloyd said.

"Well, we can do a quick check of the rest of the house while we wait for forensics to get here. Lloyd, you stay in here, see if that computer comes to life for you. Kenner, go upstairs." And she recalled the scream she thought she'd heard when she and Dave had driven past what felt like days ago now. "No, I've changed my mind. Come with me. I want to look in the garage." *What if it wasn't seagulls screeching like Dave said and there's a hostage in there?*

She left the room and glanced in the kitchen at Martine, who sat with her head down, eyes closed, soft sobs coming out of her. Dave raised his hands in a *Well?* gesture, and Carol shook her head: *Can't tell you yet . . .* He nodded in response, and she pointed to the wall behind him to hopefully get the message across that she was going to the garage. She mouthed the word to cement her intentions. He nodded again, and at the front door, she took off her booties and placed them on the floor so she could put them back on later. Kenner did the same. She led him outside, where Pitson paced the drive on his phone.

"Fair warning, I have a feeling we're going to find a woman in here," she said to Kenner then explained about the scream.

"God."

"I know. Whether they're dead or alive by now, well, that's what we'll find out. Can you put your flashlight on, please?"

At the garages, Kenner directed the beam at the door she'd indicated, the one she'd seen Martine using. Carol turned the handle, surprised it unlocked the mechanism — Martine and Harry maybe had no qualms about security as they lived rurally. Carol lifted the door, and Kenner pointed his light inside.

"What the fucking hell is *that*?" she said.

The beam didn't penetrate right to the back, only brightening the blackness to a lighter shade, but a shape that sent Carol's nerves jangling meant her instincts, at least, knew whatever was there wasn't good.

They stepped inside, and the farther they went, the clearer the shape became.

"Jesus Christ, it's another one of those doll things," she whispered.

"I don't think they're dolls, boss."

She didn't either, didn't want to acknowledge they were somehow *people*. Stuffed people. Who'd skinned them? Because that must have been what had happened. Where were the innards, the bones, the remains of the three deceased? And who was this? A man, that much was clear by the obvious extra parts between its legs, although . . .

"That's been cut and sewn at the end." She pointed to the penis. "It looks like Harry's stump. Why would they have done that?"

"Maybe Harry had a complex about the size of his todger when he saw this fella's." Kenner laughed nervously.

"You might laugh, but you could be right."

She left us, went off with this man called Tim. Never contacted us again. Have you come to say she's . . . she's dead?

Martine had been lying, trying to throw them off the scent, to stop them from coming in and discovering those things in the chairs.

Carol swallowed a tight ball of emotion — she'd bet her last quid this was Tim and the younger body in the living room was Martine's mother, but who was the old lady?

Something caught her eye above the chair. "Point that torch higher, will you?"

Kenner did that, revealing a wooden plaque with words carved into it crudely: Tim Dougan — Fornicator.

"Blimey," Kenner said. "This is some messed-up shit going on here."

"You're not wrong."

Her phone rang, her screen showing Michael. She answered quickly, eager to have a breather from this poor bastard who had glass eyes, sewn lips, a wig and those bloody earmuffs. She turned her back on him.

"Yep?" she said.

"I've got a few things."

"Throw them at me, then."

"Nabruah Panjib operated on Harry Smith's arm — Alton passed me the info as you didn't answer your phone. He has no family in the UK; they live in India, according to the lady at the hospital. No known partner. The officers who went to his flat found the front door ajar and blood on the hallway rug — a lot of blood. There was a rock in the communal garden with blood on that, too."

"So he was likely killed there."

"Right. Vincent Marsh, no other relatives, wife deceased. One incident on file for alleged indecent assault, brought to our attention in ninety-one — a historical case as the actual incident happened in the early seventies. Woman dropped the charges."

"So he was a possible pervert. I'll read the full file tomorrow. Go on."

"Harry Smith, married to a Josie Smith, no record of their divorce or her death — her car is still registered as hers and in use, tax and insurance up to date. Red Ford Focus."

"Does the number plate have a twenty-one in it?"

"Yes. So, Harry's mother. Louisa Smith, no record of a marriage, divorce or death — but she was the lady who filed the assault charge against Vincent Marsh."

"Bloody hell, so his death is making more sense now, a connection."

"Yep. For Harry, no father listed."

"Could be Marsh if the alleged assault was in the seventies. Matches Harry's age or thereabouts."

"I thought the same. Okay, Martine Smith, resides at Smithy's Cottage as we know, works at Cuttersby Clothing."

"Do a quick search for me now on a Tim Dougan."

She waited, listening to the taps of Michael's keyboard.

"Reported missing. His wife, Sally, called it in. Case is still open."

"I think it's safe to say we've found him, although only his skin."

"What?"

"I'll get you up to speed tomorrow. Continue with gathering info for all of these people until five a.m., in case there's a link we need to know about. Martine has intimated she knows who the killer is — unless she's hiding the fact it's her and her father, which is highly likely. After that, go home, get some kip and don't come back in until after lunch. Katherine can take over from you first thing. Leave her a note so she's aware of this shitstorm that's erupted while she's had her weekend off — mind you, she can get up to speed from the whiteboard if you wouldn't mind adding to it."

"Won't she already know from the news?"

"Nope, she was having a media blackout for a couple of days, and I can't say I blame her."

"Okay, catch you tomorrow if we don't speak before."

"Thanks for stopping on."

"Wouldn't want to be anywhere else."

Carol put her phone away and turned back to stare at what was left of Tim Dougan. She asked herself what the hell went through some people's minds for them to even think of stuffing corpses and displaying them like this.

She'd never understand it. Never.

"Let's close this up and go and look in the other side." She walked out and waited for Kenner to shut the door and open the one beside it.

He shone the light on the contents.

A red Ford Focus.

"Gotcha," she said.

* * *

Martine was well and truly fucked if she didn't pull it off that Guest was the killer. Carol Wren stared at her as if she thought she was the biggest liar going, which she was, but whatever, Martine would give it one last shot.

Forensic people walked around the cottage. Dad wouldn't like them poking about or touching his nice things, stuff bought with the money from the sale of Mam's house. Would they look into it and discover what Dad had done, getting her to sell up in Scudderton so he could do the cottage up with the proceeds?

That was on him, not Martine, so she was safe there, and anyway, Mam had sold it, signed all the papers, so it was legal.

She thought about her father, who was dead when she'd come home from Gary's. The pain she'd experienced upon finding him had been mixed with a spasm of relief — she was free now, free of the bad boy, and only had the bad girl to contend with.

The bad girl currently whispered in her ear to enter the biggest chameleon phase ever and act like her life depended on it, which it did, because if she had to go to prison, she might get shanked in the shower and die.

She held back a giggle. Morphed into "I'm innocent" mode.

"Please take the cuffs off. It wasn't *me!*"

"Why is there a padded suit upstairs, then, in your bedroom?" Carol asked. "That explains the large woman people have reported seeing."

Fuck these coppers, snooping around. "Guest made me put it on."

"Guest?"

"The person who really killed all those poor people. Oh!" She let out an anguished cry. Congratulated herself for the performance.

"Am I supposed to believe that rubbish? Everything points to you and your father, although I will admit there's a thin woman we're looking for — but you were seen in the same vicinity at the same time, so you or Guest had the suit on."

Carol must be bluffing, saying they'd been seen at the same time, or maybe those next-door neighbours at the Cove house had spotted her and Guest earlier. *Shit.*

Martine smiled. "I've got proof it wasn't me."

"What proof?"

"A tape recording."

"And where is that?"

"In the longest sideboard in the living room, there's Dad's old Binatone cassette player. He recorded Guest on there. They kept visiting, saying shit about Gary, riling Dad up about his hand so he ended up—" *Whoopsy-doo, almost got myself in poo. Hahahaha.*

"Ended up what?"

Could she throw her father to the wolves along with Guest? He was dead, so nothing could hurt him, but how would she explain being in the padded suit at Gary's? She'd already blamed Dad for the stuffed bodies. Fuck, she'd loved skinning Mam and Tim so Dad could create their new forms to match what he'd done to Nan. She'd learned to tan the skin, and he was so handy with that sewing machine, making them back into people again. What she hadn't liked was carting Mam about as though she were still alive, taking her upstairs to sit her on the loo, for God's sake. Dad's mind had gone with regards to her, and he'd wanted to play out the fantasy that Mam was infirm, couldn't do anything for herself, and that a routine pretending they were still a happy family was the best way to go.

She'd buried their innards and bones by Nan and Baby Smith. *Tweet-tweet.*

When she'd got back from Gary's earlier, before she'd gone up to check on Dad, she'd found Nan in her old scabby chair, sitting next to Mam in her corner. Dad had only gone up in the loft and brought it all down while Martine was out, hadn't he? Nan had sat on the floor up there for years beside the Christmas tree and all the baubles, so why had he wanted to bring her out again? Had he known he was going to die and it was his way of telling Martine to get rid of the dollies? Had him carrying the heavy chair down puffed him out, and he'd gone to bed and choked on his blood and those ugly clots and the grey blobs?

"Ended up *what*?" Carol repeated.

Martine sighed. Forced tears out. "He ended up agreeing to everything Guest said because they'd threatened to kill us both if me or Dad didn't do what they wanted. Yes, I was in the padded suit, but I didn't kill any of them. I was there at all the scenes because Guest forced me into it."

"What if we find blood on that suit?"

Shit.

Carol pressed on. "Why didn't you inform the police about your mother, and Tim, and whoever that old lady is?"

"That's my nan. Guest said they were going to kill my grandad as well."

"Who's that?"

"Someone called Vincent Marsh. I don't know him. He got my nan pregnant then fucked off."

Carol released a long breath. "So, if I'm to believe what you're saying, you must at least have known having puppets of them in the house and garage was illegal."

"Dad needed them, and I loved him so turned a blind eye." She barked out a round of sobs. "I'd already lost my mother, I didn't want to live without him, too, and I would have if I'd told. He'd have been in the nick."

"This evidence you claim to have. I'm going to have a look for it now."

"I swear, you'll see it wasn't my fault."

Martine smiled inwardly. She'd probably only serve a few years for failing to report three murders with Mam, Nan and Tim, plus knowingly keeping their skin, plus being at the scenes of crimes. But murder?

On your bike, Wren.

* * *

In the living room, Carol pressed play and watched the reels churning through the transparent square in the cassette player. Dave stood beside her, rubbing an eye with his wrist. They'd left Martine in the kitchen with Oliver, who'd arrived after a quick check at Cove — no point in being in charge of house-to-house when there were only three and Carol had already spoken to the neighbours.

The tape crackled.

"So you'll kill Gary for me?" a woman said.

"No." Harry. "I will *not* kill Gary."

"What am I supposed to do, then? I can't cope if he isn't dead. Can't you ask Martine?"

"No!" Harry shouted. "What on earth's the *matter* with you? No one can go around willy-nilly just killing people. I know he's done what he's done, but you should have moved on like I have. I lost a hand, for God's sake, yet you don't see me bleating about how hard done by I am. Can't you get therapy?"

"I've tried. *Nowt* will help me."

The tape clattered as if someone had trouble pressing the stop or pause button, then went silent.

Carol took her phone out, rewound the recording and pressed play again to make a copy on her mobile. She shook her head — *I know that voice.* She thought of the last time she'd heard it. The *day* she'd last heard it. Trawled through the conversation in her mind.

She finished the recording.

"Martine might not be lying, then," she whispered to Dave.

"Hmm."

She sighed. "Looks like we're going on a little trip. We'll take Pitson, shall we? He can go in your car with you. Kenner and Lloyd can take Martine down to the station."

* * *

Undisclosed Address

They had come in two cars, Carol Wren and Dave Waite, plus a man in uniform. Guest stared down at them from the bedroom window, partially concealed by a curtain, and knew the shit had hit the fan. Had Martine messed up, left some evidence behind? Had Guest? What if their boots had made an imprint by the bush at Cove? What if the people in the house next door had actually seen them properly — taken a picture, even?

Unless there was evidence like that showing Guest had anything to do with it, they'd blame it on Martine, Harry as the mastermind. Going to prison wasn't a step they were prepared to take, so now was the time to get all their ducks in a row and ensure that never happened.

But what will I do if they have evidence?

* * *

The living room was just the same as before, the scent of it somewhat familiar. "Guest" sat on the sofa and hugged themselves, something Carol had seen them do on their previous visit.

"You know why we're here, don't you?" Carol said.

Dave stood by the window, and Pitson had taken up residence in the doorway to block it. People ran sometimes when they knew the game was up. What would this person do?

"It wasn't me," Guest said. "I didn't kill anyone, I can promise you that."

"Maybe not, but you wanted to, didn't you?" Carol assessed them — stiff posture, eyes bleary and lined with shadows beneath. She'd bet they hadn't slept well with everything going on.

"I did *not*!" A twitch of the mouth. A lie.

"Let's just listen to this, then I'll ask the same question again if need be."

Carol took her phone out, accessed the recording and pressed play. The short conversation sailed out, if a little hazy secondhand, but it was clear what was being said. It ended, and Guest shuddered.

"I didn't know he'd done that, recorded it."

"I don't suppose you did, but it's definitely your voice. We can always put it through a test if you dispute that — we've got some good officers adept at that sort of thing. They study soundwaves and nuances. Clever people."

"Okay, I'll admit I said that, that was me, but he's recorded it out of context. I was *joking* when I said about killing Gary, and Harry got all up in arms about it, which was weird because he'd never done that before. He'd said he'd like him killed, too, for his part in what he referred to as the Bad Time. But what he *didn't* record was the bit afterwards, where he changed his mind and said someone he calls the bad boy would want him to help me out."

Bad boy . . . Martine slipped up with that earlier. "Who's that?"

"His inner voice thing. I don't know. Martine's is called the bad girl. I'm telling you, the pair of them are mad. I went there, the day I saw you two before, and there were these . . . people things in the garage. One was a man with his willy cut in half, and this woman in a wheelchair — it was Martine's *mam*! I *know* her. She used to work at the factory. They were *dead*. God, they were dead, and it was so disgusting."

"Why didn't you inform us of that?"

"Because Martine put a knife to my neck in the garage and said she'd kill me." Guest showed a small scab on their throat.

I know why I didn't see that before . . . clothing in the way. Makes sense now. "Why would you want Gary dead? I'll play the hypothetical game with you. Let's pretend you wouldn't have wanted him dead in the real sense, that it's something we've all said at one time or another: *God, I could kill them!* Or *God, I wish they were dead.*" Carol's chest tightened. *Been there, done that with Dad.* "What would your reason be?"

"He's a pervert."

"We're aware people have that view of him. Is that all?"

"I used to work at the factory, did you know that?" Guest got up to walk to the window, realised Dave was there, then sat again. "I had to leave because of what he was doing. He came on to me, touched me on the day Harry lost his hand. It was *me* in the cutting room with Gary when it happened. Harry had a thing about getting rid of everyone involved, and I shit myself because *I* was involved, although Harry had never mentioned it, so maybe he hadn't seen me? But if he had and he just wasn't saying, if he wanted to kill Gary for being there, why not me, too? I told Gary afterwards to stop pestering me, touching me, that I'd tell Sue."

"Did he stop during the time you were in the cutting room?"

"Of course he did, Harry's hand got sliced off!" Guest's voice went up in a shriek.

"Do you think he'd have stopped if that hadn't happened?"

Guest pouted. "If I'm being totally honest, yes, because he's backed off when others have said no. He's a perv but isn't someone who wouldn't take no for an answer."

"So what did you do?"

"I left the factory. Couldn't work there anymore. Made sure all the younger women knew what he'd done to me, that I hated him, because if it meant others stopped letting him paw them, then that was for the best, wasn't it? Except I had nightmares, what he did played over and over — all those years is a long time to keep being tormented. He violated me, doesn't matter whether he didn't manage to have sex, but he had his hand on my breast, up my skirt . . . Sue would have been mortified if she'd known."

"Did you tell him to stop before he touched you like that?"

"No, I . . . I liked it until I didn't . . . then I was about to say get off but Harry screamed."

"What I'm trying to establish is whether this was a sexual assault."

"No, but my brain has turned it into one, I know that, it's just . . ."

"So you got another job and tried to move on?"

"Yes, and I had therapy, which showed me because I didn't get to *say* no, Harry's scream cutting me off, I told myself I was being violated. It's too much to explain, there's a name for whatever happened to me, something to do with my brain creating the scenario. I still saw Gary from time to time, in Scudderton town centre, which set me off again. Then there was this other time. He had this scruffy dog, a white one with a black nose and eyes. A terrier."

Carol raised her eyebrows and looked at Dave. Edith and Frederick Majors' dog? Why would they even allow him to go anywhere near it if they hated the father of their granddaughter?

"Um, what was the dog's name?" Carol asked to confirm.

"Taffy."

"And why did Gary have him?"

"Because he was with another woman one Thursday. The woman was babysitting the dog and it took sick. God, what are you going to charge me with?"

"I have no idea yet until I've interviewed Martine, but what I will do now is caution you and take you down to the station, because whatever part you've played here, it isn't legal."

Carol would get to the bottom of this eventually, find out the name of the condition Guest was suffering, see if it would make a difference in how, or if, she was charged for possibly trying to get Gary Cuttersby murdered — she could get away with it on diminished responsibility. But in the meantime . . .

"Tanya Bedford, you do not have to say anything. But, it may harm your defence if you do not mention when questioned something which you later rely on in court. Anything you do say may be given in evidence."

The vet's assistant cried.

CHAPTER TWENTY-FIVE

Interview Room One

Much to her surprise Monday morning, a tired Carol, running on fumes, had got somewhere with Martine, who had admitted defeat and told her version of events — which, as it turned out, gelled perfectly with Carol's and Dave's suspicions on how this had all played out. They'd sat up until 5 a.m. in her flat, going through it all, piecing things together, then they'd crashed out on the sofa until seven, and with a quick shower and breakfast — Marmite on toast and coffee on the go — they'd rocked up to the station to face the interviews.

Martine had initially denied it all, but then Carol had shown her damning photographic evidence that had been found by digi on her father's computer and Martine's phone earlier that morning — dead bodies and a few of Martine after she'd killed her mother and Tim Dougan. In them, she held up an eyeball on some kind of spiked tool, her eyes gleaming with utter madness.

Four eyes had been found in the back of the freezer. What appeared to be dried faeces preserved beneath clingfilm had been discovered on the chair in the garage after Tim

Dougan's doll had been removed. Carol could only assume, when he'd been alive, he'd shit himself and they'd left him to sit in it.

Martine had said she'd killed her mother and Tim in the living room. Josie had watched while Tim was tortured to death. What a God-awful thing to have to witness, knowing you were next.

Now Carol wanted to clear some things up, loose ends that dangled and tickled the irritation section of her brain.

Pitson stood by the door, hands clasped over his groin. He looked as knackered as Carol felt, but he'd asked to pull a double shift so he could be in on this interview and the one with Tanya Bedford: "Seeing it through to the end, like."

A solicitor sat beside Martine. Blonde, skinny, an upturned nose. Lily Bradshaw, a quiet sort who preferred to sit and listen, only offering whispered advice if she felt it necessary instead of barking "my client" this and "my client" that. She'd shaken her head a few times during the telling, appalled by what had come from Martine's mouth.

Dave sat beside Carol, opposite them. Martine leaned back with her arms folded as if she'd resigned herself to prison — although she didn't look too unhappy about it, which was odd. In her holding cell throughout the night, she'd apparently been babbling that she couldn't face prison because of the showers, whatever that meant, and that she wouldn't step foot in anything with HMP in the name. But now? Seemed she'd had a change of heart.

Carol sipped some of the tea she'd just had brought in by an officer as they were all thirsty from so much talking. So far, they'd sat here for two hours.

"If I can just ask a few questions so I can get it straight in my head . . ." Carol's shoulders and neck burned from tiredness.

Martine nodded.

"Your nan got pregnant by Vincent Marsh, who refused to acknowledge the baby — your father, Harry Smith. We have a report here of her accusing him of sexual assault,

239

pertaining to around the time she'd have become pregnant. Except she didn't file this complaint until ninety-one, when your father was an adult. Do you know owt about that?"

"Of *course* I do. Dad liked to have a good chinwag: 'Feed the bad boy and girl, Mart!' That's what he liked to call it. She wanted Vincent to stump up the cash for looking after Dad, payment owed for all those years she hadn't seen a penny. That's what Dad told me anyroad — Nan had told him all about this a while later when he'd asked her who his father was. She'd never said so before, see? When Vincent didn't cough up, she said she'd get him for rape and that Dad was the proof."

"Yet she dropped the accusation."

"Because Vincent threatened her with all sorts, didn't he?" Martine sighed. "It was okay in the end. Like I told you, I strangled the bastard. There's this thing called biding your time. You should know all about that, what with being a copper."

Carol refused to give Martine the satisfaction of knowing how much it annoyed her when people thought they *knew* her, just because she'd featured a lot in the news. "So there was always a plan to kill Vincent?"

"Can't remember."

"When was the decision made?"

"See, that's the brilliant thing. Vincent wrote those silly comments on that thread, and Dad saw them. I was meant to go to the pub where Dad had last seen him, find out where he lived, get him after I'd done everyone else on the list. Except he was right there outside Betty's, and I'm telling you, it was karma stepping in and showing him to me. I thought I may as well nip in another murder before that Nab fucker, made no odds." Martine shrugged in the universal "couldn't give a fuck" sign.

"Why did you kill Tim Dougan? I can understand your mother to a degree, but her lover?"

"I wanted to just rough him up, you know, scare him, but Dad didn't trust the bugger. Said Tim would leave ours and call the police about being assaulted, which is what I suggested we do to him. But with Dad harping on about murder, the bad girl said: *Martine, what's one more alongside Mam?* So I plucked their eyes out, rammed an awl in their ears and cut out their tongues."

"Why did you do those specific things?"

"It was what Dad wanted."

"*Why*, though?"

"He didn't want them to see, hear or speak anymore."

The glass eyes, the sewn mouths, the earmuffs. "Why did he keep the dolls?"

Martine rolled her eyes. "I get Mam because he wanted to pretend they were still married, but Nan? I don't know why he kept her. And Tim, well, Dad liked to go into the garage and laugh at his little willy."

"Why had it been cut and sewn?"

"Dunno."

"Where's the rest of those people, the remains — your nan, mam and Tim?"

"On the moors out the back. I'm not getting done for Nan, that was Dad, but I buried the other two. I'd say I'll show you, but it's easy enough to find. I've been out there so much I've worn a path from our back garden to the spot, plus there's fresh flowers down for the firsts."

"The firsts?"

Martine nodded, animated. "Dad said our first kills should be honoured, remembered, so there's Nan and Baby Smith—"

"*Baby* Smith?" *Dear God, no . . .*

"Don't have a heart attack, Wrenny, it's only a *budgie*."

Carol hid her relief that they wouldn't be finding a baby out there. "You didn't mention where you killed Betty, just said on the moors."

"Same place as the innards and bones. She'd actually laid near them when she wanted to feel the vibrations from the earth. I'd taken the flowers away earlier, see? A different bunch to the one I put there after I'd been to Cove, *ob-vi-ous-ly*, because I knew she'd be coming to dance."

"You befriended her at work, you said."

241

"Yeah."

"Why the padded suit?"

"A *disguise*, thicko. Bigger boots, too, but then your SOCO people have probably already worked that one out."

"Why did you take her to the vet?"

"A connection to Sue. Thomas Lines. She went out with him years back, Dad said."

"Was that the only reason?"

"Yeah. I thought it was a bit obscure, but Dad, he reckoned the police would figure it out in the end."

"Why did you leave ID on her when you told us you were aware Betty visited the vet a lot and he'd recognise her anyroad?"

"I wanted to make it easier. I'm not a *monster*, you know. I do have *some* compassion for you lot having to deal with the outcome of Dad's plan."

That's debatable. I don't think you're compassionate at all. "If that's the case, why did you skew your boot print in Sue's garden?"

"The bad girl told me to do it."

"Is it a coincidence that Thomas Lines lives in the same street as Nabruah Panjib?"

"A bloody good one, don't you reckon? God, fate is a funny bastard."

"Was there anyone else on the list?"

"Some physiotherapist who bugged Dad, offended him. Suggested he'd do rude stuff with his hand like his dad would."

"Anyone else?"

"Only Gary's dad, but he died all by himself, and Gary, although that was a late addition. He was supposed to suffer without Sue, but Dad decided he had to go because he'd told you about the Bad Time — a step too far, that was. Or we played it safe in case he had, because we didn't know that for sure. He did, didn't he?"

Carol wasn't prepared to admit that. A few women who'd come forward at the factory this morning, those Gary had approached for his fumble addiction, were being spoken to at the minute to assess whether any charges of assault had to be brought up. She'd check after this whether anyone wanted him prosecuted, although she suspected it was all consensual. Tanya Bedford had even said it was, yet her poor mind had turned afterwards — maybe the trauma of seeing Harry's hand sliced off?

"Do you have any remorse, Martine?"

"Only that I have a bad girl at all. I wish I didn't sometimes. I used to like her, like it that I got to talk to Dad about bad girl and boy, but halfway through doing all this . . ." She blew out a long breath. "I just wanted it over. Knew Dad was on his last legs. Thought I'd give it a go and try to be normal."

"How were you going to manage on just your wages?"

Martine smiled. "Dad got the ball rolling on that. Changing his bank account to my name. I'd get Gary's payments and the DWP ones. Fraud, I suppose you'd call it. I'd have told people Dad moved away, but really I'd have buried him on the moors."

"Do you feel bad about that?"

"No. Thought I was owed something for all the hard work I'd put in. Waste of time anyroad, because here we are."

"You could have continued to deny it, blame it on Tanya Bedford."

Martine shrugged. "Like I said, I wanted to see what life was like without the bad girl. Maybe this is the way forward, going to prison so I'm watched — although I will say, I've thought about being shanked in the shower, so those prison guards or whatever better keep a sharp eye out, make sure I'm okay."

"What do you class yourself as?"

Martine frowned for a second or two, then a big smile came, and she threw her head back and laughed. The moment was short-lived. She snapped her face down again to stare at Carol, all hilarity gone, a blank mask tightening it. "Nutty as a fruitcake, Wrenny. Which reminds me, I'm hungry. Got any Snickers?"

Carol glanced at Dave, who raised his eyebrows. The wrappers in the bush hadn't just been placed there by one of the Cuttersby boys after all. Some of them belonged to Martine.

Carol made a mental note to see if they were still in evidence or if they'd been binned when news of a twin throwing them in the bush had come out. If they were lucky, some would have Martine's fingerprints all over them. Another point in the police's favour, as was the surgeon's blood in the boot of the Ford Focus.

It was all coming together nicely.

* * *

The Incident Room

Prior to any interview, Tanya Bedford continued to blame the Smiths from her holding cell. She'd been for an assessment with the duty doctor, Carol thinking it wise to cover their backsides, considering what Tanya had told them at her house.

Carol sat at Michael's desk as he wasn't in yet. Dave flopped into his chair and closed his eyes.

Katherine walked in holding a large brown folder. "I think you're going to have to shelve any interview for now. This was left with Joy at the front desk, from the doctor." She showed Carol a report on Tanya. "She's not fit for questioning. She's had three mental breakdowns in the time since Harry's hand was cut off, one around every three years."

After she'd left the factory, Tanya had gone on to study to become a vet's assistant. This was during a period where she'd been functioning fine. The new assessment from today's doctor was in agreement with the therapist, that Tanya suffered from a form of fictitious or induced illness where she'd convinced herself Gary had sexually violated her when she knew he hadn't — the fact she'd been prevented from saying no had burrowed into her mind and skewed her thinking.

"She mentioned Munchausen to us on our first visit to her home," Carol said, "as though she wasn't sure what it meant, yet clearly, she does know because she has it or something similar. There was me, telling her the proper name for it, and she was already aware."

"A ruse," Dave said, eyes still closed. "I've been picking over our initial visit to her, trying to come up with some tells, something we missed. If you recall, she told us she'd been to see the Smiths just before we went there the first time. We'd taken a half-hour break after seeing Liz at the Co-op, then we went to Tanya's. If we'd have gone straight there, she wouldn't have been back, because according to my notes, she told us she'd only got back twenty minutes before our arrival."

"I do remember the smell of disinfectant," Carol said. "It was there again when we went the second time."

"It's on the assessment." Katherine pointed out the section on the form where the doctor had written.

"She used it as shower gel to get the feel of Gary's hands off her, to wash him away, plus she used it like air freshener." Carol paused. "Why would she tell our duty doctor this?"

"Maybe it came out in a rush?" Katherine suggested. "There's quite a bit she said, so she obviously needed to talk."

"Then there was her wearing Lycra, as if she'd been jogging," Dave said. "When you asked her where she'd been, she said, 'Just out', yet she could have said she'd been on a run and we wouldn't have been any the wiser. Then she asked if the cases were linked. All she'd known about was Gary — finding out Betty was dead must have been a shock, and she might well have realised why the old girl had been killed because Martine told us Harry talked about everyone involved to Tanya."

"The Lycra. The top had a polo neck," Carol said. "And that's why we didn't see the nick from the knife on her throat. Damn, I remember she rubbed a finger down it at one point."

Dave *hmmed*. "She talked us through her movements when she went to see to the bulldog and the canary at the vet's. She could well have seen Martine there, been involved, yet she told us nowt out of the ordinary had happened."

"It's got chronic insomnia on this assessment. She mentioned waking more than usual, even said the word insomnia to us herself, yet neither of us queried why that was. Do you think she'd have told us if we had?"

Dave opened his eyes. "Nah. With Sue dead and Tanya knowing Harry and Martine had arranged it, she wouldn't have wanted to bring Gary up." He took his notebook out and thumbed back a few pages. "Here, look. You asked her if she knew Gary and Sue. She evaded a definite answer with: 'I heard their names on the news.' Classic deflection. When you pressed her again on knowing them, she didn't answer. Not long after, she said it was all a bit much and asked us to leave. Then there was the bit where you told her to change her times when going to see the animals overnight, and she said something like: 'Oh my God, do you think they've been spying on me?' We took it to mean the unknown killer, but she'd have thought it was Martine and Harry."

"I wonder why she got so uptight when I suggested she could go and live above the vet's."

Katherine jabbed her finger at another section on the assessment.

Carol read it out.

Tanya wanted me to include the following in my notes:
She feels her home is almost ready to fully relax in. She has been cleaning it in disinfectant ever since she moved in. This continual cleansing is a result of her thinking, whenever she breathes out or touches something, that the place is tainted by Gary. His essence, which she believes seeped inside her when he touched her, is transferred through her skin and by exhaling, thus infecting her home. With Gary dead, she feels she would no longer harbour the idea he'd violated her; therefore, when she touches anything or breathes out inside the home, it would no longer be tainted. As Harry and Martine refused to kill him, Tanya felt she had no other option but to do it herself. She went to the Cove house to do this, but Martine appeared and said she would do it. Tanya returned home and waited for news that he was dead so she could not only clean her mind of him but her home, too, one last time.

Tanya needs a more thorough assessment, and not just with a therapist, as I believe she has a mental illness that could be managed with the proper help.
She says she is sorry for her part in this "mess".

Carol sighed. "Katherine, can you arrange for that, then, please, as I don't want her in a holding cell any longer than she has to be. She needs help as soon as we can get it for her — and to be honest, I think Martine could do with some help, too, so sort something for her as well."

Katherine went off to her desk.

"Poor cows," Dave said.

"I just thought the same." Carol sighed. "The mind is a brilliant thing, but it can also be your worst enemy. Reality skews. You take steps you never would have if you were well. It's a bloody sad thing all round, to be honest."

"But it's over."

Carol nodded. "Yes, it's over."

CHAPTER TWENTY-SIX

Seaview Heights — The Cliff

A week after Martine's interview, Carol stared out to sea Monday night after work. She waited for Gary, who'd been cleared of any wrongdoing with his sexual tendencies as all the women questioned at the station had said they'd been "up for it", as well as women going back through the years. It had been a long week of interviews, but Carol had been unable to let it rest until she knew for sure whether Gary was a complete and utter sex pest or not.

The shush of footsteps through grass had her turning towards Seaview Heights. Gary walked over his front garden, crossed the road and strode along until he stood beside her to the left. He and his boys had stayed in a hotel until SOCO had finished, and now they'd returned to live at Seaview permanently. Or so she assumed.

"Lovely out here, isn't it?" she said.

"It is, although it's still so bloody hot."

It had been another scorching day, although rain was due from tomorrow. This evening, mugginess at its most unbearable since the summer began, had a stillness to it, a sense of impending change — not just the promised rain but for Gary, too, and maybe Carol if she could just get her act together and tell her lover she didn't want anything permanent. He'd been bugging her via phone all week, staring at her Wednesday night in The Lord, his black eye from that scuffle going yellow at the edges.

"Have you thought about it at all?" he'd said.

Her sarcasm had reared up. "I've had more important things to deal with, like murder."

"You need to put your job and home life into compartments like I do."

"Seems everything about you has a compartment. You've only got to walk into your home to see that."

"It's a good thing. If everything is in its place, you know where to find it."

"You can't put me in place," she'd said. "I don't belong in a box and I don't want to be found."

"But it could be a pretty one with a pink bow . . ."

She'd got up, walked out and hadn't seen him since. She'd ignored his calls, his texts, his WhatsApp messages.

Why did she always attract the weirdos or the sort who couldn't hack the fact her job meant she was so busy? She thought of the "type" people usually went for, specific to their needs and chemistry. Sue had chosen a type in Gary and Thomas Lines. Both could be acerbic, although Carol thought Gary had mellowed a lot since his wife's death. According to Pitson, before Carol and Dave had arrived at Flora's that Saturday morning, Gary had been quite the rude bastard to her, snapping, sarcastic.

Yes, people had a type.

Maybe I should try a new one, then. I'd better put my itch man out of his misery. Later.

Work would always come first.

"How are you, Gary?"

"Been to see my mother today."

"How did that go?"

"She knew who I was at least, which is a miracle in itself these days, but I told her about Sue, and she got confused.

Thought I meant a woman she used to know from work, and she argued until she was blue in the face that Sue had died from sepsis, not a murder. Still, I've told her, got it off my to-do list."

"Have you had many people dropping by to ask if they can help? I know Whitney isn't with you anymore."

"A few. The strange pair next door have been surprisingly attentive, bringing food and whatnot."

"Watch them. I think they like being involved in drama."

"I got the same impression." He chuckled. "Shit, why do I always feel guilty if I laugh?"

"It's a thing. A part of grief."

They looked out to sea for a moment.

"I spoke to Charlotte," he said. "Came to my senses and thought it was best to get that bit over and done with instead of tormenting myself for a month over how things would pan out."

"What did you decide?"

"To tell the boys."

"When?"

"Already did it. Yesterday after a Sunday roast."

"How did they take it?"

"Well, it finally ended their silence, put it that way."

She could well imagine the scene. "Oh. Lots of shouting?"

"At first, from Jack. Joseph just seemed stunned."

"How on earth did you broach it with them?"

"I got there with the name-calling before they could. Said I was a bastard, wanker, you name it, and I didn't deserve their mother. Told them I was the worst of the worst to keep playing away. Said things like that come back to bite you in the end, and God do I wish I'd never done any of it, especially knowing how it affected Tanya. Whitney told me."

"She was a unique case with the way she dealt with it. Almost like her mind took over and she had no say in what it said she had to think."

"How is she?"

"Getting help, same as Martine."

"I can't help but feel sorry for her. I know she killed my wife but . . ."

"I know. I know."

They lapsed into a quiet period for a while, Carol contemplating life without anyone to scratch her itch, and it was a relief to be fair, to put an end to that and concentrate on doing a bit of healing herself. She had her childhood to pack away properly, and until she'd cleared her mind of the abusive clutter, she wasn't fit to be anyone's lover.

Gary poked at the grass with the front edge of his flip-flop. "Sue's being buried next week."

"Are you ready for that, emotionally?"

"No, but I can't put it off forever. The boys needs closure. So does Flora."

"How are they doing with regards to their mother?"

"Whitney suggested a therapist, and they've agreed. As for Flora . . . it's best I stay away from her as much as possible. She's always going to blame me for Sue's death, and she'd be right. I'm owning it. If I hadn't fucked about so much, she'd still be alive. And yes, I know I can't control other people's behaviour, but if I hadn't been busy with Tanya, I'd have seen the cutter guard was up and prevented everything."

"True. Will Jack and Joseph be meeting the baby?"

"*Starbell*," he admonished.

And she smiled, because she'd done the same to him last week. "*Starbell*."

"Yes. After the funeral, a few days later. Without Charlotte."

"Probably for the best."

"Hmm."

A gull swooped at them, reminding her of when she'd stood here with Gary before, the time she and Dave had told him about Betty.

"Fucking things. Size of cats, some of them," they said at the same time.

"You remembered," Gary said.

"I remember too much, unfortunately. Still, we wake up each morning and get through another day, don't we?"

"You've been through something?"

"You could say that." She paused. "Live a better life now, Gary. Promise me that. No more fumb—"

"No, no more."

They watched the gull swoop and crest, swoop and crest, tears burning Carol's eyes. Sometimes, the simple things were what gripped the heart the most. The heat of the lowering sun, the beauty of the pink-and-orange horizon, the scent of the sea, its constant, calming shush.

Yes, tomorrow was another day.

THE END

THE JOFFE BOOKS STORY

We began in 2014 when Jasper agreed to publish his mum's much-rejected romance novel and it became a bestseller.

Since then we've grown into the largest independent publisher in the UK. We're extremely proud to publish some of the very best writers in the world, including Joy Ellis, Faith Martin, Caro Ramsay, Helen Forrester, Simon Brett and Robert Goddard. Everyone at Joffe Books loves reading and we never forget that it all begins with the magic of an author telling a story.

We are proud to publish talented first-time authors, as well as established writers whose books we love introducing to a new generation of readers.

We have been shortlisted for Independent Publisher of the Year at the British Book Awards three times, in 2020, 2021 and 2022, and for the Diversity and Inclusivity Award at the Independent Publishing Awards in 2022.

We built this company with your help, and we love to hear from you, so please email us about absolutely anything bookish at feedback@joffebooks.com.

If you want to receive free books every Friday and hear about all our new releases, join our mailing list: www.joffebooks.com/contact

And when you tell your friends about us, just remember: it's pronounced Joffe as in coffee or toffee!

Made in United States
Orlando, FL
03 June 2023

33780987R00157